JET V

LEGACY

Russell Blake

First Edition

ISBN: 978-1484814888

Published by

Reprobatio Limited

Books by Russell Blake

Co-authored with Clive Cussler

THE EYE OF HEAVEN

Thrillers by Russell Blake

FATAL EXCHANGE

THE GERONIMO BREACH

ZERO SUM

THE DELPHI CHRONICLE TRILOGY

THE VOYNICH CYPHER

SILVER JUSTICE

UPON A PALE HORSE

The Assassin Series by Russell Blake

KING OF SWORDS

NIGHT OF THE ASSASSIN

RETURN OF THE ASSASSIN

REVENGE OF THE ASSASSIN

BLOOD OF THE ASSASSIN

AUTHOR'S NOTES

JET V – Legacy was a tremendously fun book to write, coming as it does after the favorable reception of the first four volumes in the series. The goal was to continue in the vein I mined when writing *JET IV – Reckoning*, and have the story unfold over a relatively short period of time – a week or so. I wanted to keep up the pace and the sense of momentum as, just when it seems Jet is finally going to catch a break and have a shot at a normal life, her world is upended and the poop hits the fan, yet again.

I hope you enjoy the latest installment in Jet's saga. I've had a ball recounting her story and seeing where it ultimately leads. It's always a wonderful feeling when the character takes over, and I can honestly say that for the last few books I've had literally no idea where the plots would wind up or what she would get into next.

That's a fascinating feeling, and a little scary; but it seems to be working, so now probably isn't the time to change anything.

And so, without any further delay, I proudly present this fifth installment in Jet's ongoing drama. Strap in – it promises to be another hell of a ride.

CHAPTER 1

Four weeks ago, Genoa, Italy

A cold rain fell from the gunmetal sky, driven by a relentless wind that carried with it the distinctive smell of the sea. The Mediterranean was unrecognizable as the placid, azure depiction on the tourist-shop postcards, instead an angry snarl that battered the breakwater of the Genoa harbor with startling intensity. The overcast brooding over the city flashed with bursts of lightning as dusk released its hold and night settled in, the celestial pyrotechnics illuminating the hulls of massive cargo ships secured to the concrete piers that lined the waterfront. Rivers of murky water streamed down the ancient gutters, spilling over onto the cobblestones that jutted through the asphalt where it had worn away, a casualty of the near-constant procession of overloaded semi-rig wheels that carried cargo to and from the busy port.

Two security guards in black slickers patrolled near the access gate for the B section, reluctantly making their slow rounds, inured to the deluge and reconciled to slogging through whatever nature threw at them, fortified by strong black tobacco cigarettes and the knowledge that payday was right around the corner. The yard was empty, the shifts of rowdy longshoremen having departed for the day, and other than the token security presence and an occasional scurrying wharf rat desperate to find shelter, the area was deserted.

Across the boulevard from the ships, a long line of bars and inexpensive restaurants stretched endlessly, their shabby, weather-beaten façades offering a promise of rough seaport hospitality. Working girls shook water off their raincoats as they entered the saloons, sizing up with scant enthusiasm the pickings on a weeknight: the typical assortment of thieves, fishermen, and seamen huddled around the bars, drinking in earnest as they eyed each other morosely, hunkered down for a long night.

Above a particularly glum watering hole boasting a faded sign with a stylized caricature of a cutlass-brandishing mallard sporting a pirate's hat, dim amber light glimmered through a set of threadbare curtains that were closed to preserve the privacy of the walk-up apartment on the second floor. Sixty yards down the street, parked where it had been most of the afternoon, was a robin's egg blue Volkswagen van with windows tinted so dark they were opaque. To a casual observer the van would appear empty, but in the rear two men were hunched around a set of flat-panel monitors, the black-and-white screens flickering with a ghostly glow.

The object of the men's attention was the stairway that led to the apartment over the bar, and they had been peering at the screens, checking to verify that the feeds from the concealed cameras and the laser mics were picking up as much as possible given the short notice of the operation and the rain. Word of the meet had only come in that morning, and considerable resources had been mobilized to get the two of them into position and a few microphones in place. The storm had been a bit of bad luck, but after countless operations they had learned to play the hand they were dealt – there was no point in bemoaning the absence of ideal conditions. They were professionals, seasoned and hard, and if there was a way to make it work, they would find it.

Bringing the local intelligence personnel into it had never been considered – the Italians were leakier than the wooden skiffs that dotted the wharf, and wouldn't be used even as a last resort. Despite a supposed environment of cooperation and peace, the civilized veneer of the current climate masked a perennial adversarial nature inherent to the game. The men trusted no one but their own; and even then, with trepidation born of habit. They were used to operating alone, undercover, for weeks or months at a time, and had been stationed in Italy for over a year, eavesdropping on an ostensibly friendly regime.

Both wore navy blue wool pea coats over their coarsely woven sailor's sweaters. Outwardly they were indistinguishable from the rest of the denizens of the seedy waterfront underbelly: Corsicans, Italian Mafia, Russians, and now freelancers from North Africa and the former Soviet satellites vied for dominance in a constantly shifting criminal stew, where allegiances and rivalries were decided in blood – and the fish regularly dined on the losers of the myriad power struggles.

The smaller of the two, his three-day growth of beard dark on his swarthy face, tapped one of the monitors with a stubby finger, its screen intermittent from an electrical short somewhere in the wiring.

"How are we supposed to get anything when they give us crap to work with and no notice? This is bullshit," he groused, sticking to Italian, as agreed.

"Adam, I swear, do you have to complain every time we do one of these? Come on. It could be worse, eh? We could be doing this outside, getting soaked. I'll take this any day," his companion Samuel muttered softly, scratching his chin stubble before raising his arms over his head and stretching.

"I thought the party was supposed to have already started," Adam said. His eyes never left the image of the doorway being broadcast into the van from the concealed array on the roof, the cameras and microphones disguised as a luggage rack and an old television aerial from the seventies.

"Sorry if the intel wasn't precise enough. Do you have a hot date tonight I don't know about?"

"I just don't like these kinds of loose operations. The whole thing's been rushed. That means there's a bigger chance of mistakes."

"Thanks for the capsule summary on the dangers of inadequate preparation. I'll remember to include it in the Surveillance 101 textbook I've been working on," Samuel said dryly. The banter was expected and familiar, a way of reducing the tension that went hand in hand with the duty.

"This has been a waste so far. That's all I'm saying. And it's forty-five minutes past the witching hour and nobody's appeared. It's bullshit."

"Yes…it's bullshit – as you keep stating – but the lights are on, so they're expecting someone. Patience, my friend, patience. We're here for the duration. Let's see what shows up as the night progresses, shall we?"

"Probably only more toothless hookers and drunks. Seems like they're the only ones stupid enough to be out in weather like this."

"Since when did you have anything against either?"

"I didn't say I did. I'm just jealous. Everyone's inside enjoying their drinks while we're sitting out here freezing our asses off. It stinks, is my point."

"Noted. I'll make sure that the report conveys your lack of enthusiasm when alcohol and prostitutes aren't included with the job."

"Make sure of it. Maybe we can get some welcome changes made. About frigging time."

Both men stopped their chatter as a tall man in an obviously expensive overcoat made his way up the sidewalk from a black Lexus that had pulled to the curb, his umbrella shielding him from the worst of the weather. Adam and Samuel exchanged glances as the man walked past them. They flicked several switches on the console next to them, and then Samuel began recording the feeds for posterity.

"I can't make out much. The damned rain and the umbrella aren't doing us any favors," Adam griped, turning a knob in an effort to increase the sensitivity of the primary camera.

"See if you can get his face. That was one of the top priorities, besides recording whatever we can pick up on tape."

"I'm trying. But I'm not a miracle worker. We don't have a lot going for us here. The lighting is getting all but wiped out from the rain…"

"Just do the best you can," Samuel snapped, eyes boring into the monitors.

"He's going in," Adam said in a hushed voice, as their quarry punched the button on the intercom and stood, waiting.

"Are you getting anything decent?"

"The umbrella is in the way. I can deal with the lighting, but I can't see through fabric."

"What about the microphones?"

"Until they start talking inside we're not going to know. But it looks positive. Check out the signal strength on the audio," Adam said, pointing to a graph on a scope and adjusting the gain. "Picked up the door buzzer pretty well."

The directional microphones were designed to detect vibration from the window panes and convert them into sound. The gear was highly accurate under normal circumstances, but in a squall like tonight's the efficiency was going to be severely tested. Both men knew it, but they didn't have a lot of options. They'd considered posing as maintenance workers or custodians in order to position some bugs, but had nixed the idea when they'd seen the layout of the building – it was too risky, and they couldn't chance being detected. Their orders had made that painfully clear. They were to avoid engaging the target under any circumstances.

The occupants of the flat hadn't left the building since the van had taken its position – thankfully close enough to use at least some of the equipment. Samuel had circled around the long waterfront block a dozen times before a spot had freed up as workers left for home. Once wedged in, he'd made the best of the situation. They had recorded a few murmured phone calls over the last hour, but other than that, however many people were upstairs, they weren't speaking to each other.

Adam made another minute adjustment to one of the microphones, and when the street door lock buzzed to admit the new arrival, it sounded like a siren in both men's headphones.

"Did you get anything?" Samuel asked, and Adam ignored him as he concentrated on the camera's signal.

"Not great, but I think we got a good enough shot of him to send in and get a head start," he finally said, still listening intently.

"Okay. Let her rip," said Samuel, eyeing the indicator for the wireless signal strength.

"Give me a second," Adam replied, sliding a keyboard toward him and tapping in a series of instructions.

Both men stopped what they were doing when the crack of the upstairs door slamming boomed in their headphones.

"Sounds pretty clear," Adam whispered.

"Shhh."

A brutal gust of wind pummeled the building with sheets of rain, interrupting their vigil as the van rocked from the force. Inside the little vehicle it sounded like someone was pounding on the roof with a jackhammer.

Murmured voices faded in and out as Adam toyed with the equipment knobs, bringing up a screen on the computer at his side and adjusting some faders on a digital filtering system. He was recording everything real time, but he also had the ability to equalize the signal and remove some of the background noise the storm introduced.

Samuel cursed when one of the two cameras went dark and then displayed static.

"Damn. The wind must have knocked it out," he complained, eyes searching over the equipment for evidence of a malfunction inside the van.

"Great. How does this get any worse?"

"Don't ask those kinds of questions."

"You know what you have to do."

Samuel nodded, resigned. He'd have to get a visual on the camera array and see if he could make out anything obvious that had gone wrong. The night had just gotten more unpleasant – it was blowing at least forty knots, and the heavy rain was peppering the van like a hailstorm.

Samuel reluctantly pushed aside the heavy curtain that separated the rear of the van from the cab and grimaced as he took in the torrent of rain cascading down the windshield. He was just turning to utter a curse to Adam when the smaller man saw a red dot play across Samuel's face, then settle on his temple.

"Look out–" Adam screamed, but it was too late. Samuel's head exploded as if he'd swallowed a grenade, spraying the back of the van with blood and bone, and the windshield collapsed inward as the wind caught the bullet-weakened glass and tore part of it away like a kite in a hurricane. Adam was groping for the assault rifle by his feet when another volley of rounds tore into the van, narrowly missing him. He was raising the rifle to return fire when he registered a burst of flame on the periphery of his vision, and then time stood still as an RPG-7 rocket-propelled grenade with a thermobaric warhead streaked through the windshield and detonated in a fireball, killing him instantly and vaporizing the interior in a molten blaze.

Pieces of the van, which was now distorted beyond recognition, had blown twenty yards into the street. When the first police arrived seven minutes later the chassis was smoldering, the gas tank having exploded when the grenade detonated, further contributing to the destruction.

Nobody who'd remained in the vicinity to answer questions had seen anything, and after an all-night investigation, the preliminary assessment was that an organized crime hit had taken place – not uncommon when territorial disputes flared up.

No one remembered the occupants of the apartment silently melting into the night, nor was the pick-up truck with the shooter noted by anyone. The carnage made the papers for two days, but after all was said and done, no perpetrators were arrested, and the event joined the hundreds of others that would remain unsolved in the ongoing war on organized crime upon which the latest administration had embarked with negligible results.

CHAPTER 2

Three months ago, 250 miles east of Hobyo, Somalia

Salome's massive bow plowed through the churning swells, the waves rolling four to six feet high in slow sets, the breeze confused and directionless. Conditions were unpredictable at best in this stretch of the western Indian Ocean, and the pre-dawn sky was inky black, with only an occasional star glimmering through the fog and no moon to speak of. The freighter's diesel motors rumbled with a throaty roar as she surged against the prevailing wind toward her ultimate destination of Jeddah, Saudi Arabia.

Salome was a veteran cargo ship who'd plied the coasts of Africa, India, and Pakistan for almost two decades – grim duty, to be sure, but profitable. Her crew was a mixed bag of merchant marines from all over the world, and she was flagged in Liberia, as were many of the vessels that roamed the infamous stretch of sea, the tiny nation's almost non-existent regulations a powerful draw that attracted a maritime register of over thirty-five hundred under its flag – eleven percent of the world's ships.

Up on the bridge, the watchman nudged the mate with his elbow. "What do you think?" he asked, sipping at his steaming mug of coffee, eyeing the radar screen with a fatigued gaze as he stabbed at a glowing blip with a grimy finger.

"Looks like a fishing boat to me. What, maybe a sixty or seventy footer? Making all of nine knots, if that," the mate replied.

"How far off?"

"Six miles."

"We should wake the captain," the watchman said, taking another draw of the strong brew he drank by the bucket, thick and black, the hotter the better.

"He'll be up soon enough. We'll keep an eye on it and if it gets much closer, then we can sound the alarm. At the speed it's moving, it doesn't pose much of a threat. Let the captain get his beauty rest, I say."

The watchman scanned the horizon in the direction of the offending craft with a pair of binoculars, and then dropped them back onto his chest. "No lights."

"A lot of these old scows don't run them. Damned Chinese and Thai boats that are so old they barely float. Not a lot of money being spent on replacement bulbs. Doesn't necessarily mean anything."

"True, but still, makes you wonder. I'm thinking we rouse those two security men. Let 'em earn their keep."

The armed guards, mercenaries from an Israeli company that specialized in maritime anti-piracy precautions, ran ten hour shifts, leaving four hours every day where the watchmen were told to wake them if anything suspicious occurred. Sighting a slow-moving fishing boat didn't really qualify as particularly alarming, but neither man was much liked by the crew – they kept to themselves and made a big show of toting around their rifles, the only guns on the ship.

Commercial craft were historically banned from carrying weapons, but because of the spike in piracy off the eastern coast of Africa, a number of countries had changed their rules, which had introduced a new opportunity for enterprising security firms. Increasingly ships that routinely made the run hired gunmen to stave off hijacking attempts and to act as a defense against pirates, who were typically after easy targets, not gun battles; although lately, as an international naval presence had massed in an effort to curb piracy, reports had surfaced of more aggressive attacks where the pirates had engaged, using automatic weapons and rocket-propelled grenade launchers.

The mate grunted assent as he left the bridge to wake the guards. *Salome* was cutting along at eighteen knots, and the other boat chugging through the seas at scarcely half that, so he felt no particular urgency as he wound his way down the stairs to where the security men were slumbering.

He roused the two sleeping gunmen with barely concealed delight and stood at their cabin door as they quickly pulled on clothes. Both donned Kevlar vests over their shirts and then scooped up their Kalashnikov AKM assault rifles before following him to the bridge.

"What have we got?" Ari, the taller of the two, asked the watchman.

"Doesn't look like much." He pointed to a bright spot on the glowing radar screen. "This guy, right here. No lights, on a heading that shouldn't get much closer than a couple of miles. But I figured you'd want to know. Earning your keep and all. Maybe get to fire off those popguns."

Ari ignored the jibe. His job wasn't to get into a pissing contest with the crew. This was just another boring gig, one of hundreds of voyages he'd made, where nothing had ever happened – almost disappointing, given the buildup the company had given him when he'd applied for the position. He'd had visions of exotic ports and clashes with pirates on the high seas, not a virtually endless supply of diesel fumes and seasickness.

He looked at Barry, his partner, and grimaced.

"Not a lot to get excited about. You want to stay awake for this? I'm going to go back and try to get some more sleep. At the snail's pace they're moving, it'll be like watching ice melt…"

"Sure. I agree. Won't take two of us to keep an eye on the situation."

Ari shook his head and trudged back to the narrow stairwell that led to the main deck level, carefully ensuring that his gun barrel pointed down at all times. Another false alarm in a long string of them. Every time a ship saw anything other than another tanker these days in the waters around Somalia, it was a fire drill – but at this point in his two-year-long career it had been a wash.

He had mixed feelings about that – some of the other men he worked with had been in firefights with pirates, and those had always ended with the attackers turning tail the second anyone shot back at them. They were opportunistic, extremely poor, and uninterested in doing battle to make their money, which was why the deterrent value of his company was undeniable. A few bursts across the bow of a pirate vessel and it would veer off in search of more benign prey. At least that's what he'd been told, and he had no reason to doubt it.

Up on the bridge, Barry set his rifle down and moved to the coffee pot, resigned to spending the last hour of darkness staring at the screen and trying to stay awake.

⤜⤛

Jiang Li, a thirty-year-old steel-hulled Chinese fishing trawler, had been hijacked three weeks earlier, and the crew held aboard as the leaky tub was used as a mother ship for the pirates who had taken her without a fight. Two fast skiffs trailed the boat, towed by stout rope, and over time the fifteen Chinese crew members had grown apathetic about their lot; they weren't paid enough to risk their lives fighting the pirates, and it was unlikely that their owner would pay much of a ransom for their return, so they were just taking it day by day as the twenty-one armed Somali gunmen kept them on the deck where they could be used as human shields if any warships approached – which, so far, none had shown any interest in doing. A multi-national coalition force had sent ships to patrol the area, but it was a vast ocean, and the sector the pirates operated in was bigger than all of Europe, making the effort largely hit or miss.

Two ebony-skinned gunmen heaved the ropes and brought the skiffs to the stern as the pilot cut power, and in a few minutes eighteen of the heavily armed fighters had loaded aboard. The target was *Salome*, a medium-sized freighter hauling cargo to the Middle East. An accomplice with internet access in Mogadishu had alerted them to its passage, and their leader had decided it was a viable target.

Salome was operated by a prominent Israeli shipping company with offices in most major European ports, which made it an excellent candidate for ransoming – the value of the cargo alone would be worth many millions, perhaps over ten, so a ransom of a few million could be in the offing, rewarding them handsomely even after their financial backers had been paid. Pirating had become a booming cottage industry, and opportunities were now traded on an ad hoc exchange in Harardheere, although the market was down since the success rate had dropped – a function of the increased military presence now patrolling the area.

The powerful outboard motors cranked to life, and a few moments later the boats were slicing through the waves, bound for where *Salome* was moving inexorably north, oblivious to the magnitude of the threat headed its way.

܀܁܀

"Damn. Two bogies, small, just separated from the fishing boat. Looks like they're headed straight for us," the watchman said, eyes following the glowing dots on the screen as they moved away from the larger blip that was the Chinese fishing vessel.

"Speed?" Barry asked, standing, his heart rate accelerating at the prospect of an attack. Ribbons of red and orange were just beginning to light the sky as the sun fought its way over the horizon, and if it hadn't been for the approaching small craft it would have been another breathtaking sunrise at sea to behold.

"Fast. At least twenty-five knots. They're moving at a ninety-degree angle to our position, so they'll be on top of us in just a few minutes. The fishing boat is only a couple of miles away from us now, so you can do the math."

"Get someone to wake Ari. I'm headed down to the deck to set up a firing position. I don't really even need them in range. Six hundred meters out I should be able to throw a few bursts their way. That should send them running," Barry explained, grabbing his rifle from where he'd stowed it in a corner of the bridge.

"All right. Consider it done," the mate said, rising from his swivel chair and preparing to follow him. "I'll go get the captain, too."

As they entered the stairwell, the mate cleared his throat. "Why don't you shoot at them from up here, on the superstructure? Wouldn't that give you a better position? Shooting from the highest possible point?"

"Flexibility. I want to be able to cover both sides of the ship, as well as the bow and stern. I can't do that as easily from up top because of the railing and the configuration of the walkways — and there's less cover." He paused as his foot hovered over the next step. "Look. Just do me a favor and get Ari. We'll need all the time we can get. And tell him to bring some more ammo, as well as our sidearms," Barry snapped, perfunctorily dismissing the mate. With his first real-life pirate attack imminent, he wasn't in the mood to play twenty questions.

Once outside, the salt wind lashing at his face, he looked around until he found a suitable spot where he could lie on the deck and fire while presenting as small a target as possible, as he'd been trained. It had been seven years since his service days, and a maritime exchange was different than firing at fighters in the desert, but the basics remained the same. A gun was a gun, even on a moving platform like a ship under way, and maintaining rigid control over your reactions was still essential, regardless of the turf.

Ari was by his side three minutes later, an excited expression on his face, and handed him two spare magazines and a pistol.

Barry raised the neoprene-sheathed binoculars, scanned the water, and pointed into the distance. "There they are. I can just make them out.

They're definitely hostiles. Boats are bristling with guns. And it looks like they've got binocs, too. Shit. They're splitting up now. Probably going to try to get one on the starboard side while the other one takes the port. Tricky bastards, I'll grant them that. They'll try to approach more toward the stern. That's what all the latest reports say is the standard M.O. What's the range?" Barry asked.

"About nine hundred meters. I'd give it another minute and then let them have a few rounds. That should put the fear of God into them. Oh, wow. They also have RPGs. Nice."

"I wouldn't worry about the grenade launchers. Those things are all but useless over a hundred yards. Two hundred would be a prayer," Barry said.

"You want me to move to the other side?"

"Nah. Not yet. I have a feeling this'll be over before it starts."

"I wish the cheap pricks at the company had equipped us with Barretts and scopes. This kind of sucks. There's nothing I hate worse than a fair fight," Ari griped.

"The scope wouldn't have done you much good with the seas like this. They're bobbing around pretty good, and we're not exactly standing still. Besides, it won't matter. Once they hear my rifle and see the bullets shredding the water around them, they'll back off."

"Be nicer if we had a .50 caliber machine gun. That would make short work out of them."

"Or ack-ack guns. Like the Navy. Kaboom. Party over."

They waited as the ship continued plowing north, their nerves hyper-tuned by the prospect of their first real engagement. Barry squinted down the barrel of his assault rifle and prepared to fire.

"Range?"

"Maybe six hundred, but closing fast."

"That's my guess too. All right. Let's get this show on the road."

The stuttering report of the AKM echoed off the topsides as Barry fired four bursts at the nearer of the two boats, breaking his promise to himself to try to avoid hitting them with the warning volley. Once he was actually trying to sight the bucking rifle on the boats, he realized that he would be lucky to get within a dozen yards of the bouncing skiff.

Ari peered through the glasses and then swallowed hard. "They aren't turning."

"Shit. Dumbasses. Well, time to open up on 'em, then…"

"Damn. And they don't just have AKs. Now that they're closer, I can make out some other weapons. Looks like at least one sniper ri–"

A rain of slugs hammered the metal around them as the lead boat opened fire, eight guns blazing on full automatic, hurling hundreds of rounds at their position. Most slammed harmlessly above and below them, but one caught Barry in the neck and ripped through the side of his throat, sending a spray of arterial blood onto Ari's face. Barry grunted as he dropped his rifle and clutched at the wound, his eyes surprised and then panicked, his life burbling through his hand as he groped blindly for his weapon.

"Oh, God, Barry–" Ari's expression had changed from eagerness to horrified fright, and for a few seconds he froze, torn between doing something to help his friend and continuing to fire at the rapidly approaching boats. Barry groaned as he weakened, deciding the priority – Ari needed to repel the pirates before he did anything else, otherwise they were both going to wind up dead.

He drew a bead on the closest skiff and fired, his weapon now on full auto, and saw two men collapse in the lead craft as three of his rounds found home.

That was the last thing Ari registered. A ricochet shattered the back of his skull, instantly liquefying his brain, killing him before he even realized he'd been hit. Slugs continued to pepper the ship, and another bullet shredded through Barry's chest, ending his agonized struggle as his limp, blood-soaked hand fell lifelessly at his side.

The mate watched the gunfight from one of the bridge side windows, and when he saw the two guards get shot he made a snap decision and abandoned his position with a yell to the watchman and the pilot.

"They're hit. I'm going down. No way am I going to spend months in some Somali shithole," he warned, sprinting by them.

"Wait. That's not your job. Don't get involved or they'll shoot you too," the watchman cautioned. "This is bad enough as it is. Two already dead…"

"The only way we're going to avoid being taken hostage is if we keep shooting. I'm not about to be tortured for months before they kill me. I've heard the stories," the mate said, ending the discussion, and then he ducked through the door and descended the stairs at a run.

When he reached the deck, the two pirate boats were only a hundred yards away. Ducking to present a smaller target, he bent down and picked

13

up one of the rifles, taking in the carnage at his feet with a determined expression. He'd spent time on the battlefield years before in the military and was no stranger to death, but the slick blood pooling on the deck was a stark reminder of its reality. The pirates spotted him, and three of the shooters began blasting away at his position. He dropped to the deck next to the dead men and returned fire, and then watched in horror as one of the attackers shouldered an RPG and launched the grenade directly at his position.

The shell went wide, but the blast rocked him, destroying his hearing and blowing a hole in the metal superstructure. He blinked dust out of his eyes and then the pain hit – his leg was bleeding where errant shards of shrapnel had torn through it, leaving a burning mess of mangled flesh and oozing blood in their wake.

He fought to keep the rifle steady as he fired again and again at the approaching boat, and grinned with satisfaction when two more of the assailants slammed backwards from his bullets; and then his expression froze as a row of slugs shredded his torso from his shoulder to his ribcage. The Kalashnikov fell from his grasp as he convulsed in shock. He watched helplessly as another RPG hit the top of the superstructure above him and detonated, blowing all of the communications antennae and radar arrays into the sea and showering the bridge below with a rain of deadly debris.

The first skiff reached the port side of the ship, near the stern, and one of the pirates swung a grappling hook at the end of a knotted cord and let it fly. It clanked against the deck until it found purchase on the steel rim. After a cautionary pull on the rope, the first gunman climbed up the ship's side, followed closely by three more. The second boat repeated the procedure, and two minutes later ten heavily armed pirates stood on the deck, surveying the destruction. One of the men approached the fallen security guards and the mate, and after toeing them and confirming they were dead, confiscated their weapons, sliding one of the pistols into his belt with a leer before passing the remaining guns to his fellow pirates.

The crew stayed inside. Nobody wanted to risk the wrath of an angry boarding party that had sustained casualties by doing anything that could be construed as defiance. A merchant seaman's duties didn't include taking on armed murderers, and not a man among them wanted to join the dead.

When the leader of the pirates reached the bridge, the watchman and the captain were lying amidst the wreckage, bleeding from their noses and ears, the second grenade's detonation having wreaked as much havoc inside as it had above. The pilot's body was a shapeless heap in the far corner, his neck broken, eyes staring sightlessly into eternity. The leader pulled his newly acquired pistol from his waistband and grinned malevolently, and after a quick perusal of the wheel and transmission levers, turned and shot both men in the head.

"Open the engines up, full throttle, and head for land. We should be able to make the cove before dark tonight. We'll drop anchor and then deal with the crew. Maybe they'll be worth something more than the ship, maybe not. Nadif, you take first watch. The rest of you, go gather the crew and search them, then lock them in one of the storage rooms and mount a guard outside the door. I don't want any surprises," he instructed, and his men rushed to obey.

The leader was a different kind of pirate than those who had come before: born in the war-torn south, brutal, vicious, and completely remorseless. While many plying the trade were ex-fishermen or local villagers fallen on desperate times, he was a new breed of professional criminal who had sought out his current vocation for the riches it could bring – and as he'd just proved, he was willing to kill and be killed to achieve his ends.

The big ship increased speed, edging to twenty knots as Nadif set a course for the eastern shore of Somalia – a windswept desert pounded by huge surf and plagued by radiation from the toxic waste that European and Indian firms had been dropping in the coastal sea for years, unhindered by any Somali naval force and unmoved by the blight of disease their deadly refuse left as its legacy leaked out along the poisoned coast. One of the men radioed to the fishing boat and it set a course for land as well, its usefulness for the time being at an end, the fate of its crew uncertain as the reluctant owner negotiated with the pirates for its return.

CHAPTER 3

Ten years ago, Baghdad, Iraq

Rifle fire chattered as fires burned out of control from the battles that had been fought for the last five days between Iraqi forces and invading troops. A pall of black oil smoke hung over the city from wells that had been ignited to hide troop movements, and the fighting raged from street to street as the Coalition forces advanced through the city. The night was a near-constant series of explosions and gunshots as soldiers loyal to Saddam Hussein battled with the invaders in fierce building-to-building fighting. Whole tracts of the city were out of control, with looters running unchecked through the streets as gunfire erupted in sporadic bursts.

Three men wearing civilian clothes, toting American-made M16 rifles, sprinted toward a bunker on the outskirts of the downtown area, Coalition forces only blocks away. The surrounding structures belched fire from the latest bombing runs and occasional stray tank rounds. An Iraqi scooted past with a television on his shoulder, and two young boys followed him carrying stereo components, their faces alight with the excitement that only great adventures can bring.

Two of the men exchanged a grim glance while the leader checked a handheld GPS transmitter, peering at the small backlit display. He pointed two fingers at an entrance on the far side of the large concrete building in front of them.

The leader flipped night vision goggles down over his eyes as they approached the darkened edifice, one of countless official strongholds now abandoned yet still possessing the peculiarly menacing quality that prisons did even decades after closure. The other two men did the same, and the trailing man turned to face the street as the other two edged along the side of the hulking structure, down a dank alley that reeked of human waste and rotting garbage.

At the far end, two oversized iron doors stood bolted shut, the entryway pocked with bullet scars from a skirmish only a few hours earlier as loyalists had moved through the district, doing their best to inflict as much damage as possible on the better-equipped Coalition soldiers. The lead gunman patted his companion's backpack and both stopped, the third man sweeping the vicinity with his rifle, which was equipped with an infrared scope. The distinctive rattle of Russian-made weapons sounded from the near distance, down the street, answered by a barrage from the higher-pitched smaller caliber M4s of the U.S. troops.

"This is it. Ready to get to work, Joseph?" Solomon, the leader, whispered through clenched teeth.

"Let's do it," Joseph replied.

Solomon waited as Joseph reached into the backpack, pulled out an explosive charge in an adhesive pack, and swiftly moved to the door and mounted it in the center, where the bolt would be. He flipped a switch, and a red LED light began blinking, at first every three seconds, then accelerating to one blink per second. Ten blinks later the charge detonated, the doors buckled, and then the right one swung open with a groan.

Two loud explosions sounded from the ongoing battle down the street – grenades – and then the heavy stutter of a large-caliber machine gun joined the fray. After a final look around the alley, the three men ducked into the building. The last pushed the door closed and positioned himself further inside, from where he would be able to defend the entry should anyone try to come in. The other two stopped, looking around, and then Solomon pointed at a stairway descending into the bowels of the building.

They took the stairs cautiously, leading with their weapons, prepared for anything. When they reached the lower level, two stories below the street, Solomon switched on a PDA and stared at a hand-drawn diagram on the dimly lit screen. Pausing to orient himself, he looked down each of the three corridors before choosing the one on the left and pacing off a measured distance. He paused at the fifth door and signaled to Joseph, who was still at the landing. When Joseph approached, his Vibram-soled boots nearly silent on the rough concrete floor, he hesitated as he arrived at the door, and then, after a nod from Solomon, reached out and tried the lever.

Locked, as they'd been told it would be.

Nobody but a few trusted confidants of Saddam Hussein's regime knew what was stored behind any of the doors, and even fewer knew the truth about this one. The construction of the lower levels was more akin to that of a bank vault than a military bunker, the walls six feet of high-density concrete reinforced with several inches of Russian steel plating and enough rebar to be able to sustain direct hits from all but the most advanced "bunker buster" bombs. None of which was evidenced by the recessed steel doors, deliberately anonymous and unassuming.

Their source had given them detailed instructions in return for his life, safe passage out of the country, a new identity, and five million dollars – a paltry sum by his current standards among the Iraqi elite, but the promise of a new life on a beach in Malaysia was more than adequate compensation, considering the circumstances. His captors were waiting for a confirmation call from the incursion team to spirit him away, never to be heard from again – on pain of death.

Joseph shrugged out of the backpack and placed it on the floor. He set to work, first removing a heavy steel case and then another, larger package. He opened the case and removed two glass vials from the form-fitted foam interior, unscrewed the cap of the first one, and poured the contents onto two of the three heavy metal hinges. He repeated the process on the final hinge with the second vial and stabbed a button on his digital stopwatch, waiting patiently. The acid emitted an acrid chemical smoke as it weakened the barrier's structure.

Three minutes later, he opened the pack and removed what resembled long tubes of modeling clay, taking care to form the charges so they would do maximum damage at the hinge joints. They had been warned that the door was deceptively innocuous, and that it would take hours with a torch or a diamond-bit drill to cut through the lock, but the hinges had a possible weakness – one they were about to put to the test.

Stepping back to inspect his work, he next set detonators into the putty and edged down the hall, followed by Solomon. Joseph compressed two foam plugs and jammed them into his ears before holding up a tiny remote trigger and pressing the button.

The charges ignited in a white-hot blaze, and both men squeezed their eyes shut until it had dimmed. Joseph flipped up his night vision goggles and approached the door. He surveyed the damage, and then mounted an explosive charge to the center hinge position, flipped the toggle switch, and trotted back to Solomon, who joined him in a hasty return to the landing, where they could take shelter around the corner.

They could feel the force of the blast when it detonated, and once the concussive wave had passed, both removed flashlights and returned down the hall, which was filled with smoke. The doorway resembled a wall that had taken a direct hit from a tank shell; the door had blown inward off its hinges. Holding their breath, they trained their beams into the dark expanse. Another set of stairs stretched down into the gloom. Solomon nodded before he began descending to their ultimate destination five stories below the Baghdad streets.

The final landing was anticlimactic – just a ten-foot-square area with three more steel doors. An electric keypad glowed, still functioning from the battery backup power they'd been assured would last for up to six months. Solomon reached for the nearest one and entered a series of six digits, reading the PDA screen where the numbers were scrawled in shaky script on the same document as the crude blueprint.

The door opened with a hiss, hydraulics easing it inward, and Solomon shined his flashlight beam inside. A single black Anvil road crate sat on casters in the middle of the small chamber, Cyrillic script emblazoned on its side in white paint, a heavy electrical cable running from its base to a junction box on the far wall. Joseph approached on hesitant feet, then unfastened the two latches on the lid and opened it. Inside were two blue aluminum cases, no more than thirty-six by twenty-four inches, without markings. Both bore strong black nylon straps fastened through sturdy eyelets to make carrying easier, the rugged single center handles being inadequate for transporting their heavy mass for any sort of extended distance. Thin, flat cables were plugged into special sockets near the bases, running from a surge-protected transformer built into the Anvil housing.

Joseph carefully lifted one of the cases from the neoprene-lined road crate and then, as Solomon trained his flashlight beam on it, flipped open the clasps and slowly opened it. Both men stared in silence at the contents for a few moments, and then Joseph softly closed the lid and moved to the next one. After repeating the process, he unplugged the cables and whispered to Solomon.

"Bingo."

When they had removed both from the chamber, Joseph handed Solomon two grenades from his shoulder sack and turned to begin his walk back up the steep stairway. Solomon pulled the pins on both, tossed them into the room, and swung the heavy steel door closed. The six locking bolts engaged with an audible clunk, and he spun and hefted the remaining case as he dropped the night vision goggles back into position for the long climb back to the street.

At ground level, the eerie silence of below was replaced by the dissonant reports of automatic weapons shooting no more than a hundred yards from their position – the Coalition forces were on the move, and Iraqi resistance was giving way. Like the fall of Hitler's Berlin, everyone involved knew that the outcome of the struggle was pre-ordained even as the battle was joined, but there would always be soldiers willing to die for the ephemeral ideas of duty and honor and country. As one set of young men, barely more than boys, charged forward, sacrificing their lives as though the taking of the next block was worth trading for the only time they would ever have on Earth, another set of young men, equally patriotic, defended their native territory with the conviction of the truly righteous – the resulting carnage an oversight of a leadership that hadn't factored in the cost of taking on an army of willing martyrs.

The three men crept out of the building and took a final glance down the narrow passageway to their left, away from the nearest gunfire, and then darted into the night toward the crumbling tenements a few blocks away.

They'd cleared a block when gunfire erupted and bullets pounded into the walls around them. Without breaking stride, two of the three fired efficient bursts at the muzzle flashes in the windows of the nearest buildings, driving the shooters back into the relative shelter of the rooms from which they were firing at anything that moved.

A round struck the pavement a few yards to the side of the third man, and the ricocheting slug gashed his hamstring. He stumbled but then powered on, firing up at the gunman who had wounded him. When he reached the corner of the nearest building he stopped, out of the field of fire. He whistled; his two companions slowed when they heard the distinctive sound and turned to see that he was lagging behind.

"I'm hit," he hissed, as Solomon circled back to check on him.

"Where?"

"Leg."

"How bad?"

"If we had a car, not that bad. But to run out of here? Aghh…!" The wounded man winced as the full extent of the pain hit him.

Solomon reached into the pocket of his cargo pants and retrieved a syringe. He injected half the contents into the wounded man and knelt down to look at the damage. After a few seconds he stood.

"You'll make it, but we need to get you to a vehicle. Let's move another block, and then we'll see what we can find. I'm not going to abandon you here."

"No. Leave me. You know the stakes – this is far too important. I'll be fine. Worst case I'll get three squares in a POW camp for a few months. Get the hell out of here. Now."

Solomon hesitated, and then adjusted his grip on the aluminum case he was carrying and nodded. "Good luck. We'll see each other again soon. I'm sure of it. Keep your head down, and surrender to the first Coalition troops you see. They'll treat you better than your own mother."

"Easy for you to say. And Mother hates me…"

Solomon grinned, but it was forced. "She's not alone. Take care. The shot will keep the pain at bay for awhile."

"I know. Here. Take my credentials and the NV gear," the wounded man said. He fished out a wallet and handed it to Solomon, then pulled the goggles off his head and tossed them to him.

"See you around, tough guy. I'll dispose of these," Solomon said.

"You too." The wounded man hesitated. "If…something happens, let Mom know I love her, would you?"

"Nothing's going to happen, but all right, little brother, I will." Solomon's eyes were sad but hard behind the night vision goggles. "Don't do anything stupid. This isn't our war. Keep quiet, lie low and wait for the inevitable. And shoot any locals who come near you – they'd just as soon cut your throat as give you a sip of water."

"Yeah. I know the drill. Now go. You know what you have to do."

Solomon stood to his full, considerable height, shifted the shoulder strap on the heavy suitcase, turned without looking back, and jogged with a fluid gait away from the battle, his precious cargo now the priority above all others.

CHAPTER 4

Three weeks ago, ten miles south of Eyl, Somalia

A harsh wind blew in from the ocean, shifting *Salome*'s hull around in the cove so that it pointed at the shore like an accusatory finger. Camouflage netting covered the superstructure and most of the deck, except for the area where the pirates gathered near the bow. Korfa, their leader, raised his AK-47 over his head as he addressed his men, who were mostly in their late teens to early twenties and also toting Kalashnikov assault rifles. He had a resonant speaking voice and an air of authority that was undeniable, even among the rabble that were his men. Nobody dared to interrupt him or jeer in the manner typical of their interactions among themselves. They stood listening respectfully as he outlined the progress to date.

"The company negotiator is still insisting on concessions, and has taken the stance that because members of the crew were killed, he's hesitant to negotiate with us."

An angry murmur ran through the group. Korfa held up a hand, commanding silence.

"This is all posturing. They know that the longer they wait to pay, the more likely we are to accept less than our initial demand."

"How much are they offering, sir?" one of the fighters nearest the front, a favorite of Korfa, asked.

"We demanded five million dollars. They countered with one. This has now been going on for over two months, and we're still no closer to collecting. I think that the company has the impression that we'll gladly accept whatever they offer if they wait us out. To which, I say, we must send a message they'll understand."

The men managed a glum cheer, but were far from happy. They'd been expecting their part of a big payday, and each week that dragged on made them increasingly agitated and impatient.

"To that end, I want you to go below and bring up three of the remaining crew members. Any three. I don't care which. Whoever is the sickest or has been the most troublesome. Nadif, I want you to film this.

We'll have our conduit in Mogadishu send the footage to the company and see if that creates urgency. Because I'm tired of waiting for the rich shipping company to decide what price they put on their ship and their crew's lives."

The men cheered again, this time with more enthusiasm, as five of them peeled off and moved to fetch the crew members. Nadif, Korfa's second in command, withdrew an old digital camera from his pack and checked the batteries while they waited.

"I have enough to film for maybe a minute. At most, two."

"That's all we'll need. I don't plan on making any long speeches," Korfa said with a smirk.

The three unfortunates were herded onto the deck, the relentless sun beating down on their pasty skin disorienting them after months in the stinking dark belly of the ship. They looked nothing like the men who'd been aboard when the vessel had been taken. The effects of starvation and abuse had left them little more than walking skeletons, their shambling gait and confused, blinking, unfocused eyes adding to the impression that they were something other than human – alien, nocturnal cave dwellers caught unawares by a hunting party.

Korfa nodded at Nadif and pulled a rusty machete from his belt.

"Tie their hands behind them," he ordered.

One of the pirates trotted to a pile of line and quickly returned, slicing it into sections with his dagger. He tossed two pieces to his mates and then roughly jerked the first crew member's arms behind him and tied his wrists. One of the other crewmen still had some fight in him and resisted, struggling, but was quickly convinced of the error of his ways by a hard slam in the head with the wooden stock of an AK-47. Once all three were bound, Korfa told Nadif to start the camera.

"These men are three of the remaining twelve crew. Several have died in captivity. These men today will die because of your stalling. We told you a week ago that you needed to meet our demands or dire consequences would ensue, so this is on you. Each week you delay, three more will meet the same fate. You were warned. Now, see what your games have brought," Korfa said in his native Somali, confident it would be translated and his meaning made clear.

Korfa approached the first man, who had been knocked to his knees, and without preamble swung the heavy machete blade, chopping through half his neck and eliciting a gushing torrent of blood. He stepped back as the crewman's heart continued to beat for a few seconds, pumping more spray into the sunlight, and then the body fell forward into a growing puddle of crimson. The pirates hoisted their rifles over their heads in triumph, shaking them and dancing impromptu little jigs as Korfa moved to the next wide-eyed man, who closed his eyes and was muttering a prayer when the blade ended his life.

The final crew member glared at the pirate, who now had blood spattered across his face and shirt, his strong arm muscles bulging from his grip on the machete, and then hissed a curse at him before spitting in his face. Korfa grinned again, and with one hand wiped the phlegm from his cheek as the other brought the machete down, this time on the man's clavicle, shattering the bone and slicing six inches into his rib cage. The man screamed in agony as blood poured from the wound. Korfa repeated the blow on the other shoulder, watching impassively as the man shuddered in agony, shock beginning to drain his face of color, but his body still alive even as his life seeped slowly away.

"Untie his hands and throw him overboard. Let him try to swim faster than the sharks," Korfa instructed, and then gestured to Nadif to stop filming.

The men hoisted the dying crewman by his feet, his arms ruined, and dragged him to the side of the ship. One of them severed his bindings and another kicked him in the head, and then three of the pirates pushed him to the edge and over into the water two and a half stories below. Money exchanged hands as the gunmen bet on how long he would last before one of the big marine predators caught his scent and came in for the kill, and for a moment, the men's faces were animated by the game and the ability to wager on its outcome – or rather, the timing of it.

Korfa didn't remain on deck to see who won. He wordlessly signaled to Nadif to follow him, and then retreated to the relative cool of the superstructure.

"Get this to our friend in Mogadishu as soon as possible. I want it sent to the company so they know what it means to trifle with me. And have the blood cleaned up – I don't want to have to deal with the flies."

"Yes, sir. I'll leave immediately. But...no disrespect...isn't it going to increase the odds of the military getting involved? I mean, the countdown to more killings?"

Korfa shook his head, considering whether to strike his subordinate or try to explain his reasoning. He opted to teach rather than punish, so the young man would make similar decisions when the time came.

"As you know, we enjoy a certain protection from the local government, such as it is. We pay well for that, and it ensures that nobody violates the sovereignty of Somali territory – it would be considered an act of war. And as long as we don't broadcast the executions, the company isn't going to want to tell anyone. It would correctly be viewed as their having engaged in brinksmanship with their crew's lives in the balance – all to gain a financial advantage. Tell our contact to make clear that if anyone leaks a word about this to the press or to any government, the entire crew will be butchered the day I find out, and the cargo destroyed, and that I'll make a special point of targeting their ships from here on out. Whereas if they cooperate, I'll give their ships safe passage from our group. The combination of a threat of future reprisals with more bloodshed and a benefit if they comply should keep them quiet. And our negotiating position will have strengthened."

Nadif considered Korfa with new admiration. Besides being ruthless, he was incredibly smart. His strategy was simple and yet foolproof. Any communications with the authorities would result in everyone being killed and the nightmare happening all over again with another of the company's ships. It was brilliant – much more so than the typical demands the simple leaders of other groups issued. This elevated the process to a new, more profitable level, at a time when the effectiveness of piracy had dropped by sixty percent due to the constant coalition naval presence in the region.

Nadif joined Korfa in smiling, and then a cry went up from the pirates on deck.

The first shark had arrived for lunch.

CHAPTER 5

Three weeks ago, Jerusalem, Israel

Four men dressed in expensive business suits watched the video in stunned silence. When it was over they sat back, faces drawn, and the dignified, gray-haired man at the head of the table, Jacob Weinstein, president of ARCA Shipping, leaned into his chair and took a deep breath.

"I thought these pirates always took care of their hostages," he seethed.

"It's true. This appears to be something completely new. They're generally only interested in the money, and they lose their negotiating leverage if they start knocking off the hostages, so it's usually avoided. It's…unprecedented, frankly," David Cohen, VP of Operations, confirmed.

"Something new? They're killing the crew while we dawdle because you felt like it would buy us a lower ransom amount, and when they send us footage of this…butchery, all you can say is that this is something new?" Jacob spat.

"Jacob. We can't anticipate everything these psychos are going to do. This has never happened before. We're just playing the same game every other shipping company has had to play when it happens. It's a cost of doing business, but you don't want to leave any money on the table. We didn't invent this, but we have to do the best we can under the circumstances. It's just bad luck that we ran into the pirate equivalent of Genghis Khan…"

"You heard the translation. He intends to execute another three in" – Jacob consulted his watch – "four more days. I think everyone can agree that we need to do something. They want five million. I say we give them three, and move on."

David shook his head.

"I disagree. If we cave, we can expect that this will become the preferred new approach for the pirates, which will lead to many more casualties over time, and far greater cost. With all due respect, we can't just hand them millions because they went on a rampage. It sends the wrong message."

Jacob pointed at the monitor. "*The wrong message?* Are you not getting this through your head? They're going to kill three more innocent men in five days. What do you think those men would think about parsing 'messages'? What would their families think? Good God, if this gets out…it would be a disaster. Think about the lawsuits. We'd be ruined," he sputtered.

"Gentlemen, I think it's safe to say that this must stay within this room, yes? Could we have a moment here? I'd like to speak with Jacob alone," David said to the other two attendees, who nodded and rose, more than willing to comply. Jacob might be the president, but David ran the company. Jacob was a political gadfly and tremendously powerful – he'd built the network of contacts that had made the company successful over the last thirty years – but it was David who attended to the day-to-day details, and it was David who wielded the real clout.

"Of course, David. I'll just go back to my office. Abner? Some coffee?" the stockier of the pair said.

"Sounds like a good idea. David, Jacob, I just want you to know that whatever you decide, you have my full support. This is a regrettable incident, but we need to keep our eye on the big picture, too," intoned Abner, the Chief Financial Officer. By big picture, he of course meant the purse strings.

Once the two had left, David stood and began to pace.

"This is a more than regrettable debacle. We need to throw them a bone and call it a day," Jacob began.

"I'm not so sure. I'm thinking that's exactly the wrong thing to do. Let's work this through. Seriously. There might be an opportunity in all this," David said thoughtfully. "The ship and the cargo are fully insured, so if we had never heard from the pirates, it would be a write-off. True, our premiums will go through the roof, but they will anyway now, whether we get the ship back or not."

"That's the economic side, David. What about the human cost?"

"Look, you didn't kill those men. These animals are savages. They're doing the unthinkable, no more than common thieves and murderers. I may not have all the answers, but I know it's a bad idea to negotiate with murderers."

"We can't just not pay them, David. Word would spread, and it would be the end of the company, as well as to our personal stakes. The suits would bankrupt everyone. And our reputations…"

"Word won't spread. They aren't going to tell anyone. They can't afford any publicity, or the entire naval group policing the area will come down on them like a ton of bricks, and it will be game over. The coalition naval force would scorch the earth to make an example out of them. So they're not going to talk. Remember, they're the murderers, not us."

"I'm not sure I like the direction you're going, David."

"Hear me out. Even if we coughed up the money, at this point, we would still be subject to an inquiry. People would want to know why we didn't move faster, and whether there was something, *anything*, we could have done. Enter the lawsuits, this time from the families of the crew that have been lost so far. Only it would be worse, because there would be witnesses. The surviving crew."

"So either way, we lose. How the hell did we allow this to get this far out of control, David? Why didn't we just pay them?"

David regarded Jacob impassively, his arms folded. "Calm down and try to see the sense in it all. We have an opportunity here. One that will solve a number of issues for us. Think about Sodom for a moment."

At the mention of Sodom, the code name for something so secret it was never spoken about, all the blood drained from Jacob's face.

"Are you out of your mind? Mentioning…that? What the hell are you thinking? Besides which, you lost me – I'm not following."

David lowered his voice. "Jacob. We have a situation that will ruin everything you've accomplished in your entire life, and could destroy you personally as well. That would destroy both of us. It would also put an end to everything we've worked for, and that your father worked for. That's not acceptable. As regrettable as it is that these crewmen have been put in this position, we can't change that. But we cannot allow this crisis to destroy decades of effort and countless millions of investment in…changing the future. We're too close."

Jacob's eyes narrowed to slits. "What are you saying, David?"

"I'm just thinking out loud. What's been the biggest hurdle on Sod…on the project? What have we been fretting over for the last two years?"

"Viability."

"Exactly. Providence might have just handed us a chance, here. The solution to our problems. I think it's time to convene a Council meeting. The sooner the better."

"The Council?" Jacob whispered the words with reverence. "What does our pirate situation have to do with…with that?"

"Everything," David said, and then he pulled out the chair next to Jacob and sat down, speaking in hushed tones. Explaining.

Ten minutes later Jacob strode from the conference room, feeling both fatigued, and yet, paradoxically and simultaneously, energized. He moved to his palatial corner office with an incredible view of the city and made a call on one of several disposable cell phones he kept locked in his safe.

Within half an hour, he'd reached everyone. Schedules would be rearranged, excuses made, and a location selected based on which of the agreed-upon meeting spots was available.

And then The Council would meet to discuss their problem, and the opportunity David had brought up. There was merit to his logic – this was potentially the chance they'd been waiting for. It remained to be seen whether it truly was, but Jacob felt stronger after hanging up on the last call and dismantling the phone, its parts to be discarded in garbage cans around Jerusalem.

Yes, tomorrow night The Council would meet.

And its decision could change the shape of their world forever.

Jacob sighed as he sat back down in his executive chair and looked out at the waning day, the late afternoon light fading as dusk approached.

Tomorrow, they would meet.

And the Earth would tremble.

In his bones, he felt a tingle of anticipation. Perhaps David was right, and had seen what he'd been too blind – no, too *frightened* – to see for himself.

Perhaps it was finally time.

He would know soon enough.

CHAPTER 6

One week ago, ten miles south of Eyl, Somalia

"They've agreed to our demands," Korfa announced with a triumphant smile. His audience of gunmen went wild, dancing on the deck of the ship, firing their weapons into the air, ululating and yelling primal sounds of joy and victory. He let them continue for a few moments and then raised his hand for silence. Their grins were ear to ear, and the men looked more like jubilant boys than hardened cutthroats.

"When, sir?" Nadif asked, the question that every man was wondering.

"In three days."

"How is it to occur?"

"I gave them coordinates for a drop a few miles from here. A vehicle will be left there with the money in the back. Once the funds have been counted, we'll divide it up and then they'll send in a small crew to pilot the ship to the nearest port for repairs. By which time we'll be long gone."

Another rousing round of cheering erupted from the men, accompanied by more gunfire.

"After all expenses have been calculated and we've paid back our supporters, your shares will be worth a fortune – you will all be wealthy men. And it proves that my approach is a valid one. These industrialists only understand the blade of a knife or the barrel of a gun. Not so different from our brothers, really. They posture, but in the end, they bow to force. I see a bright future ahead of us. Truly, a bright future."

The rest of the afternoon was spent celebrating, the end of a long and arduous campaign finally at hand. Already the men were discussing what they would do with their impossibly large cuts of the take, and what the next project would be. In a country where the average person made no money, and lived off whatever animals they could raise, the prospect of earning tens of thousands of dollars apiece was almost unimaginable. Korfa hadn't burdened them with the knowledge that the total take was actually four million dollars, and that even after restituting his backers, he would pocket half a million himself. All they needed to know was that they were all rich men because of his vision, and he had no doubt that the next mission would bring even higher rewards and a virtually endless stream of candidates eager to follow his lead.

He had executed another three crew members a few days earlier and sent the video on. That had clearly made the difference. Their contact in Mogadishu had reported that within twenty-four hours of receiving it, the shipping company had agreed to the renegotiated number, eager to put an end to the massacre.

Sheep. It didn't matter what country they were based in, all men were the same. When the wolf appeared and demonstrated its willingness to do the unthinkable, the sheep flocked to offer the wolf whatever it wanted in order to leave them safe – for the present. He had learned much growing up in the southern region, where the civil war had broken out over two decades earlier, and his stint first as a child soldier and then as a feared lieutenant for one of the country's most ruthless warlords had taught him everything he needed to know.

After much backslapping and congratulations, Korfa retired to the captain's cabin for a nap, to dream about what he would do with his half million dollars. The sum seemed so abstract; he couldn't imagine that amount of wealth. How many camels was it? Visions of a life elsewhere, a speedboat tethered off the beach from his home, a bevy of comely young women at his beck and call, drifted through his imagination as he made his way to his quarters. If his next few missions were as successful as this one, he could retire a millionaire, the lord of everything he saw. Maybe he would move to Italy, a wondrous place he'd heard glowing stories about from the few remaining immigrants who were left over from when Italy had ruled Somalia.

Yes, a villa off the coast of Italy sounded perfect.

Soon, he would be able to afford it.

❧❧

Four days ago, Mahe, the Seychelles islands

The Cessna Caravan waited on the Mahe airport runway, engine warming up as the pilot went over the last-minute details with the three passengers he'd be ferrying on this trip. Fuel topped off, the plan was to fly to the African mainland, with the estimated travel time just over six hours to reach the Somali coast — allowing for headwinds and any unexpected weather — and then to continue on to Yemen.

Dawn had broken a few minutes earlier, and the passengers had wasted no time loading their gear into the plane. The pilot didn't speak much, nor did the men, which was for the best — all were extremely good at what they did, and had learned not to ask questions. The pilot had no reason to want to know who his passengers were or what they were going to be doing once they were on the ground in Somalia. All he cared about was the large paycheck he was collecting — easily two years' worth of cash, if not more.

"I am Henri, your pilot. So, you are ready?" he asked with a token smile, his French accent coloring his English with a musical lilt.

"Never more," the tallest of the three replied, not returning his smile, his English also accented, but only slightly, and not with French. "You can call me Sol."

"*Bon*, Sol. Then we go, yes?"

Sol nodded and then made for the plane, the pilot following more slowly. He recognized the effortless economy of movement all three shared, but didn't comment on it. The less he knew, the better. He had made a small fortune running discreet flights for a select group of special clients, in addition to his air tour business, and this wasn't the first time he had received unusual instructions that weren't strictly legal. Then again, a man had to do what he could to make his way in the world, and legality changed from country to country and depending on what day it was, so what did he care of the rules men arbitrarily imposed upon one another? None of it much mattered at twelve thousand feet — they all looked like ants once at a certain altitude, going about their busy chores, scuttling across their domains with single-minded determination. Flying above it all had given him a certain perspective many earthbound mortals couldn't appreciate, which enabled him to take delicate jobs without any qualms – as long as the money was sufficient.

At forty-nine, Henri Jacquot had seen much in his life, first as a member of the elite French Foreign Legion, later as a jack-of-all-trades entrepreneur plying his skills in Africa, where the siren song of boundless treasures to be had for men of grit – and the paucity of rules – appealed to his free-spirited nature. As a natural part of his orientation, he had gravitated toward jobs that involved considerable risk to offset their outsized rewards, and over the last twenty years had been involved in too many questionable operations to count. Whether flying blood diamonds north or arms south, Henri was a survivor, and one of his great skills was the ability to forget what he needed to, virtually instantly.

The plane taxied to the end of the runway and he paused, waiting for clearance from the tower. When it came he pushed the throttle forward, and before they were halfway down its length he was pulling up into the clear sky, only an occasional white cloud floating in the seemingly endless blue. He climbed to a cruising altitude of ten thousand feet, and once he had leveled off, engaged the autopilot, the engine droning its familiar purr as the passengers gazed out the windows with uninterested expressions. He settled into his seat and shifted, trying to get comfortable, his bones feeling old on days that began like this, and adjusted the headset to better monitor any radio chatter.

When the Somali coast loomed like an endless brown smudge on the horizon, Henri turned from the controls and called out to the men.

"Hey. We're going to be there in a few minutes. Up and at 'em, *non*?"

Three faces stared back at him blankly, and then the men began going through a routine familiar to Henri – the sorts of things men who killed for a living had been doing for as long as that vocation had existed.

They began their descent, Henri plotting the course according to the GPS coordinates he'd been given, and within another ten minutes they were dropping into a desert wasteland, all sand and barren emptiness save for an occasional desiccated stream bed. The plane bucked as it was buffeted by thermal updrafts from the rising heat of the arid land, tossing it around as if it was being swatted by a bored deity's hand.

The Cessna lined up on the road, if a dirt track could be described as such, and then set down on a wide stretch, dust billowing behind as its wheels skidded along the hard-packed sandy soil. Once Henri had slowed to a taxi speed he continued until he came to a wash where two vehicles sat parked in an adjacent flat area – an ancient Toyota SUV, at one time in its existence white, but now more rust than anything else – and a seventies-era Datsun pickup truck.

Henri pointed the plane at an empty spot near the cars and eased the Cessna to a stop. Behind him in the cabin the passengers were already moving, passing out assault rifles and pistols from one of the oversized rucksacks they'd brought aboard. Under normal circumstances that would have been alarming to any pilot, but this was Africa, and Henri was open-minded. He didn't bat an eye when the youngest of the three swung the fuselage door open, rifle in hand, looking like he was going to war.

The men leapt out of the plane and waved at the three Somalis standing by the vehicles, also toting Kalashnikov AK-47s – the ubiquitous accessory for any well-dressed local – who waved back and beckoned them to approach. Sol went to greet the welcoming committee while the other two opened the cargo hold and dragged a large green canvas pack out of the Cessna's belly, placing it carefully on the ground next to the door.

After a brief exchange, two of the rail-thin Somalis moved to the plane to help the new arrivals with the heavy cargo, and the four of them lifted it into the rear of the Toyota. Sol nodded, and the two natives climbed into the Datsun truck bed while the driver ambled to the front cab and slipped behind the wheel. Sol and his companions squeezed into the Toyota with their silent Somali driver, and a few moments later both engines roared to life in a cloud of blue smoke and pulled onto the road that traced the outline of the coast, headed north.

Ten miles later the little convoy slowed, and Sol consulted a handheld GPS. He turned and murmured to the driver, and the vehicles rolled to a halt as they reached the rendezvous point. Sol squinted at the harsh terrain, his eyes roving over the surroundings – he could just make out the ocean in the distance, maybe two miles away over a slight rise created by sand and wind, but desolate, like everything they'd seen up to that point.

Satisfied there were no obvious threats, he checked his watch and issued a few brief instructions to his companions. After grabbing their rifles, the pair quickly exited and moved to the rear of the vehicle where the pack was nestled.

At Sol's prompting, the driver got out with him and headed toward the pickup truck, a hot gust blowing sand across the road, no sound marring the windswept tranquility of the landscape but that of the open desert and the burble of the truck motor. As they approached, the Somalis in the truck bed opened an old cooler and fished out bottles of water, their weapons resting easily in their laps, their dark skin seemingly impervious to the sun beating down. A few minutes passed, and then Sol's men approached from the Toyota, walking slowly in the heat.

"Let's get the hell out of here," the younger one said, eyeing the horizon before exchanging glances with Sol. The two Somalis in the bed shifted over, making room, and everyone clambered aboard for the bouncing ride back to the plane.

When the truck returned to the Cessna, Henri stepped from the wing's shade and wiped sweat from his face, eyeing Sol behind the wheel, only his two men sitting in the truck bed.

"Where are the lads?" he asked as they hopped out, all three covered in a fine layer of tan dust.

"They decided to walk," Sol said, his expression neutral. "Let's get going."

Henri took the cue — it was none of his business. The men boarded the plane, stowing their weapons in the now empty cargo hold, and then took their seats in the sweltering interior.

Henri cranked the engine over and it roared to life, and he coaxed the Caravan onto the dirt track. He fought to keep it under control as it bounced along, picking up speed, and when he saw a long, relatively straight stretch he firewalled the throttle, the sudden torque pushing everyone back in their seats. The big motor revved up effortlessly and soon they were airborne, the ravaged, drought-plagued Somali coast disappearing beneath the wings as Henri made a long, slow bank over land and then pointed the nose toward Yemen as they became a solitary dot in the lonely sky.

CHAPTER 7

Korfa watched through binoculars as the truck drove away, leaving the Toyota unattended at the agreed-upon spot a kilometer away. He waited a few minutes, scanning the road with the glasses, and then lowered them and turned to Nadif, who was waiting next to him with three of his most dependable gunmen.

"Come on. They're gone. Let's go get our money," Korfa said, rising from his position behind a large rolling dune. The small group began trotting toward the waiting SUV, and in fifteen minutes they were at the vehicle, eyeing it suspiciously. Korfa gestured to the rear compartment, and Nadif moved to the cargo door and swung it wide.

The men's eyes widened when they saw the rucksack in the back. Nadif stepped back, making room for Korfa, who took hold of the bag and unzipped it, pausing for a few moments as he eyed the contents before closing it back up. He shrugged off his backpack and ferreted around in it before extracting a device that had arrived the prior day from Mogadishu, along with instructions for its operation. Taking his time, he powered it on and then moved it slowly over the bag, watching the dial intently, and then stood back and methodically went over the entire vehicle. Satisfied, he switched the scope off and handed it to Nadif with a nod.

"It's clean as far as I can tell. Are the keys in the ignition?" he asked.

Nadif hurried to the driver's door and opened it. "Yes."

"Start the engine," Korfa ordered as he edged away from the vehicle. Nadif's brow furrowed, and then he nodded and hopped behind the wheel as Korfa continued to distance himself from the truck, his assault rifle held loosely by his side.

The motor rumbled to life and everyone visibly relaxed. Korfa strode to the SUV and climbed into the passenger seat, while the three remaining men squeezed into the rear.

"Get us back to the ship. I feel exposed out here. We'll count the money, and assuming it's all there, we'll clear out by this evening," Korfa commanded, raising the glasses to his eyes once more as they bounced over the ruts and beat a trail across the dunes to the sea. He never stopped sweeping the horizon, on the alert for any trickery.

Their Mogadishu contact had provided the gizmo he'd assured Korfa would catch any transmitter or locator chip, but he knew nothing of these things, even after being coached to watch the lights and the meter, and was inherently distrustful of technology. This was the largest ransom he'd ever collected, and his experience had taught him that nothing worth having ever came easily.

The heavy SUV crossed the blighted expanse at a crawl, and took half an hour to reach the ship, anchored in the shelter of the large cove. Half the men were onshore, waiting, and when they saw the Toyota they began whooping, jubilant, the tension of the long standoff finally dissipated.

The old vehicle stopped at the shore and Korfa got out, followed by Nadif and his men. As the others gathered around, Korfa and Nadif moved to the rear of the truck and watched as the pirates hoisted the rucksack between two of them.

"Come. Let's get the bag to the ship. We'll count it and then I'll radio for the others to bring the trucks," Korfa said. Once the money was verified, on Korfa's orders transportation would be dispatched from the village of Eyl, and then the pirates would disappear, the surviving crew turned loose to fend for themselves while they waited for their ordeal to finally end.

The men cheered again as their compatriots lifted the sack over their heads, carrying it like a holy relic to the shore and the waiting skiffs. Korfa grinned as he saw the excitement in their eyes – this was the kind of take that would be legendary, and his name would be whispered in hushed reverence for years to come.

He supervised the passage to the boats, reveling in his moment of triumph while keeping his expression somber. All the men boarded and the outboard motors revved as they cut across the natural harbor to the ship, looming in the water in silent witness.

Nadif had the two men carry the money to the captain's cabin, where a cash counting machine sat waiting on the table. He and Korfa ducked into the room with the money while the two trusted gunmen framed the doorway, guarding the quarters as their leader went about his joyful task.

In the Toyota's tire compartment, a red LED under the floor cover blinked for five seconds, and then switched to green.

The detonation vaporized the vehicle in a white-hot blast, and in a nanosecond the searing explosion spread, enveloping the ship and everything around the truck for half a mile. The distinctive shape of the mushroom cloud would have been wondrous to behold if anyone had lived to see it, but that wasn't to be – everything in the vicinity was immediately killed, metal melting from the searing heat, the ship blown out of the water like a child's toy by a chain-reaction that for a brief moment approached the temperature of the surface of the sun.

❧

The men in the Cessna saw the fireball in the far distance as the explosion shot skyward, visible even though they were already sixty miles away. Henri's eyes betrayed a flicker of shock as he craned his neck, and then he drew a controlled breath and focused on concealing his reaction. A hint of a smile tugged at the corners of Sol's mouth, and he removed a satellite phone from the bag next to him and entered a number. A voice answered after a few seconds and he whispered several words in a foreign tongue, then switched the phone off and turned to look at the three packs stowed in the rear of the plane.

"How long until we're over the Gulf of Aden?" he asked Henri, moving to the front of the plane, grabbing the seats for support as the craft bounced through a patch of turbulent air.

"No more than half an hour and we'll be over water. Why?"

Sol retrieved a slip of paper from his breast pocket and handed it to him. "Change of plans. Head to this point. We're going to make a little detour on the way to Yemen. My boys and I will be saying goodbye before we get over land again."

Henri nodded warily and entered the coordinates into his GPS. "That's northwest of our flight route."

"Correct. Just fly the plane. Drop down to a few hundred feet above the terrain so we don't get picked up by any of the longer-range radars."

"You're the boss. But there aren't any in these parts — at least not around here."

"Humor me. Hug the ground until we're over the water. Once we get closer to the coordinates, we'll ascend to where we can safely do a low-altitude jump. Have you ever done this before?"

The pilot grinned humorlessly. "There's not much I haven't done."

"That's what we were told. What's our time till we're in position?"

Henri consulted the GPS and performed a quick mental calculation. "Hour and a half, maybe an hour forty-five."

"Good." Sol reached over and jerked the headset cable out of the radio. "If you don't mind, I'd just as soon not have any communication."

"What about if we're pinged by one of the naval vessels?"

The passenger took the seat behind Henri as they began their descent. "Let's hope we aren't."

❧

An aide pushed through the doors of the conference room and cleared his throat, staring at the balding man seated at the head of the table. As chief of the Middle East division of the CIA, he wasn't unaccustomed to being pulled out of meetings for one crisis or another, but by the look on the underling's face, whatever had happened warranted serious and immediate attention.

"Gentlemen, would you excuse me for a minute? I'll be right back," he said to the assembled men, rising and making his way for the door before anyone had a chance to comment.

"What is it, Jackson?" he barked once the door had closed behind him.

"This is big, sir. NSA just informed me that a nuclear detonation occurred on the coast of Somalia twenty minutes ago."

"What? Are you serious? Jesus. Somalia? What the hell…"

"Exactly, sir. It got picked up on satellite, and there's no mistake. The signature is definitive."

"Who the hell would nuke Somalia?" he asked, almost to himself.

"Unknown at this time, sir. What's odd is the size of the blast. Preliminary estimates are that it's in the five kiloton range."

"That…that's small. I mean, really small…"

"Yes, sir." The aide was waiting for instructions.

"Call a crisis meeting in conference room C. I want everything we can get on the explosion, real-time feeds, the works. See if they can reposition a satellite so we can get visual. Do we know anything else besides it was a small nuke? Where in Somalia did it go off?"

"That's the weirdest part, sir. It's the middle of nowhere, on the coast. There's literally nothing there. Closest town, if you can call it that, is eleven miles away — far outside the blast zone. Although there could be small amounts of fallout depending on the wind direction. But there's nothing strategic there. Not that there is anywhere in Somalia. But still. It's the ass end of the planet, literally."

"So you're saying that someone nuked a bunch of goats and scrub...?"

"I know. It doesn't make much sense, sir. Unless it was some kind of a test..."

"Get everyone into the conference room. I'll be in shortly."

❧

News of the explosion reverberated through the world's intelligence communities, including those most proximate to the blast in the Middle East. Reaction was immediate as regimes in the region raised their alert levels to high, but after a few hours more questions remained than answers. Why had the first use of a nuclear weapon outside of a known test and those dropped on Japan during the Second World War been on a remote stretch of African coast — and who had detonated it?

❧

Sol patted his two companions on the head and swung the door of the Cessna open, the plane having slowed to nearly stall speed, barely sixty miles per hour. It was holding level at a thousand feet, flying toward Yemen, and there was nothing in plain view other than a dot in the water in the distance — a super-yacht steaming toward the Red Sea.

"All right, gentlemen. Bombs away," he yelled, and the two waiting men hurled themselves out into space, their parachute packs securely cinched for the low-level drop. Sol returned to the front of the plane and flipped the toggle on the explosive pack sitting by Henri, his head lolling to the side at an impossible angle, and after a final glance at the autopilot and the bomb timer, he edged to the open door and pushed himself out into the open sky. He waited two seconds before pulling the ripcord; the chute deployed and the harness bit into his thighs and chest, and then he got his canopy under control and steered himself toward the others, already well on their way to the waiting yacht that had slowed for their rendezvous.

CHAPTER 8

Present day, Moscow, Russian Federation

The contingent of soldiers stiffened to ramrod attention as two uniformed officers strode down the long hall to the ornate wooden double doors; both men bore insignia identifying them as generals in the Russian army. The taller of the two stopped and knocked, rapping twice, and the pair waited silently as footsteps sounded against the polished granite floor in the interior chamber.

The right-hand door swung wide and a thin man with severely cropped silver hair, wearing a dark gray suit and round steel-rimmed spectacles, offered them a permanent expression of a man who'd just swallowed something repellent as he stared at them for several seconds before motioning for them to enter.

"Generals. Right this way. The minister will see you now," he said in a sandpaper voice, nodding to another doorway at the far end of the reception area. Moments later they were marching into the office of the second most powerful man in the Russian Federation – Alek Sureyev – who was sitting behind a desk the size of an aircraft carrier, with two morose-looking men seated in front of it.

"Generals Esina, Malerov. You know our colleague from the GRU – Tomkin, and from the FSB...Grigorovich?" Sureyev asked, not so much a question as a statement. Both generals understood that the presence of both the FSB, the *Federal'naya sluzhba bezopasnosti Rossiyskoy Federatsii* – the successor agency to the KGB, and the GRU, the *Glavnoye Razvedyvatel'noye Upravleniye* – the military intelligence agency, spelled huge trouble. To see the heads of the two rival groups sitting in the same office was more than disconcerting – it was unprecedented.

"Yes, of course," confirmed Malerov, the older of the two generals.

"Good. Then, please. Take a seat. We have much ground we need to cover." Sureyev paused, waiting for the officers to take the proffered chairs, and then resumed the ongoing discussion he'd been having with the GRU and FSB men.

"The implications of the explosion are not good. Already questions are being raised about where the device could have come from. I don't need to remind everyone of the possible consequences, do I?"

"No. Which is why this has always been a concern. It does not take a genius to figure out that whoever got their hands on the devices did not do so because they wanted to collect hazardous waste. We have followed up on every lead to surface since the invasion, but they have all turned into dead ends," Grigorovich said. "There were rumors that the Iraqi regime had acquired them from the black market, but this was pure speculation. I think it is safe to say that if there were any WMDs in Iraq, we would have heard about it by now. God knows the Americans turned over every cursed rock in the place."

"May I point out that there is nothing implicating the Army in any wrongdoing here?" General Esina interrupted. "It's not as if we sold suitcase nukes to anybody."

"Nobody is pointing fingers. We are trying to understand how two nuclear weapons can disappear without a trace, so we know what we are up against. Because make no mistake – if the Somali detonation was one of ours, it will eventually come out. And, heaven forbid, if it was a Russian-manufactured device, and there is another one floating around to be used in some sort of a terrorist attack, it *will* ultimately be traced back to us, and then, regardless of what explanation we offer, there will be a backlash like nothing you've ever seen," Sureyev warned with a scowl.

"Are we sure about how many are...unaccounted for?" Malerov asked.

"Two. There can be no doubt," Sureyev snapped.

The GRU man nodded assent. "We hoped that by now they wouldn't be usable. The devices needed to be kept under power, and the components used and the battery backups were...primitive. All our experts assured us that at this point they were no longer a threat. I think it is safe to say, based on yesterday's detonation, that assessment was, mmm, overly optimistic, at best."

"Just how long have we known about this?" Esina asked.

"We have been aware of the missing units for two decades. But that is not the issue at this point. What matters is that we are finally sure – after the Army, the GRU, and the FSB wasted massive amounts of time pointing fingers and stating categorically that the danger was long past – that one of the devices was used, albeit for unknown purposes," Sureyev said, glaring at all four men. "But now that one has exploded, there can be no higher priority than locating the final missing device. We can run for cover and insist that we are not behind this, and considering the strange detonation site, that point is plausible; but further denials will not be accepted if the other one is used on a populated target. All that anyone will care about is that the bomb originally came from Russia. Which makes it your problem. All of you. Let us not forget that we are still living down the Litvinenko poisoning. The world does not trust us, and this would give it every reason to justify that stance."

"My people tell me that all of the units have been inoperable for years. The batteries dead, beyond salvaging, and many of the parts degraded to the point of obsolescence," Grigorovich said.

"True," Tomkin said. "But with the right kind of expertise, alternatives have obviously been found. Technology has come a long way since the mid-eighties. In light of yesterday's event, we have to assume that someone was able to fashion a workaround."

"How difficult would it be to retrofit one?" Esina asked.

"That is debatable," Tomkin said. "Let's just say that it is more than achievable. I think we can agree that this isn't theoretical any longer. A skilled technician with the right equipment and expertise could arm one. Fundamentally, the technology is not really so complicated. It is a relatively straightforward device."

"But limited, correct? Five kilotons?" Malerov asked.

"A third of the size of Hiroshima," Tomkin said.

"Not so large, then," Esina observed. "More effective to achieve shock and awe than total destruction."

"Depends on who you ask, I would say," Sureyev remarked, his tone icy. "Imagine one being detonated in Vatican City. Or downtown London. Or Moscow. Never mind the initial fireball and blast damage – consider the radiation and psychological effect as well. Does anyone want to argue that would not be an unparalleled disaster?"

"No question it would be…problematic," General Esina conceded.

Everyone fell silent.

Eventually, Tomkin shook his head. "It would be big enough," the GRU man said quietly.

Sureyev shifted and then leaned forward, glaring across the desk. "We need to track it down. You are here to tell me where and how we must begin. It is not as though we can just shrug our shoulders and wait for the other one to go off. What steps can be implemented, immediately, to locate it?" he demanded.

Twenty minutes later the only thing the gathering had agreed on was that the situation was potentially catastrophic, and could not only bring down the regime, but cause global chaos.

Suitcase nukes – portable tactical nuclear weapons – had been dismissed by the western media as a non-issue, a red herring, the stuff of overactive imaginations, largely due to a sustained public relations campaign by the Russian government stemming from the discovery of the missing devices in the early nineties. But now that one had exploded, all that expensive spin would quickly count for nothing, and the first country everyone would suspect would be Russia – for very good reason.

During the Cold War, the Soviet Union had built dozens of the portable nuclear devices and shipped them into the field, so-called "suitcase nukes" because they were compact and weighed only sixty pounds. The instructions had been clear – if war broke out, the devices were to be detonated near strategic targets, the obliteration of which would materially disrupt the U.S.'s ability to fight. The same had been done with a variety of biological warfare agents, to be dumped into the nation's rivers and reservoirs.

When the Soviet Union had started coming apart in the late 1980s, the units were recalled from not only Europe and the U.S., but also the satellite countries where they had been deployed for use against the civilian populations in the case of widespread rebellion. But two had failed to materialize – the pair that had been in the Ukraine. The base where they had been stored had been presumed impenetrable, but as the regime lost its grip on the region, larceny had resulted in a security breach the likes of which had never been encountered before.

When the smoke cleared, the devices were deemed missing without a trace, leaving the deteriorating Soviet administration without a clue as to who might have taken them. Originally, it was suspected that the new Ukrainian government had secreted them away to be used as a bargaining chip; but after a multi-year investigation, that was deemed a dead end. For Russia, it was every nuclear-equipped government's worst-case scenario, but one that had faded over time as the usable life expectancy had expired. Until now.

Esina and Malerov exited the meeting with considerably less spring in their steps than when they'd entered, and as they stalked from the minister's offices, both men had scowls on their faces that would have been enough to send their subordinates running for cover. One thing was obvious as they emerged into the cold gray light of late morning, pausing on the steps of the Kremlin, eyeing the soldiers in the light snow standing rigid as statues in their dress uniforms.

Their lives had just changed dramatically, and they'd now devote every waking moment of their existence to locating the missing bomb – or die trying.

CHAPTER 9

Present day, Tucson, Arizona

The freeway exit resembled countless others Jet and Matt had passed during their marathon drive from Washington, D.C., but the Explorer needed gas and they were near enough to their stopping point in Tucson to justify pulling off the road and finding a hotel for the night. Tomorrow would have them crossing into Mexico, and then, with any luck at all, driving to the first airport and catching a flight to Mexico City, from where they could get to Uruguay so Jet could finally reunite with Hannah and put the entire ordeal of the last weeks behind her.

It was already dark, the sky clear as only the high desert night can be, the twinkling tapestry of stars breathtaking and immediate. They filled the SUV with gas and drove down the frontage road that paralleled the freeway until they came to a two-story strip motel that looked no worse than anything else they'd passed.

"This'll do. How are you feeling? Up for some dinner?" Matt asked, eyeing the dreary stucco façade and anonymous styling as they pulled into a parking slot near the office.

"Sure. I'll tell you what, being cooped up in this rattlebox is already getting old. Let's get a couple of rooms and then see if there's a downtown where we can stretch our legs a little while we find a restaurant," she said.

"Sounds like a plan. I'll go book the digs. Be back in a second."

Jet watched as Matt strode to the office, which she could see through its picture window was filled with glossy brochures and factory-manufactured art exuding plastic cheer. She closed her eyes. Only another day or two and she'd be back with her daughter Hannah, finally able to begin her new life. But one completely different than the one she'd envisioned a week ago, when Alan had been alive and everything had seemed possible. How quickly things could change, she mused – in the blink of an eye she'd lost him. And then Matt, whom she'd believed dead, had suddenly reappeared...

She'd spent much of the last forty-eight hours thinking about that abrupt reversal in her fortunes. There had always been a powerful attraction between herself and Matt, but she'd presumed him dead in Thailand; and then Alan had entered her life and everything had gotten complicated.

A few minutes later Matt swung the glass office door open and stepped outside. She studied his face as he approached – strong jaw, definitely handsome, but shopworn in an interesting way – the face of a man who had lived, who had spent time outdoors, and who had seen joy as well as horror. But most of all, right now, a man who looked tired, with several days' growth of stubble and a preoccupied air, the sort of daze usually seen on passengers disembarking from transatlantic flights. They could definitely use a little rest. Neither had slept much the night before, and their driving day had begun at dawn.

"*Voilà*. You have the honeymoon suite. Hot tub in the bedroom, pink champagne on ice..." He opened the door and handed her a room key. "Ground floor. Number eighteen. I'm in twenty-two."

"Champagne? More like one of those vibrating bed things that costs a quarter, by the looks of this place," Jet said.

"Don't knock those. I once went through five dollars before I figured out it wasn't a slot machine. My teeth are still loose from the experience."

She smiled and peered past him at the motel. "How long do you need before we go for dinner?"

"Maybe half an hour? I really want to take a shower," Matt said, moving to the rear of the truck and opening the cargo door. "That work for you?"

"You bet," Jet said, and hopped out of the passenger seat to join him. She grabbed her overnight bag and shouldered it. "Which way?"

"Down at the far end, looks like."

"Did you get any dining recommendations?"

"There's an area downtown that has a bunch of southwestern places. That seems to be the draw here."

"Southwestern?"

"Expensive Mexican."

"Ah. Enchiladas with attitude."

"Exactly. Twenty-dollar mango margaritas with almost no tequila in them."

"Sounds heavenly..."

They found their rooms, and Jet collapsed onto the bed before forcing herself back upright and into the bathroom. After a long hot shower she felt more human, and she took her time, enjoying not being in a headlong rush for once. Washington and all the killing seemed a million miles away now, and even though they'd only left two days earlier it could have been an eternity – part of another life, a chapter thankfully closed for good.

As she towel-dried her hair, her thoughts lingered on Matt. He'd just naturally accompanied her. It had never even really been an option to go their separate ways again after the assault on Arthur's compound…and Alan's death. Ostensibly, he was going with her to recover his diamonds, but they both knew that there was more to it than that. At least they had time, now, with no deadlines or pressure. Time to explore the energy that crackled between them whenever they were close…

She knocked on his door, her hair still damp, and he greeted her, barefoot, wearing jeans and a dark blue button-up silk shirt with a stylized martini glass and brand name boldly embroidered on the back. Very American, she thought fleetingly as he welcomed her in.

"I'll just be a minute," he said, gesturing to the two chairs by the window.

"No problem. So…do they pay you to advertise stuff on your clothes?"

He laughed, his face lighting up at the unexpected question. "No, but now that you mention it, they should. These things actually cost more because of the design…"

"The American consumer is never short of things to spend his money on, is he?"

"More the global consumer, nowadays. But yes, it's amusing that we've had to invent ways to spend a hundred fifty bucks on a ten-dollar shirt. I'm told it's good for the economy, though," Matt said, sliding his shoes on.

She noted he had shaved, and again remarked to herself that he was a good-looking man. "Then why does the economy suck?"

"I haven't bought enough shirts, I guess."

"Selfish bastard, aren't you?"

"You don't know the half of it. This is a knockoff I got in Thailand."

Jet held his gaze and they both smiled at the same time. "What's for dinner? You going to keep starving me?" she asked.

"After the mastodon steak in Dallas, I'd have thought you'd sworn off food for a month."

"Nonsense. I'm just getting started. Got to keep my strength up."

"Excellent. I figured we could head downtown, park, and walk around till we see something promising."

"Lead the way. I've got all my stuff locked in the room safe. You have money?"

Matt patted his pants. "Big wad of green so I can show the lady a good time."

"Now you're talking."

They spent twenty minutes strolling along the sidewalks with the other evening pedestrians, ambling with no particular destination in the balmy night air, the temperature perfect. Eventually Jet took Matt's arm and pulled him toward an upscale restaurant with a Mexican courtyard theme, and in moments they were at a cozy table near one of the oversized windows, surrounded by well-heeled diners. Music seeped softly from hidden speakers, a sultry melody with a crooning male singer just loud enough to embellish the backdrop of chatting patrons. After studying the menu for a few minutes, they made their selections and settled back into their seats.

"So *mañana*, huh? We're headed down Mexico way? Kind of exciting, don't you think?" Matt asked.

"I'll never be happier than when we're across the border. Let's just say I don't have particularly fond memories of the U.S."

"No, I don't expect you would after the last week. Frankly, I've been away for so long that it seems more of a foreign country to me than Thailand. I guess you acclimate to whatever you're around, and that becomes your norm..."

"That has to be weird for you. I mean, this place is so...big. Everything's big. Big roads, big cars, big malls, big portions, and big people. Almost the polar opposite of Thailand."

"Yes, and everything is clean, have you noticed? We're obsessed with hygiene. Most everywhere we've stopped has been spotless by Thai standards."

"By Mexican standards, too. Wait till you cross the border. Have you ever been?" Jet asked.

The waitress arrived with their drinks and deposited them before turning to take another order at one of the tables across from them.

"Years ago. At least twenty."

"Wow."

"You probably hadn't been born yet."

"Tell me what it was like back then. Did they have electricity? Did everyone ride horses? Were you raised in a mud hut?" Jet teased, taking a sip of her drink – something red with a fruity name.

"It was primitive. People listened to music on these disks called CDs, and the former vice president still hadn't invented the internet, so people still talked to each other. And cell phones were becoming a big deal – but they didn't do anything but call other phones. It was like living in caves," Matt explained.

"Wow. Had they invented Viagra yet?"

"They were dark times, young lady," he intoned solemnly, taking a pull on his artisanal beer. "No joking matter. There was no reality TV, and it could take hours to get a message to someone. You would actually have to write something and put it on a scanner and then send it across phone lines using a primitive device called a fax machine."

"I think I saw one of those in a museum, next to the stone axes."

They were interrupted by an elaborately coiffed server carrying their meals, which he placed on the table with a flourish before automatically asking whether they would like anything else. Jet shook her head and the young man threw her a wan smile and then sashayed away to care for other diners.

"It's kind of funny, isn't it? I mean no matter where we are in the world now, technology is there. Even in the jungles of Laos or Myanmar, you'll see a smuggler with an iPod," Matt said, taking a taste of his chicken. "Wow. This is pretty good."

"And there's a lot of it, I see. Do they make the chickens here lift weights or something? That looks like a turkey breast in cheese sauce. It's the size of your head," Jet said, then took a bite of her soft taco.

Dinner passed with agreeable banter, Jet and Matt enjoying each other's company, already easy together, as if he hadn't just reappeared from the dead after many months of absence. When the bill came, he paid it and then they strolled down the street, Jet clasping his arm, as naturally as if they'd been an item for years.

"I called Hannah earlier. Everything's fine. I told Magdalena I'd be back soon. She seemed relieved," Jet said as they watched ostentatious luxury cars glide by, tinted windows safeguarding the occupants' anonymity.

"I would be. Everyone's been through a lot. Ferry explosions, attacks, manhunts…it'll be good to get home, won't it?"

"It'll be good to get back to Hannah. But home? I'm not sure where that is anymore. We can't stay in Uruguay. We'll need to move someplace else and start over again."

"You keep mentioning Argentina. I heard there were pretty dramatic economic problems there," Matt said.

"There are. But if you have money, it's a great place to live. It would just suck to have to try to earn a living or run a business."

"Ah. Which you don't have to do."

"Exactly."

"And is it safe?"

"Depends on where. Mendoza is incredible, from what I've seen, and seems extremely quiet. Maybe not Buenos Aires – there's a lot of poverty, and it's a massive city. I suppose that's more like asking if New York or Paris is safe – it would depend on what part."

The ride to the motel was short, the evening traffic light, and they sat side by side in silence, tired after the cross-country jaunt. When they arrived, Matt walked Jet to her room and then hesitated. Jet stood on her tiptoes and kissed him, her full lips soft and yielding, and the moment stretched into a minute before they pulled apart.

"Good night, Matt. Sleep well," she said, and then unlocked her door.

He wasn't going to press the point. There was no rush, and it wasn't the right time. "You too. See you bright and early."

Jet listened to the sound of his footsteps echo off the walkway, and then his door closed with a finality that made a small part of her sad. She moved to the dresser and slipped out of her clothes, changing into an oversized T-shirt, and then padded to the bathroom to brush her teeth. She felt exhausted, the hours, meal and the drink all seeming to hit at once, and minutes later she was on the bed, the lights out, the only sound the muted purr of the air conditioner and the distant rumble of traffic on the freeway.

CHAPTER 10

Jet awoke with a start, something in the room's atmosphere different, triggering an unconscious alarm. Her pulse rocketed as she sensed a presence by the door – she wasn't alone. A soft scrape sounded from near the window, and she threw herself at the barely discernible shape of the intruder, hearing him grunt with surprise as she went from being fast asleep to an attacking wildcat in under a second.

A muffled cry met her elbow's connecting with a face, and she was rewarded by a gush of warm blood from his crushed nose. She was just about to follow the strike up with another using the heel of her hand – a fatal blow – when her entire body went into convulsions and her legs buckled, her limbs refusing to obey the commands her brain was sending.

She hit the carpeted floor and her vision dimmed, the room's darkness replaced by a starburst of exploding synapses, and then the lamp on the night table next to the bed illuminated as sensation returned slowly to her body. A man wearing dark slacks and a black windbreaker leaned against the wall by the window holding his face, blood streaming down his arm from his brutalized nose, and another stood by the side of the bed, a stun gun in his hand.

"Don't try anything, or I'll shock you again," the man with the stun gun said.

Panic greeted his warning, and it took a moment in her disoriented state to register why his words caused such a strong reaction. He regarded her, lying on the floor, and nodded as understanding registered on her face.

"Okay, you can get up, but don't attack us. We're not here to hurt you," he assured her, taking in her expression as she groped for support from the side of the bed, trying to move.

Jet slowly got to her feet and stood, legs apart, defiant, glaring at her assailants.

"Why is the Mossad sending agents to break into my room?" she asked, hating the tremor in her voice and the sudden wave of nausea that threatened to overwhelm her. The Hebrew sounded thick on her tongue, the words fuzzy and unfamiliar.

"Ah, good – you know who we are. The answer is very simple. Someone needs to talk to you. Somebody important."

Jet glanced at the agent whose nose she'd broken. "Get a towel from the bathroom. Put pressure on it and hold your head back. You know the routine," she said, her voice sounding stronger to her own ears as she recovered from the jolt. She returned her attention to the other agent as she pulled the stun gun barb from her shirt and tossed it onto the bed. "You could have knocked."

He smiled humorlessly and secured the weapon, then walked over to the small circular table by the television and took a seat. "I'm sure you would have answered. *Knock knock. Who's there?* Yes, I can see that playing out well." He gestured to her, inviting her to join him, but she sat on the edge of the bed instead.

"So you're here. I'm listening. What do you want?"

The other man returned from the bathroom and stood in the doorway with a towel pressed against his face, his head back.

"I have a phone in my pocket. My orders are to get your attention and then place a call. I would say we have your attention, no?"

"You're partner is lucky he's still alive," she said, her tone flat.

"Yes, well, probably. But that's neither here nor there," he replied, reaching into his coat and extracting a cell phone. He jabbed at one of the speed dial digits and then, after listening for a moment, handed it to her. She leaned forward and snatched it from him, eyeing him warily, and then listened as a deep male voice spoke.

"I trust they didn't hurt you?" it asked in Hebrew.

"I think they got the worst of it."

"Hmm. I have no doubt." The voice paused, hesitating. "Do I need to tell you who this is?"

"Let's make it official, shall we?"

"Very well. This is the director."

"What do you want?"

"A good question from the start. I have a situation, and I require an operative with your unique skill set."

"Run a classified ad. I don't work for you anymore."

"Yes, that's right. You're dead. It's hard to keep that straight sometimes." He cleared his throat. "I wouldn't have reached out to you if it wasn't a dire situation. If there was anyone else…well, with Rain dead, I'm afraid I don't have anyone left who possesses your level of expertise. He was the last of the select few. I'm sorry, by the way. I was told that you were with him."

"You know about...about that?"

"You'll find I know about most things, young lady."

"How?" The word was like a slap.

"I have eyes everywhere."

"Then you know that I'm out of the game, forever, and...disappearing," she said softly. "Again."

"I wish I could allow you to do that. Believe me. But I'm afraid it's not that simple. As I said, there's a situation..."

"And as I said, I no longer work for you."

"May I remind you of the oath you took?" The director's voice hardened.

"I remember it. But you got your money's worth, and then some. We're even."

"That's not how it works."

"It is with me."

The director sighed, sounding tired, and tried a different approach. "Have you seen the news?"

"What? No. Why?"

"If you watch it, you'll see that the biggest breaking story right now is the detonation of a nuclear device in Somalia. It happened yesterday."

"A nuke? Somalia? Why? What's in Somalia, and why do you care? And why should I?"

"That, my dear, is a long story. The short version is that I believe it's only one of a pair of devices. The second one is still out there."

Jet took a few moments to process that. "Fair enough. But why do you care about an explosion in Africa?"

"Now we're at the essence of why I need your help. If I'm correct, that was a test. To verify that the devices still worked. It's not like you can just set off a nuke these days and say, 'excuse me, my bad.' I believe that test confirmed viability, and that the second one will be used sooner rather than later. And not on a remote stretch of coastline nobody cares about."

She nodded as the scenario sank in. "You think that they intend to use it...in Israel?"

Jet could hear the director's heavy breathing as he formulated his response.

"It's more complicated than that." And then he told her a story. He went on for five minutes, without interruption, and when he spoke the final words, her entire world had shifted.

Both Jet and the director sat silently for a few moments, the faint buzz of static on the encrypted line hanging like the pause before a guilty verdict.

"What do you need me to do?" she asked, afraid she already knew the answer.

"Isn't it obvious? You need to find them and stop this."

Her eyes darted to the man sitting at the table, who was studiously examining his nails, doing his best to appear deaf and dumb.

"And if I refuse?"

"There are some things you cannot refuse, my dear. As you know, by this point in your life."

"What's your proposal?"

"You help me, and I forget you exist. You go on to lead whatever life you were hoping to, and we're even."

"What if I say no and then kill your men, and then disappear forever?"

"Do you really believe that would be possible now? I know you're alive. I discovered it only a short while ago, when we began surveillance of Rain in Washington. It took a while for us to place the face – there are no records to speak of. But some of us have long memories. Still, I shared your opinion – you'd done enough, paid your dues. Then Rain was killed, and this situation developed. It forced my hand. I have no other option."

"You could send someone else."

"Like the two you see there? Please – don't waste my time. The team no longer exists. I don't have access to resources like that at present – it would take years to rebuild it, to train, to find candidates that can successfully graduate and survive their trials by fire. My problem is time. I don't have any. And I need to solve this problem now, or it will mean the end of the world as we know it. Was I unclear on the stakes?" the director growled, his voice an ominous rumble. "Do you not understand what will happen if this isn't stopped?"

"How did you find me?" she asked quietly.

"A tracker on the car. We had trackers on yours and Rain's, and when this man met with you at your hotel, we tagged his as well."

"How did you find Ala – Rain?"

"He called from an internet phone. That left an IP address we could trace. From there, we were able to track his identification – I'm sure he believed that not all of his IDs were known to us, but he was wrong. Again, there is very little I don't know."

"If that's the case, then where are the...where are the men who are causing you this problem?"

"Ah, another good question. We have suspicions, but nothing concrete. I'm working on that as we speak. Look, let's not play any longer. I need you to do one last mission. For the sake of your country. For the innocents who will be slaughtered in the war to follow if this device is detonated as I believe it will be. You can name your price. I don't really care at this point. But I cannot accept a no."

Jet thought about his words, and then sighed to herself. "There is no cost beyond my freedom at the end of the mission. You will forget I ever existed, and our business will be concluded. That's the price. No exceptions. But I don't need to tell you that if you're even half right, there's no guarantee of success, and you'll need to provide a full support group for logistics and surveillance." She let that sink in, then shifted on the bed and looked over at the standing man, his nose now clotted. She raised an eyebrow and got up, went to the TV, and tuned to a news channel. After muting the volume, she moved to the dresser, pulled on a pair of sweat pants, and returned to her position on the bed, lifting the cell to her ear like it was radioactive.

"So what's your plan?"

CHAPTER 11

When Matt knocked on Jet's motel room door the following morning, bearing two cups of coffee on a makeshift tray with a bag of fast-food croissants, he was immediately struck with a sense of unease when she opened it, wordlessly standing back for him to enter, and then turned to continue what she was doing inside.

"Good morning, sunshine. Are you ready to hit the road?" he asked, setting the food and coffee on the table and taking a seat.

"Yes and no. Have you seen the news?" she asked as she packed the last of her things into her bag.

"No. Why? Are we on there?"

"No, but...I had visitors last night."

"Visitors?"

"Yes. In the middle of the night. Former colleagues of mine." She went on to tell him the story.

"I...I'm really not sure what to say. Obviously we need to switch cars..."

"I don't think that'll be necessary. I've...I've given the situation a lot of thought. They wouldn't have tracked me down if they weren't in a bind."

"So they're in a bind. It happens."

She finished packing and fixed him with a frank gaze. "I've got to do this, Matt. I don't have any choice. They really need my help, and time's running out even as we sit here." She moved to the table and sat across from him, then pried off the plastic lid from the coffee and took a long, appreciative sip.

"You don't *have* to do this at all. You can walk away. They can't force you." Matt's tone was strained.

"Well, that's debatable."

"I think you need to take some deep breaths and think this through."

Jet looked around the room. She took his hands in hers and gave them a reassuring squeeze.

"Matt, I spent most of my adult life in the service. This is the biggest threat I've ever heard of. They've come to me looking for help, and I can't just say no. Frankly, based on how it was described, they may be right that I'm their best chance of stopping it in time." She saw the look in his eyes and shook her head. "I can see your brain churning away at this. Don't. It's a mission, I've accepted it, and that's that. It's not your concern." She stood and went to her bag. "So come on. Time to move. Getting out of the country is still the same issue. Once we're in Mexico, I'll have more options. We both will…"

Matt stood, obviously struggling with an internal debate, then grabbed the croissants and his coffee. "I suppose there's no point in arguing, is there?" he asked.

"Not really."

"Do you need any help with the bag?"

"No, I'm good. Let's get going. I have a feeling it's going to be a really long day."

Matt turned in their room keys at the office and returned to stow her carry-on in the back of the Explorer next to his. In a few minutes they were motoring along Highway Ten on the way to the intersection that would take them south to Nogales and then into Mexico. Neither spoke as the endless procession of malls and industrial buildings flashed by. Matt finally broke the uncomfortable silence.

"So where are we going?" he asked, his voice normal again as he kept his eyes on the road.

"Mexico. We'll hop a flight to Mexico City, and split up from there."

"Split up? Whoa. I thought we were sticking together."

"That was before. And we *will* stick together. Just not until I go keep the Middle East safe for another generation. Or at least safer." Jet studied his profile, his jaw muscles clenching. "Matt, I need to do this alone."

"No, you *want* to do it alone. There's no reason I couldn't help you."

"I…I appreciate it. I really do. But there are a million reasons you can't help."

"Try me. Remember I've got at least a decade, maybe more, of operational experience on you."

RUSSELL BLAKE

She appraised him, her expression neutral. "Oh, right. I keep forgetting what a hard ass you are. Okay, let's start with some obvious questions. Do you speak Hebrew?"

He hesitated. "No."

"How about Arabic?"

"Not that, either. But I speak a mean Thai, and some of the regional dialects…"

"Which is all good for the area of the world you were in. But it wouldn't do squat where I've got to go. Matt, you no speakee, and you're a poster boy for white guys. Is why this isn't a great idea starting to sink in? Why you'd be more of a liability than an asset?" She deliberately softened her tone so the message wouldn't seem as harsh, but she needn't have bothered. The words had the effect of a slap.

"That's it? That's your whole pitch? You're going to try to confuse me with facts and logic? What the hell kind of strategy is that?"

"Look, this isn't a dig against you, and it's not a reflection of your tradecraft or your skills. But this is a different operating theater. This is my back yard. You would stick out like a sore thumb, and I can't afford that. Besides which, I honestly work better alone. It seems like whenever I have a partner–"

"They wind up dead," Matt finished for her.

"It's true. First David on the Grigenko incursion, then Rob in Thailand, and finally, Alan. I don't like my recent track record, and frankly, I'd rather not lose the only man in my life," she concluded in a quiet voice, almost inaudible over the road noise.

"You're trying to protect me? *Me?* A guy who spent forever living in the wilds of one of the most dangerous places on the planet? *You* need to shield *me* from danger?"

"Have you been listening to anything I've said? It's about my odds, not about you. I'm safer, and my chances of pulling this off are much higher, if I work alone." She took a sip of the coffee she'd been gripping with white knuckles. "This isn't a democracy, and you don't have a vote in it, Matt. I'm sorry, and I don't mean to ruffle your feathers, and I really appreciate your offer to help, but this is one of those times where there's nothing you can do except let me go do what I do best. I'm sorry, but that's the truth." She drew a long breath. "There's no point arguing about it. I need to leave."

He paused as he changed lanes. "What about Hannah?"

60

"That's below the belt, Matt."

"No it isn't. It's a fair question. You're a mother now, not a super agent, and you have a responsibility to her. You deliberately opted out of the covert life for that reason, and now you're going to jump back in?"

Jet stared into the distance for several seconds before turning to face him. "You're right, Matt. And under any other circumstances, it wouldn't even be a question. But this is big. Way bigger than anything that's ever threatened Israel. I don't like that I'm the one who has to risk my life to stop it, but that's the way it's played out, and there's nothing I can do about it. So Hannah will have to stay with Magdalena for another week or so while I deal with this. There's no other way. God knows I wish there was." She took a final pull on her coffee and thrust the cup into the holder. "The situation is terrible, no matter how I slice it."

More silence, the anxiety in the air palpable. After another mile Jet inched closer to Matt and took his hand.

"Matt, I lost you once, on Koh Samui. I don't plan to do that again. Just be patient for a little longer. I know you don't like this. I don't either."

He seemed to relax with her touch, but his eyes never left the road. "I just don't trust them. Any of them. All governments lie and cheat and steal, convincing themselves that they have to for the good of their populations. And intelligence agencies are the worst of the worst. Maybe it's just my bias, but it always seems very one-sided. You need to sacrifice everything, possibly even your life, so that some mission or objective can be accomplished. From what you've told me, that's probably what's driving whoever has the bomb, too. It's always an ends-justifies-the-means thing, and it always involves the faithful dying to advance someone's agenda. I don't see any congressmen volunteering to spend a month on patrol to save the life of a soldier, and I don't see any clerics strapping bombs to themselves to bring terror to the masses. It's always you who has to sacrifice, not them. This is just more of the same." He shook his head in frustration.

"Hey, Mister Bitter, lighten up, huh? I'm a big girl. I know that they're all a bunch of conniving weasels. But if a nuke goes off in a populated area, much less a big city, even the most cynical can figure out that's going to be bad all around. If it was anything else, I'd have refused, and they could spend the rest of their lives trying to find me. I'm no neophyte. I get it.

Now, is there some reason you're driving like a grandma? Do you want me to drive?"

"Hey, I'm doing the speed limit."

"I think we just got passed by a woman in a wheelchair."

They both chuckled, and the tension seemed to defuse. Matt wasn't a stupid man, and given his history, Jet could understand his feelings. And he wasn't wrong – but there wasn't anything she could do about it. Fidgety, she stabbed the radio on, stopping at a Mexican music station out of Tucson.

"It just seems like every time we get a chance to spend some quality time together…something happens," he groused.

"I didn't get blown up on the beach. Let's just remember that, shall we?"

"Good point. But it still sucks, as you're so fond of saying."

"You don't see me arguing, do you?" She reached for the volume, turning it down. "What are you going to do, since we're not going to Uruguay yet? You going to stay in Mexico City until I get done? This is your big chance to travel, see the world as a single man. No ball and chain to drag around…"

"I hadn't thought about it, but now that you mention it, I might want to go get some of my diamonds out of the vault in Bangkok so I have some mad money for the foreseeable future. Because you know how I cherish my lavish lifestyle."

"Then it's off to Thailand?" Jet asked.

"Seeing as I'm not going to get an invitation for an all-expenses-paid junket to wherever the hell you're off to. It's either that or hang out in Mexico, and that doesn't really have much appeal for me. Do you know where you're headed?"

"We agreed I'd go to Israel first, via Spain, and then they'll brief me once I'm there."

"And you're completely sure this is what you want to do…?"

Jet exhaled noisily and released his hand. "Oh, Matt, no, in fact there's nothing I'd rather do less. I wanted to be reunited with my daughter and start looking for a new home somewhere, spend some serious time hanging out with men who are too old for me, and maybe develop a drinking problem or start collecting cats. But that isn't going to happen yet, is it? Instead I'll be headed to a part of the world I thought I'd left forever and put myself into harm's way. Did I mention this completely sucks?"

"Stop." He turned to her and grinned. "You had me at cats."

Her musical laughter filled the car as they rolled down the road, their future uncertain and their pasts racing to catch up with them, and soon he was joining in, an easy sound that for all its mirth contained a hint of melancholy neither of them could deny.

CHAPTER 12

Mexico City airport thrived on a kind of controlled mayhem – the busiest hub in Latin America processing more travelers per day than most American big city airports during peak season. The trip from Nogales through Hermosillo had been smooth, if longer than either of them would have liked. They'd stashed the Explorer in a lot on the Mexican side of the border and taken a cab to the Nogales airport, and then a commuter prop plane to Hermosillo before the final leg to Mexico City.

Jet and Matt found the ticketing area and booked their respective flights, he on KLM to Amsterdam and then on to Bangkok, she on Iberia to Madrid and ultimately, Tel Aviv. His plane would leave first, in just a few hours, so they found a restaurant and ordered dinner, then spent the entirety of it trying not to discuss the elephant in the room. Eventually the server brought the bill, and Matt paid as they lingered over their coffee.

"Any idea how long this will take?" he asked, eyeing her over the rim as he took a sip.

"You sound like Magdalena."

"How did that go?"

"She was relieved to hear from me, but not happy about my not returning like I had told her I would. I assured her it would probably only be a week, and she seemed mollified. Apparently the big manhunt down there has petered out and other headlines are occupying the news. Didn't take long. She doesn't feel like she's in any jeopardy, so for now, she's fine," Jet said, but to her ear it sounded like she was trying to convince herself.

"You really believe it'll be a week?"

"I'm hopeful. The director made it abundantly clear that this is a fast-track operation and that time is of the essence."

"Help me understand it better. This group has a…device, the twin of the one detonated in Somalia…and, what else?"

"He said that the weapons were removed from Iraq during the invasion. By Mossad agents who were inserted during the battle for Baghdad for that purpose – or rather, he *believes* the devices were removed by them, and that they'd kept quiet about locating them. All three men on the team wound up leaving the service within a year or so after the mission, which was reported as a failure, with nothing found. But now, it appears the operatives weren't entirely truthful, and for whatever reason, kept the find to themselves."

"So Saddam actually did have nukes?"

"Apparently so. The intel we got was that he grabbed them during the Kuwait invasion back in 1990. Kuwait purchased them from an ex-Russian KGB colonel who ran a smuggling operation, among other things. Typical Russian mob stuff. Of course, it also might have been the Russian government selling them the devices through the back door, using a deniable cutout. Hard to tell with the way things go over there. Be that as it may, the intelligence suggested that the Iraqis got two Russian suitcase nukes before leaving Kuwait and had them secreted in a bunker somewhere in Baghdad, under heavy guard, in a top secret location. It came from a reliable source – a former party official and confidant of Saddam's who was negotiating for his life."

Matt's eyes roved over the other diners as he fished some peso notes from his pocket and slid them under his saucer.

"Wait. Ex-Mossad agents have been sitting on Russian bombs they stole from Iraq, who in turn stole them from Kuwait, who had them for unknown purposes...and now are nuking Somali scrub? Come again?"

"They don't have all the pieces yet, but there have been rumors for years of an ultra-conservative group of very powerful Israelis who believe that the country has lost its way and needs to be more aggressive. A clique that makes the hawks there seem mild in their views. About eight years ago, rumors started surfacing about that group having established a dirty-tricks arm – a black-ops division, if you will. Again, we're dealing with snippets of information and very vague, low-level scuttlebutt. But if that's the case, and if they're working with the ex-Mossad agents, and if they have the Russian nukes, well, you can see where it becomes frightening pretty quickly."

"What's the objective? I mean, I get that nukes are bad. And in any rogue organization's hands, disastrous. But what would a bunch of ultra-conservatives want with nukes?"

"That's a big question mark. The prevailing fear is that they'll decide to take out a regime they feel is a threat to their interests. That's the most obvious. Iran comes to mind. There are certainly others. Can you imagine what would happen if a nuke went off in Tehran? It would be a game-changer. Everyone knows that Israel is the only nuclear-equipped nation in the region. So that's where the blame would fall, and it would be catastrophic."

"Where are these ex-Mossad operatives located? Do they have any leads?"

"That's one of the problems. Nobody seems to know."

"Great. You're walking into a snake pit of hypotheticals, with no hard answers, and you're in charge of stopping Armageddon. Tell me there's a good part to this. Because otherwise, it sounds like you're in deep shit, and I better start looking for real estate as far from the Middle East as possible. Like maybe Antarctica. Am I missing anything?"

Jet shook her head. "No, that's about right. The hope is that by the time I get to Israel they'll have made some progress and we'll have a trail to follow. Right now, it's all theoretical, based on hearsay and innuendo."

"I wouldn't pick today to quit drinking."

"If I actually boozed much I'd probably increase my intake by gallons. I know the situation stinks. But it's the one I've been thrown into." Jet checked her watch and pushed back from the table. "Looks like it's that time. You need to get to your gate. Tell you what, big boy, I'll walk you there."

Matt nodded. They'd tried to stretch their remaining hours together and make them last as long as possible, but reality had now reared its ugly head and there was no getting around it. They would soon again be parted, with Jet having been thrown from one crisis directly into another with hardly enough time to catch her breath.

They rose, and Matt extended his hand to her. Jet took it and they slowly made their way down the stairs from the restaurant to the departure level, where a quick glance at the flight information directed them to the KLM gate, filled with travelers waiting to board. Matt had taken Jet's advice and booked a first class seat, and in a few minutes they were calling his cabin.

She threw her arms around his neck and kissed him, her soft lips hungry to consume every bit of him she could get, both oblivious to their surroundings or the watching passengers. When the attendant's abrasive voice screeched from the public address system for a second time requesting all first class passengers, it was like being doused with cold water, and they reluctantly tore away from each other, Matt taking a long moment to lose himself in Jet's glistening emerald gaze.

"Be careful. You're not bulletproof or invisible, you know," he whispered as she pulled close to him again, nuzzling his neck.

"Says you. Stay away from the ping pong clubs. You could lose an eye."

"Good counsel," he said. "Don't take any unnecessary risks. Remember that your primary job now is to get through this safe so we can pick up where we're leaving off."

She kissed him again; and then the moment was over and he was walking purposefully toward the jetway, an anonymous businessman on his way to Europe, like countless other unremarkable road warriors waiting their turn to get on the plane. She watched as he disappeared, and then without looking back, turned and made her way to her gate, with two more hours to kill on the ground and nothing to occupy her time but her conflicted thoughts and the still-tingling memory of their final parting kiss.

CHAPTER 13

Twenty-two hours later, Jet's flight touched down at Ben Gurion International Airport in Israel. As the big jet lumbered to the gate, she stretched her arms over her head and took a last swallow of water, hoping to stave off the worst of the dehydration that was a by-product of prolonged air travel. Once off the plane, she was met by two stern men who whisked her through immigrations and customs without requiring that she do anything but smile, and then handed her off to a waiting black Mercedes sedan with windows tinted so dark that she couldn't make out the driver's shape from outside.

The car wove its way onto the freeway and then toward downtown Tel Aviv. Once in the city it pulled into a massive skyscraper's underground parking garage and deposited her at the elevators, where two more somber agents waited, their earbuds betraying their purpose. One of the agents wordlessly took her travel bag and indicated that she should enter the waiting elevator and the pair followed her in, the one with her bag punching the button for the twentieth floor.

The seconds ticked by as they ascended the tower, and then the door opened with a ping. Jet stepped into a large lobby – the colorful logo emblazoned across the front of the reception desk announcing it as the headquarters of an import company, though she noted it was staffed entirely by men and women with the distinctive air of operatives. One of her escorts nodded toward the offices behind the receptionist's station, and they walked back to a conference room at the far end of the suite. The agent opened the door and handed Jet her travel bag before stepping back and speaking his first and only words to her.

"Inside. He's expecting you."

Jet nodded and entered the room, which offered a panoramic view of the Mediterranean Sea through an oversized picture window. The door closed behind her and a figure beckoned from the far end of a large conference table.

"Come. Sit over here. Don't be shy – I won't bite."

The speaker was an older man, late sixties, perhaps early seventies, with a crown of tight, steel-gray curls framing a long, heavily-wrinkled face, decades of stress and impossible decisions carved into it with indelible creases that gave him the appearance of a beleaguered Shar Pei. Only his hazel eyes, dancing with a keen intelligence from behind heavy black-rimmed glasses atop his aquiline nose, hinted at the unstoppable intellect and strength of will that permeated the room like a physical force.

"Please. Sit. I trust your flight wasn't too taxing," he said, his voice deep and gravelly, worn by countless crises and a two-pack-a-day cigarette habit.

Jet took a seat and swiveled to face him. "Well, here I am."

"Yes, indeed. I won't bother to thank you for coming, seeing as it wasn't entirely voluntary, but I want you to know that I do appreciate it."

"What's done is done. Have you made any progress with the situation since we last spoke?"

"Regrettably, nothing concrete. But I'll update you on what's transpired, and how we're planning to move forward. Feel free to interrupt whenever you have a question. Would you like something to drink? Water?"

"No, thank you."

The director leaned back in his chair. "Our people have confirmed that the bomb that went off in Somalia was of Russian manufacture. I won't bore you with how. The Russians are of course denying it vehemently, but that's to be expected, and nobody believes them. For our purposes, it's unimportant, other than that it confirms what we've suspected, or rather, feared, for some time: The two Russian RA-115 devices that we were told were in Iraqi hands have finally surfaced, and contrary to all the expert opinion, are functional – or at least one was, which means we need to assume the other is as well. That they could still be a danger was considered an impossibility; but as luck would have it, the rumors of their inoperability turned out to be misguided wishful thinking."

"Which leaves you with one more nuke floating around," Jet said, her tone flat.

"Exactly. I suppose the only good news is that it's not in the hands of Al-Qaeda or Hamas."

"But you don't seem relieved."

"No. Because the organization we believe has it is ultimately just as dangerous, if not more so. Have you ever heard of The Council?"

"No."

"They're a shadow group of very wealthy, very powerful ultra-nationalists, who have a political ideology that's incompatible with the real world. We've heard rumblings about their existence for twenty years, and frankly had put it in the same category as the Illuminati or the Templars. It turns out that was also wishful thinking. I won't belabor how we got from point A to where we are today, but the group is very real, and we believe they've joined forces with the three operatives who were sent into Iraq to find the weapons, but who claimed to have come out empty-handed. Except we now believe that was a lie. We're convinced that they located the nukes and got them out during the chaos of the invasion."

"But that was a decade ago. Why would they have waited until now to detonate one, and why in the most desolate stretch of coast in the world?"

"All we have is conjecture, but we think there must have been technical hurdles to be surmounted to render the bombs operable. They were built in the mid-eighties, so they're relatively primitive by contemporary standards. Crude. But the radioactive material – the uranium – hasn't lost its capacity to create a chain reaction, so we're really talking the wiring – the brain and the power – that would have been the problem. The basic guts of it aren't particularly sophisticated: An explosive charge propels the uranium bullet at the uranium target, and when they collide, well, boom. Conceptually it's simple. But the devil's in the details."

"And you think that they've somehow either rehabbed or changed the computer or whatever it is so that it's now viable."

"Exactly. Our experts say it could be done, though it might take years; and if there were false starts trying to locate components that can't exactly be bought at the local electronics store…anyway, the how isn't so important at this point. More so is the why."

"And the who. Tell me about these men. These operatives."

The director pushed three files across the desk to her. She opened the top one, and found herself looking at a photograph of a handsome dark-haired man with strong features, in his late twenties.

"That's Solomon Horowitz. He's the older of the two brothers. Sixteen months older, to be precise. The younger one is Peter. Both in the service for six years at the point they were sent into Iraq. Their entire dossiers are there, although the photos are a decade old, so they are unlikely to look the same. You can study their backgrounds at your leisure. The third man, Joseph Aloni, was in the same class as Peter. But he went on to specialize in explosives, including arcane devices, which is why he was part of the team we sent in."

"But I thought the Mossad didn't recruit family members?" Jet interjected.

"We stopped after these two left the Mossad. That's not important for your purposes. They were part of us – and we sent them into Iraq to find the nukes."

"And they came out, reported that they never found anything, and then…?"

"The younger of the two brothers turned in his resignation six months later. Their father had just died, so it wasn't completely unexpected. His death hit them both very hard, according to their colleagues. Four months later, Solomon quit – said it was time to move on to something else. He expressed interest in traveling."

"And you just let them go?"

"This wasn't like our experiment with your team. That was a special case. If an operative really wants to leave, we aren't going to force them to stay. There's no point. If they've lost the stomach for it, they're more dangerous to us remaining in the service than leaving."

"Apparently not always," Jet said, then bit her tongue as the director glowered. She may have resented him dragging her back into the fray, but he was a figure who commanded respect. Who had earned it, just as she had, through years of demanding duty.

"I'll let that slide. The third operative, Joseph, departed thirteen months after the Iraq assignment. Then all three of them dropped completely off the radar."

"How is that possible, in Israel? It's a small place. Everyone knows everyone else's business. How do you just disappear?"

"Under normal circumstances you'd be right. But nothing about any of this is normal. You see, all three men left Israel, and as far as we know, haven't been back. It's probable that they're using aliases and different passports, or we would still have a good idea of their whereabouts."

"Almost like they'd planned to go dark for some time."

"Exactly. We now believe that whatever scheme they concocted to abscond with the nukes was hatched before they ever left for Iraq. So it was premeditated. And required considerable planning."

"And resources."

"Yes. And that's where we believe The Council came in. Money is nothing to that group. Which is speculative; but if accurate, explains how three young men can disappear, with nuclear weapons, and stay invisible for a decade."

"What about motive? Money?"

"That's one of the big questions. Certainly, in my experience, money makes the mare run. But it could go deeper than that. One of Solomon's closer friends was interviewed when alarms sounded after they disappeared, and he mentioned that Solomon was staunchly conservative in his political views – which, given his career choice, wasn't viewed as a negative. Only we now believe that we missed a warning sign. Upon closer examination, there are hints that he wasn't just conservative, but radically so. He apparently felt that we weren't doing nearly enough to stamp out the terrorism that's been plaguing the nation for years. His friend said that he once mentioned that he thought we should take a scorched earth policy, and recognize that this was a war to the death. Those were the exact words he used. At the time, that wasn't viewed as zealotry so much as the sort of patriotism we would want. Perhaps a little simplistic and hyperbolic, but young men need big ideas to sustain them when they're being asked to sacrifice everything…"

"I remember."

"That's right. I keep forgetting how much of this must seem familiar."

"What about tracking the nukes? Don't they emit some kind of radioactivity?" Jet asked, moving past the why question to more practical concerns. When all was said and done, it didn't really matter why a suicide bomber detonated his vest in a crowd – it just mattered that he did.

"Negative. They would be shielded. If these are anything like the other designs we've studied, there's a lead sheath, and the case might also be lead-lined. That's part of their weight. The lead, and of course, the uranium."

"And you haven't come close to locating any of the three former operatives."

"Correct. It's as though they evaporated." The director paused. "Except for one possible sighting in Genoa recently, which ended with the surveillance team butchered. We had picked up some promising chatter, but the operation ended in disaster. Long story short, it was inconclusive, and we wound up with nothing but what you see here."

Jet thought about the magnitude of the problem as she read through the files, taking her time, absorbing the details for future reference. "Both devices are in the same kiloton range?"

"Yes. Roughly five. I could take you through the physics of the fireball versus the air blast versus the radiation radius, but suffice it to say that anything human out in the open within at least a kilometer will be killed. Worse, if it's detonated in the air above a target. A small plane with a warhead could cause almost twice the damage as a ground-level strike."

"Do you think that's a legitimate possibility?" Jet asked.

"At this point, anything's possible. But I think the better question is what the likely target will be."

Jet closed the files and pushed them aside. "You've given some thought to that, or have a lead, correct?"

"I wish you were right about the lead. All we have are guesses. None of which are positive. Iran. Syria. Any of a half dozen terrorist groups. Most of our neighbors, when it comes down to it, depending on how radical these men's ideologies have become. A holy place. Or a false flag attack on a location in Israel. It's a question of how twisted their logic is, and what they hope to accomplish. I would hope none of those, but from where I'm sitting, hope isn't a very good strategy, is it?"

"Not really. Imagine the fallout if a nuke were to go off someplace like Mecca. It would be a never-ending holy war. Nobody would care that these were fringe lunatics. That they were Israeli would be all anyone would ever remember."

"And any denials would be meaningless. Yes, we've considered the worst-case scenarios, and they're more horrifying than any sane person could contemplate."

"But the members of this Council – are you saying that they're insane? Who are they, anyway? Any ideas?"

"Not insane. Not in the way you or I would think of it. But reckless and fanatical, and willing to jeopardize world peace to attain their goals. Which is just as bad. Maybe worse." The director ran a hand over his leathery face and fixed Jet with a cold stare, his eyes unblinking. "At this point our chances of locating the three former operatives are almost nil. Which leaves us with The Council – and the one man we're almost sure is a member. If we can penetrate its ranks, then our hope is that we can learn where the bomb is. That's all we have."

Jet returned his gaze. "How do you do that?"

He smiled for the first time since the meeting began, more of a grimace than anything, a humorless and cold thing that tugged his skin in unfamiliar ways.

"You were always the best of the team members. I remember reading the reports. The smartest. Fearless, effective, but also brilliant. They broke the mold…"

The director flattering Jet disturbed her more than any threat or blackmail attempt would, and yet a small kernel inside her glowed from the unexpected praise. Apparently she hadn't completely separated herself from the life – all of her self-talk notwithstanding.

"I'm listening. And the clock's ticking."

"Indeed it is," he acknowledged, and then told her how he intended to infiltrate the ranks of the secretive Council – an organization that was little more than a whisper in the halls of power. By the time he was finished, she was nodding.

It could work.

CHAPTER 14

"Sir, there are two men here to see you." Jacob's secretary's carefully modulated voice sounded tense – uncharacteristic for her, even under the most difficult of circumstances.

He set his pen down and stared at the intercom speaker. "Men to see me? I don't have anything on my book. Who are they?"

"They're from the government, sir."

"The government? Tell them to make an appointment like everyone else. I'm busy."

"They're very insistent."

"They can be as insistent as they like. If they want to speak with someone without an appointment, point them to Howard. That's why we have a corporate counsel in the first place."

"Sir, I think you may want to speak with them. This doesn't seem like any sort of routine visit. They're quite adamant that it's a matter of the highest priority."

Jacob paused, a small tickle of anxiety quivering in his stomach. "Fine. Show them to conference room B. I'll be in shortly. And see if you can find David," he snapped, and stabbed the intercom off.

He was a powerful man, accustomed to having his will obeyed, and he didn't take the intrusion well. Whatever this pair wanted, he'd make them rue the day that they had shown up and tried to bully their way into his offices. He'd come too far to be afraid of any bureaucrats, but he'd also learned that it was better to play nice sometimes than to come in with guns blazing.

With a final glance at the document he had been poring over he stood, then straightened his tie and donned his hand-tailored navy blue suit jacket, appreciating the perfect fit as he always did when he wore it. Jacob traveled to Hong Kong once a year to get ten new suits made by his favorite tailor – a modest luxury for one of the wealthiest men in Israel, but one that never failed to give him a blush of satisfaction.

He stalked from his suite to the conference rooms. B was decorated in dark wooden panels and adorned with centuries-old oil paintings, creating an imposing aura steeped in tradition and big money; a room that spoke of mega-wealth and importance. When he swung the door open, he was greeted by two hard-looking unsmiling men wearing drab gray suits, seated at the opulent oval table. Both regarded him like he'd stolen their wallets, and the pulse of unease in his gut became a snare drum roll.

"Gentlemen. I'm Jacob Weinstein. You want to speak to me?"

"Mr. Weinstein. Sit down." The words of the older one were an order, not a suggestion.

"Just one minute here. Who are you, and how dare you barge into my offices and speak to me in that insolent tone? Let's see some identifica—"

"Sit down, Weinstein. I'm not going to tell you again."

Jacob was so surprised by the outrageous behavior that he was rendered momentarily speechless. He reached to his side and pulled one of the expensive chairs toward him, then eased his bulk onto the butter-soft wine-colored leather with a grunt.

"Here's how this is going to work. I'm going to talk and you're going to listen. If I ask questions, you're going to answer them. You will not ask me any. As to who we are, I'll give you this much. We're with the Mossad, and this isn't a social call. It's a matter of national security, which means that I'm deadly serious and am not going to waste any time."

"The Mossad! What the hell does the Mossad want to talk with me for?" Jacob blurted.

"To warn you."

"Warn me...," Jacob echoed, puzzled.

"A little over two days ago, a nuclear explosion occurred off the coast of Africa. Somalia. You no doubt know all about it — it's on every news program. But what isn't common knowledge is that one of your ships was hijacked several months ago. By Somali pirates."

"How do you know—"

"We looked over satellite footage of the area where the detonation occurred, and guess what had been floating in the cove that was ground zero? A ship. Camouflaged, to be sure, but still, a ship that looked suspiciously like your missing cargo ship, *Salome*."

"You found her!" Jacob said, affecting relief.

"Cut the crap. The explosion vaporized the boat, and anything that was left sank."

Jacob's eyes pretended confusion. "I...I don't understand. If she sank, then why is the Mossad in my offices?"

"Because we believe you're involved with the explosion."

"What! That's outrageous! Involved in what way? Have you people lost your minds?"

"Mr. Weinstein, I'm not going to warn you again. I'm here to give you an opportunity to change the course you're on. Because it's a bad one, and it will end in disaster. You're a rich and powerful man – a man of accomplishment who's admired and respected. But that isn't going to matter when I come back and take you in, charged with treason. You know what we can do. You can disappear." The man rose. "This is a national security matter. We believe you're involved in something that poses a threat to Israel, and if we're correct, there will be no mercy. So this is your chance. I want to know everything you know about the blast. No lies. No denials. The truth."

Jacob dry swallowed, and then his eyes took on a flinty hardness.

"Gentlemen. I'm not sure what you believe you know, but you've obviously been led astray. We lost a boat, as you know. We were in negotiations to get her back. Negotiations that were nearing a conclusion – a successful conclusion. Now, I don't know how you think the shipping world works, but we don't go around bombing adversaries. Especially not when it's over a few lousy million dollars. Not to mention that I have nothing to do with any nuclear program, nor do I have a pile of nukes in my basement, which you should be well aware of if you've done any research at all." He softened his tone. "Look, the ship is insured. Any ransom would be a cost of doing business – and not even a big cost. So you're way off base."

"Off base. Then why did a nuke go off right next to your boat?"

"Are you a hundred percent sure it was even one of our ships?" Jacob saw a flicker of hesitation in the agent's glare, and drilled home his advantage. "How would I know why a nuke went off? Maybe these same scum were involved in some kind of arms dealing? All I can do is guess. You know as well as I do that area of the world is out of control. There's no law. Anything goes. Maybe they were trying to build, or arm, a device, and they screwed up? Poof. The point is that I have no idea what this is about, and there are infinite explanations I can think of off the top of my head that don't involve me, my company, and nuclear weapons."

"I don't believe you," the agent stated flatly, his tone openly hostile.

"It doesn't matter what you believe. I'm telling the truth. You're on a fishing expedition, and somehow you got pointed in the wrong direction. Who put you up to this? One of my competitors? It had to be. One of my enemies. And you fell for it." Jacob leaned forward, matching the agent's malevolence. "Here's my suggestion. Go bark up another tree. Because there's nothing to see here. I've never been involved in the arms business, or anything even remotely connected to weapons of any kind. That's easy to verify. So I'd suggest that you look elsewhere, because this is a dead end. And frankly, if you pull another stunt like this and bully your way in, you'll be sitting across from my attorneys. This discussion is over, and if you don't leave quietly, I'll start making calls to my connections in the government, and I promise you whatever you think you have won't get you out of that hot water." Jacob held up a hand. "I know you have a difficult job to do. I can sympathize. But I'm a patriot, and an upstanding member of the community, and the notion that I'm involved in anything related to the explosion is preposterous."

The two agents stared stonily at him.

Jacob stood, more sure of himself. "I've given you all the time this warrants. This is a big mistake. Don't make it a bigger one. I'm willing to forget you were here, but only this once. If you barge in again making wild claims, there'll be hell to pay."

The younger agent put his pen down on the desk, carefully, and looked Jacob square in the eyes.

"The only mistake is the one you're making. When we come back, and we *will* come back, you'll be crying like a baby as we drag you off. That's what's going to happen. Probably soon. Very soon."

The older agent nodded, facing off with Jacob, his shoulders square. "You must think we're stupid. In a way, that will make what we have to do even more enjoyable. Mr. Weinstein, last chance. What is your involvement with the explosion?"

"I'm not going to say anything more. Shall I get my lawyer and call the prime minister?"

The two agents exchanged a glance, and then the older one shook his head and signaled to the other.

"Weinstein, you should definitely speak with your attorney. Because next time we come, it will be to cuff you and take you in for questioning. And that won't be due process questioning. At that point it will be too late, and all the king's horses won't be able to save your ass," he spat, and then pushed past Jacob to the door.

The younger one eyed Jacob like he was lunch, sneering at him as he followed his partner out.

"Have a nice day. Thanks for your valuable time," he said with a malevolent chuckle, chilling Jacob's blood, although he fought not to show it.

And then they were gone.

Jacob sat, shaken, for a full minute before heaving himself heavily to his feet, his hands trembling from the adrenaline rush. And from something else.

For all his bravado, for the first time in a long while, Jacob was genuinely afraid.

CHAPTER 15

"Just get ahold of yourself. If they could prove anything, they wouldn't have come in and tried to rattle you. That's not how these guys work," David said, trying for confidence, his voice betraying him.

"Oh, really? And how, exactly, do you know how they operate? I mean, other than that you believe it to be true? As far as I can tell, my ass is now on the firing line because of a series of bad decisions you drove me to. 'The bomb could solve many of our problems.' Really? Did that work like you thought? Because last time I checked, having the Mossad breathing down my neck is a pretty big problem," Jacob worried, pacing in front of David's desk, his last words still ringing stridently.

"Jacob. Just think about it for a few seconds. What do they know? Nothing. That maybe one of our hundreds of ships was in the area when some Somali warlord blew himself up while trafficking in banned weaponry. Am I missing something here? Did they offer anything other than vague threats, trying to get you to crack?"

"You didn't have them telling you they were going to haul you away in chains for treason."

"Jacob. That's not how things work. You're way too high profile. Seriously. This was a desperation move on their part. If they actually had anything they could act on, they already would have. As it is, they came, took their best shot, and got nothing for it. You sent them packing. The end," David said, as if by declaring their hopes out loud he could make them true.

"I disagree. We need to accelerate things. Once the second part of our strategy is in motion, nobody will care about Somalia. They'll have bigger fish to fry."

"No, Jacob. You can't go off half-cocked. Everything is proceeding on schedule. Don't panic and do anything rash."

"Rash, my ass. It won't be you they're cutting fingers off of in some back room."

David shook his head. "Again. It's not going to happen. The best thing you can do is continue on, business as usual. Don't do anything that will give them a reason to come after you, and you'll be fine."

Jacob stared out the window at the cityscape before responding. "I hear what you're saying, but it's way easier to be brave when it's someone else's head on the chopping block."

David sighed, obviously exasperated. "Please. Just give it a little time. You'll see I'm right. As of now, you've had a scare. Hell, I'd be scared too. Having the Mossad pay a visit has to be harrowing. But they've got nothing. At this point, we could be our own worst enemy. Just play it cool, stick to the plan, and we'll be fine. Come on. This is the culmination of, what, fifteen years of preparation? We've never been closer. Let's not blow it now."

"I hear you, David. But I'm not happy, and I'm worried. And if I'm worried, you should be too. These are big stakes we're playing for. Winner takes all. I don't buy that they're just going to go away."

"I didn't say they would go away. Reality is that they'll still nose around, but in a short while none of that will matter. Look, worst case, plan a trip to Zurich or Fiji and watch the whole thing play out on TV. This is now a cause set in motion, and it's bigger than you or me. Just don't lose your nerve."

"Easy for you to say," Jacob muttered, and then, after a few more minutes of David reassuring him, he left David's office and returned to his own.

҈ೂ≈ര҈

The technicians sat at a console monitoring on headphones as Jet and the director stood nearby, listening to catch any nuance over the speaker that was broadcasting the conversation so they could hear it. They heard the distinctive sound of footsteps echo on the playback, and then a door closed.

The director turned to Jet.

"Neat technology, no? We turned his cell phone microphone on without the phone indicating it's in use. Just that little conversation is enough for us to pull him in, now, and work him over for as long we need to."

"The problem being," she said, "that there's no telling just how much he knows, or how long it would take to get it out of him."

"True…," he murmured thoughtfully, and then they heard rustling, and another slamming noise from the tape. "Listen here. This is the call."

She could hardly make out some tones, and then Jacob hung up as the line began ringing.

The lead technician stopped the recording. "We're working on filtering out the background noise and enhancing it, sir. I think we can get a number within another half hour."

"Give it your best shot. Call me the moment you have something. I'll be in my office," the director ordered, and then motioned for Jet to follow him.

"He used another cell phone for the aborted call. We think he was trying to reach the operatives, or another member of The Council, and then had a change of heart," the director said.

"What are the odds are that we can triangulate the phone?" she asked.

"Depends on where it's located. The most sophisticated equipment in the world belongs to the American NSA, and I have a good relationship with them. I'll be pulling some backdoor strings once we have the number. If there's a way to pinpoint it, they'll be able to," the director said as he moved back to his office. Jet knew that the high-rise wasn't the Mossad's permanent location – just as her former control and lover David had moved his operation around periodically depending upon the mission, she was sure that the director and his support staff didn't stay in one place for very long.

"You mentioned the satellite footage. A plane?" she reminded him.

"Yes, but it hasn't helped. It was owned by a corporation based in Nigeria, which not surprisingly turned out to be a shell. We nosed around and discovered that the pilot was a crazy Frenchman who was well known in the region, but he's likely dead now."

"Dead?"

"The same satellite detected an explosion near Yemen later that day. The plane was destroyed."

"How good is the satellite coverage?"

"That's one of the problems we're having. Not very. If you asked for footage of any street in Jerusalem we would have it in seconds, but nobody really watches that part of East Africa. So it's sporadic coverage, and only bits of it at that, on the periphery of whatever the bird is focused on as it orbits over it. For this region, it's usually Iran, Iraq, Syria, and us."

"Then there's no chance of going back and doing a frame-by-frame analysis?"

"No. I mean, maybe NSA would have something, but they're not going to share it with us until they're done analyzing it and the CIA gets through with it. For something like this it's still hit or miss. But we've requested getting several of our birds redeployed for our exclusive use from the military. We'll have better visibility moving forward."

"Hopefully that will translate into an advantage," Jet said, as she took a seat in front of his desk.

"So far, we're doing better than we could have hoped. This Weinstein made a mistake that with any luck will lead us to the bomb. That's a significant break. We're fortunate we're dealing with amateurs. A trained operative would have never made that call," the director said, lighting his tenth cigarette of the day. "If it's someone here, we'll drag them in and break them — the only reason I can think of that he'd have placed a call and then aborted it is because he was panicked, which is what we wanted. So he was either calling someone high up in The Council, or he was calling the operatives to warn them, and then thought better of it. Either way will lead us to them."

"And once we know where they are?"

"Then, depending upon what country it is, you'll be in the driver's seat. If by some miracle it's here, in Israel, we have the resources to deal with it, and you'll be back on a plane to wherever you like in no time. If not, which is probably the case, I'll work with you to come up with a plan. Nobody has the sort of field experience you have. Not since the team was wiped out..."

When the intercom sounded, the abrasive buzzing was jarring. The director lifted the phone handset and listened.

"You're absolutely sure? Fine. Good. We'll be right there," he barked, then stood. "Looks like you're going to be up at bat. We at least have a country now."

Jet studied his expression and then rose to follow him.

"Where?"

He hesitated, his step slowing slightly before resuming its confident gait.

"Libya."

CHAPTER 16

Bangkok, Thailand

Matt cleared airport customs quickly, answering the few questions from the officials in fluent Thai. His carry-on was subjected to a cursory search and then he was waved on. When he stepped out of the terminal he was immediately assaulted by the heat and humidity, a near constant in the capital city. Arriving passengers thronged the sidewalk by the taxi stand, and as always, pandemonium reigned, which he found strangely reassuring. Some things could be depended on, and Bangkok's unending flirtation with chaos was one of them.

He chose one of the nicer hotels in the downtown area, having made his selection primarily for its convenient proximity to the bank where he kept the diamonds. Tomorrow he would arrive unannounced and pull a handful out, and then negotiate a deal with one of the numerous vendors he knew. He wasn't going to try to sell them all at once – a million dollars would more than cover his needs for the foreseeable future, and the other nine million worth he was intending to withdraw would fit in his pants pocket. That would still leave him almost two hundred million in stones, counting the fifty Jet was holding for him – a king's ransom, and more than enough to last him ten lifetimes.

Which got him thinking about her again, for the hundredth time since they'd said their goodbyes at the Mexico City airport. She'd been through so much over just the last weeks, never mind the rest of her life; and yet here she was again, pressed into a dangerous situation that had nothing to do with her, working on behalf of an agency she had faked her own death to escape from. He didn't see how she maintained her sanity, much less the calm she exuded. And yet through it all, she remained rational, reasoned, and effective.

No wonder he was so attracted to her. Setting aside the obvious physical beauty, she had something inside her that increased her allure for him exponentially. A combination of strength and vulnerability that he'd never encountered before. And one that he was determined to explore, whatever the cost.

Matt was hardly a teenager in lust, but for the first time in his life he had the feeling that he'd met his match – maybe more than just his match, truth be told. And the attraction seemed to be mutual, so he wasn't pining over unrequited love. But circumstances had again conspired to separate them, and there wasn't much he could do about it at the moment but attend to his business and hope that Jet came through it unscathed.

Once in the hotel room, he quickly folded his clothes and stowed his valuables in the safe, then went down to the lobby and out onto the street. It was early afternoon, and he realized that he was starving. Fortunately, Bangkok was a town that catered to discerning appetites, and after years prowling the streets, he knew better than most where to find the best food. He walked slowly, easily, taking in the smells and sounds of the bustling metropolis, waves of pedestrians moving along the sidewalks like platelets in the bloodstream of a gigantic urban organism.

Four blocks away he arrived at one of his favorite Thai food places and took a seat at a table near the window, indulging in his customary people-watching as he ordered and then consumed his meal with an icy cold Singha beer. The heat from the spices made his eyes water – something he'd been missing since leaving Thailand, but for which his digestive tract had probably been grateful.

Matt wasn't particularly worried about running into anyone he knew, but it was still in the back of his mind. His goal was to slip in and out of Bangkok with a minimum of drama. Even though the drug network he'd battled to bring down was now effectively in shambles, there was still a danger from his former colleagues in the local CIA station. For that reason, it was best to keep a low profile and avoid his usual haunts at night – the restaurant wasn't a risk, but if he went to any of his customary watering holes, there was a chance that some enterprising snitch would recognize him and complicate matters.

He didn't believe that the local Agency staff had been compromised by Arthur and his group, but he didn't intend to stake his life on it. The danger had presumably died with the scar-faced miscreant, but enough stolen diamonds to buy a small country would still exert a magnetic pull, and he didn't kid himself that he would ever be entirely safe. His customary field instincts were still sharp, and his eyes skimmed over the pedestrians as he munched, watching for any tell-tale signs of surveillance.

Once finished, he paid and then set out to get a cell phone and some other odds and ends. A mega-electronics store was all too happy to sell him a cheap Nokia, and after checking the new battery and verifying that it had at least a partial charge, he consulted his other phone, found the number he was looking for, and dialed it.

"Hello. Is Niran there?" Matt asked in Thai. After a brief pause, a male voice came on the line.

"Yes?"

"Niran. This is Ralph. I've got another bunch of stones I want to find a home for. How's your cash position?" Matt asked, using the alias he'd adopted when dealing with the diamond merchants.

"Ah, my friend, it's always too long since I hear from you. Business is challenging, but somehow I persevere. How large a transaction were you interested in?" Niran responded coyly. At no point in his history had the Thai jeweler ever admitted to doing better than scraping by, and yet he'd purchased tens of millions' worth of stones from Matt over the years.

"Nothing momentous. I was thinking around a million dollars' worth. Unless you aren't in a position to carry that kind of weight. Given the fiscal environment, I won't hold it against you if you can't. I have several others who would snap these up, but I figured I'd come to you first..."

"Always a wise move. I shall find the money somewhere, even if I need to sell a few of my wives to do it. When are you thinking?"

"Tomorrow afternoon. Say, around three? It shouldn't take long, and I'll need to get to the bank to deposit the funds..."

"Three is perfect. I shall wait to see you then."

As Matt slid the new phone into his shirt pocket, fatigue washed over him, and he realized he was beat – bone-tired from so many sleepless hours in the air. The combination of the food and alcohol had worked its magic, and it was all that he could do to get back to the hotel room before he collapsed onto the bed and was out cold, dead to the world until the following morning.

Moscow, Russian Federation

The drab gray concrete walls in the dank room reverberated with the screams of the naked man suspended by his wrists over a drain in the sloped floor, designed for easy hosing down following an interrogation session. Oleg Illyovich paced in front of the hanging figure, avoiding the congealing pool of fluid beneath him, smoke drifting towards the ceiling from his forty-seventh cigarette of the day, his suit rumpled from sitting slumped over for hours in the room behind the two-way mirror at the far end of the space as he watched the proceedings unfold.

The interrogator, Ivan Makarev, was taking a break, also smoking, having washed his hands in a steel laundry sink in the corner. He was leaning against the wall by the door, reading a gentlemen's magazine, chuckling occasionally at the amusing anecdotes in the Letters section — some of the outlandish claims by the writers really did test the limits of plausibility, even if they were funny.

The naked man's body trembled from the frigid temperature, the burns on his torso and legs heightening his sensitivity to cold. Illyovich stopped a few feet in front of the captive and spit a piece of tobacco on the floor — he preferred the non-filtered French cigarettes, raspy and strong, to the more civilized American brands that were now widely available. These were a throwback to the good old days when the Soviet Union manufactured its own cigarettes — vile-smelling creations, strong enough to etch steel; an acquired taste, and one he'd grown to enjoy.

"So you are going to stick with this absurd story of facilitating a sale to a group in Kuwait? If the devices went to Kuwait, then why aren't they there now? Why was one used in East Africa?"

The captive opened his remaining good eye, bloodshot to the point where it resembled a tomato, and blinked the ruined lid a few times, trying to focus as he croaked a feeble response.

"Please. No more. I've told you everything I know."

The words were barely distinguishable, most of his teeth now scattered near the drain, mingled with several pints of his blood. He convulsed after the last word and dry heaved. A yellow trickle of bile ran from the corner of his now-ragged mouth and down his neck, stopping on his chest near one of the ugly welts the soldering iron had seared into his tortured flesh.

"I do not believe you. You are lying. Protecting someone or something. Hoping that they will get you out of here. You have built yourself a nice network over the last twenty years, haven't you? You are a big man now in Ukraine – a big swinging dick in the new regime, eh? I bet you think any minute one of your cronies is going to pull enough strings or pay off the right person and you will be released. Well, I hate to break it to you, but that is not going to happen. You belong to me. I own you. And I will prolong this unspeakable agony for days – weeks if necessary. You *will* tell me everything. It is just a matter of time," Illyovich said, his voice harsh from forty years of smoking and prodigious quantities of cheap vodka.

"No. I swear. It's the truth."

Illyovich blew a stream of bluish smoke at the ceiling, stained yellow with nicotine from countless prior exchanges in the room, and shook his head, his wolfish features unnaturally pallid in the industrial fluorescent light.

"You have to help me. Give me something new. I have heard this story enough to last a lifetime. You are like a broken record," he complained, as if the prisoner's tortured confession was a personal affront, an insult to his intelligence.

"It is…the…truth…"

"Enough of this. Let us try the electrodes. Maybe our friend here will be more favorably disposed to veracity after a few hours of shock treatment?" Illyovich said to Makarev with a reptilian grin.

Makarev reluctantly closed the magazine and set it on the stainless steel rolling table next to the collection of saws, knives, and drills, which he then wheeled closer to the subject. On the lower shelf, next to an industrial grinder, a variable transformer trailed two wires: rubber-clad cables with an inch and a half of exposed copper at the tips.

The naked man's eye roved over the device and he screamed in abject horror as Illyovich, a look of boredom on his face, left the room, a cloud of toxicity following him out the door.

Back in the observation room, Illyovich took a seat next to two officials and stubbed out his cigarette.

"Do you think he has told us everything?" the older of the pair asked, his gray hair clipped close to his head in a crude buzz cut.

"Probably. But it has not done us much good, has it?"

"Then that is the whole story, at least as far as he knows. They did a deal with Kuwait, sold them the nukes, and then six months later Iraq invaded on a pretense. Sounds to me like the Iraqis were tipped off that Kuwait had the bombs, and either wanted them for themselves or wanted to eliminate the threat of them. Then the U.S. jumped in almost immediately, after sending nothing but green lights to Iraq and rushed to Kuwait's defense – but too late. So Iraq had the devices, but the U.S. could not say how they knew, because if Kuwait had had them, as a close ally, the U.S. probably had its hand in the matter.

"Fast forward a decade, and the U.S. is getting more nervous about the nukes as Saddam is agitating for oil sales to be denominated in gold – getting way too big for his britches and endangering the dollar's survival as the world's reserve currency. And worse yet, pushing to ignore OPEC's quotas and increase production threefold, which would drive the price of oil down, threatening to harm the Saudi cartel, and the U.S. oil companies' profits. So they use an invented WMD story to go in and get them. Only they cannot have their own people's hands on them, so they outsource it to…the Mossad."

"Yes, but that is where the trail ends. We have excellent sources within that group, and they never located the nukes. That is a dead end," Illyovich griped, tapping out another cigarette from the crumpled packet.

A hideous shriek echoed through the chamber at the first jolt of electricity to a part of the naked man's anatomy that was particularly sensitive to pain.

Illyovich turned down the wall speaker volume. "I think it is safe to say that nothing useful is going to be discussed in the near future in there. How do you think we should proceed?" he asked.

"Let us see what we can get from digging within the Mossad. At this point, it seems like all trails end there," the older man said, standing, his tolerance for the endless pall of noxious smoke in the small observation room at its limit. "Call us if you get anything more."

Illyovich watched the two men leave. He lit his cigarette, then reclined in his chair and fondled himself as he watched the torture proceed. For the last five years, the only time he ever got aroused was during one of these sessions, and he'd learned to never waste an opportunity. A few minutes later he rose and bolted the door, the speaker volume back up for his enjoyment, then returned to his seat to finish his stimulation, the anguish from the delirious captive fuel for his twisted fire.

CHAPTER 17

Jet returned to the Mossad office the following day, anxious to get going. The director had sent for the documentation team, which was working furiously on creating identification that would pass muster in a chaotically hostile and suspicious nation like Libya. Since the fall of Qaddafi, the country had been in turmoil, with various factions fighting for supremacy even as a new government struggled to take control and restore some semblance of a central rule of law. But the religious intolerance between different sects, the minority and tribal discontent, all combined with the sudden lack of a strong leadership, had resulted in many areas slipping into anarchy — yet another oil-rich nation supposedly freed of an oppressive regime by a coalition of troops under the auspices of the United Nations, which had resulted in tens of thousands of citizens slaughtered even as the country was 'liberated' to protect them.

When Jet strode into the conference room, the director's secretary was waiting for her with another pile of files. She handed them to Jet and, after apologizing for the director running late, the harried woman left Jet alone to her research.

Half an hour went by, and then another, and Jet was growing restless when the conference room door opened and the director entered, trailed by several subordinates. He made introductions and then took his customary position at the head of the table. He cleared his throat and spoke.

"The NSA has narrowed the location down to an address in Benghazi. We're trying to get a team in from Tripoli for surveillance, but they aren't the most skilled at this sort of thing. I'd prefer specialists, but one of the issues we're having is that the political situation there is in flux, to put it mildly, and so the entry requirements are changing by the day. As of right now, the only way we can get anyone into Libya is by obtaining a visa at the airport in Tripoli once the plane lands, which is problematic. But we hope to have the situation resolved in another day — we're working on developing a contact in immigration who is, shall we say, flexible. More to follow on that as we have additional information."

"We should have a passport for you by tomorrow," one of the subordinates said. "We've chosen Italian due to the political ties between Italy and Libya. The hope is that we can achieve an insertion shortly thereafter, at which point you can coordinate with the team on the ground."

Jet frowned. "I have a problem with that part – where I coordinate with the locals. In my experience it's a recipe for disaster. These are rarely people who are up to par, and whenever there's a complication in a mission, it's due to someone on the ground being an amateur. I'd just as soon leave them out of the mix and do the surveillance myself once I'm there. I suppose it can't be helped that they have to be on site until I arrive, but I want to limit their involvement to a passive support role, unless we have the good fortune to have a top-flight covert ops commando loitering around there."

"I understand your sentiment, but you need to adjust your expectations. We're working under an extremely tight schedule, and don't have time to be that selective," the second subordinate warned.

Jet sat back and eyed the man. "These men, the targets, are all ex-Mossad, with advanced training in search and destroy, infiltration, explosives, surveillance and counter-surveillance, and a list of other specialties as long as my arm. If you put amateurs up against them, I'm out. I can guarantee a disaster. It's that simple. The more well-intentioned but under-qualified personnel you have in the field, the greater the chances of the mission ending in failure."

The director held up a hand as the discord looked ready to escalate. "You have a good point, and one we should take under advisement as we pencil out a strategy. But I don't want to argue. The purpose of this meeting is to bring you up to speed on what we know and have done to date. We have a pair of operatives en route to Benghazi from Tripoli. We've acquired satellite photos of the neighborhood, which we'll have later for you to study. We're lining up weapons and gear so that once you're in-country, you'll have everything you need. In short, we're doing everything we can, but we still don't have the building under observation, which means that by the time anyone gets there, they could be gone."

"I'd say that's a pretty big problem, wouldn't you?" Jet ventured.

"It's occurred to me. But it is what it is. We have to do the best we can in light of the situation."

"So you're sending me in blind, to an unstable country in an intermittent state of civil war, supported by dilettantes of questionable competence, in pursuit of highly skilled targets who might have already flown the coop. Is that about right?" she asked, her tone deliberately neutral. "This is how people get killed."

"It isn't a perfect scenario, I'll admit, but considering that, I've asked for our most experienced field analysts and mission planners to convene here this evening, once our people are in position and can send us more intelligence, so we can come up with a strategy for taking the house – recognizing that support will be limited, and the natives will be decidedly unfriendly. I'd like you to participate in that meeting. Out of it will come our course of action moving forward."

"Am I correct that even at this moment, the targets could be walking out their front door, wheeling a suitcase nuke down the sidewalk, and we would have no way of knowing it?" she asked, ignoring the director's statement.

"We have a satellite moving into position. We should have a live feed any moment," the first subordinate said.

"Then everything since the phone call till, say, now, has happened in the dark. Did I leave anything out?" Jet gave the director a withering look. "Gentlemen, with all due respect, if you want to stop these men, you need to be better than them. To say that your performance to date has been lacking is charitable. Any advantage we might have had is largely gone, and really, as far as I can tell, we're depending on luck now – which is a lousy substitute for a plan."

"Now just wait a—" the second subordinate blurted.

"No, *you* wait a minute. This is a comedy of errors. We have a nuke, we have a location, and yet we've managed to do nothing with that information. And now, I'm supposed to go into hostile territory on a wing and a prayer in the hopes that the targets are as slow-witted as we are. Were you able to at least put a locator on the phone number?" Jet asked.

"Yes. It's a cell phone, and it's still at the house. So that's a bit of good fortune," the director affirmed.

"Which could mean they're still there, or that they decided to leave the phone when they left."

The director pushed back from the table, the meeting having gone differently than he'd hoped. "We're going to let Weinstein remain free for now. If Benghazi doesn't yield results, he's our only lead to The Council. I wish we had more solid information to go on, but everyone's doing the best they can. Please plan on attending the meeting. It'll start at six p.m. Now, if nobody has anything more that I need to be here for, I've got some other matters to attend to. I'll ask the three of you to be civil in my absence. I know this is frustrating, but we're all on the same side," he said, with a warning glance at Jet.

She nodded, disgusted and troubled at the way things were developing. But it would do no good to take it out on the lesser lights. And realistically, she needed the Mossad's support if she was going to have any chance at success, so she didn't need to start creating waves that might distract them from identifying a key piece of information at a critical time because of any confidence issues.

"I'll play nice. But I want it on the record, if there's going to be any, that this is not getting off to a good start," she said grudgingly.

"Very well. Noted. Now please use your valuable time productively, and I'll see everyone here again at six." The director took one more look around the room before leaving.

Jet tuned out the pair of subordinates as they droned on, updating her on the deteriorating situation in Benghazi and describing the various insurgent factions that had turned the city upside down. She already got it – it was as near a war zone as possible without having shock troops racing through the streets gunning for anything that moved. That didn't trouble her nearly as much as the sense that the entire operation was already slipping away from her. It would be a miracle if the targets were still at the house by the time she touched down, and she didn't like to depend on divine intervention for her plans to succeed.

She sat back, lost in thought, and fleetingly wondered how Hannah was doing, on the other side of the world with a surrogate taking care of her instead of her mother. Glancing at her watch, she resolved to slip out of the meeting and call both Hannah and Matt as soon as possible. The desire to hear her daughter's voice was almost a physical need sometimes – to reassure herself that this wasn't the real world at all, but rather an artificial construct she would soon be finished with.

And Matt. She'd spent a troubled night with him dominating her dreams, the memory of their parting replaying in her mind like a tape loop on infinite repeat. This crisis couldn't have come at a worse time, and a part of her just wanted it to be over and didn't care about the ramifications of another detonation. People did horrible things to each other all the time. It was the way of the world.

She was pulled out of her musings by one of the subordinates asking a question, and she realized that she'd completely spaced out and hadn't registered anything they'd said in the last few minutes.

"I'm sorry. Are we keeping you from something important?" he asked, a thinly veiled insult in his tone.

Jet looked daggers at him, and then decided that this battle wasn't worth fighting – there was no point in antagonizing the director's underlings. She sat forward in her chair and offered an insincere smile.

"Actually, yes, but that's not relevant. I don't think I caught that last bit. Sorry. Have you figured out where the bomb is?" she asked, then focused on the task at hand and put Hannah and Matt out of her mind, at least for the moment.

CHAPTER 18

Jerusalem, Israel

Ben Roth left the restaurant with his young girlfriend hanging from his arm in a dress that was little more than a skin-tight T-shirt pulled down over the uppermost reaches of her long tan legs, leaving little to the imagination and even less to modesty. The nightspot was a trendy place, expensive, with small portions and big attitudes, the heady smell of pricy cologne and exotic perfume blending with the palpable scent of money in the air. Ben secretly hated places like it, but his companion loved nothing more than seeing and being seen, and he was willing to play along in order to keep her happy.

He had met Rachel two months before, at another high-end bar, and had been delighted when she'd seemed interested in him – no doubt a function of his buying Rachel and her girlfriend a bottle of champagne before sidling up to them and making conversation. From that encounter had come a date where he had lavished delicacies upon her at one of the hottest restaurants in Jerusalem, and then spent the evening dancing at an impossible-to-get-into disco that he'd read about in magazines – the trick to entry being the right denomination bills surreptitiously slid to the doorman, who had palmed them as adeptly as a magician before sweeping the velvet rope aside and welcoming the guests like royalty.

Ben was in his late thirties, average-looking, tall, his dark hairline receding, a kind of geeky man who had, of late, stepped up his game with a new wardrobe and an upgraded attitude – courtesy of a recent financial windfall that had been as unexpected as it had been welcome.

Rachel giggled, alcohol being her preferred social lubricant, and pulled closer as she teetered down the sidewalk in impossibly high heels that showcased her dancer's calves, which in reality needed no help. She was twenty-three, with jet black hair and hazel eyes, all white teeth and easy laughter and good times – a wannabe actress between jobs since her receptionist position had been phased out, and in no hurry to find another now that Ben had appeared in her life and generously agreed to help her make ends meet with her small apartment while she considered opportunities more in line with her ambitions. Ben didn't mind – he, more than most, understood that everything in life had a cost, and the charms of a woman fifteen years younger than he was were no exception.

They slowed as they approached his new white Mercedes coupe, gleaming at the curb. He opened her door for her in what he imagined as a chivalrous manner, and watched with admiration as she slipped into the passenger seat, her toned body as lithe as a serpent, and wondered to himself again at his good fortune.

When he'd been approached by an old university acquaintance and offered the opportunity of a lifetime, he had quickly jumped at the chance. He'd run into hard times with his corporate security business – when he had started it, he'd imagined an infinite demand from companies looking for the very latest electronic countermeasures to safeguard their secrets from corporate spying. However, the reality had proved far less lucrative than he'd hoped since leaving the army, where he had been an explosives specialist with the bomb squad. Being arguably the best hadn't translated so easily into a stellar civilian career, and he had been scraping by for the last few years.

All that changed when he had been offered a chance to do what he did best for a client for whom money appeared to be no object – his friend had hinted that it was the government and that the budget was virtually limitless, but said he couldn't discuss his work with anyone because it was beyond top secret. Ben had agreed, and after signing a sheaf of official documents, he had been taken to work on a device that he had only heard rumors about – a suitcase bomb from Russia that the government had been trying to get operational again.

It had taken many months in a sequestered location, but he had finally been able to develop a new arming and timing system that incorporated the obsolete one and solved the problem of the power supply and battery, in return for which he had been paid a small fortune, after being again reminded of the dire consequences if he breathed a word to anyone. He had crafted a second system for the other device, and warned his hosts that both were extremely delicate – there were limits to what he could achieve without a specialized factory to harden the gizmo and make it shockproof.

One million dollars had been transferred into an offshore account with his name on it, and he'd been cautioned not to alter his life lest he attract undesirable attention – the nation's enemies were everywhere, and he was now a valued asset. Ben had done his best to control his impulsive nature, but in the end had lost the battle, and bought the car, leased a penthouse in a desirable area of town, and set out to have some fun, for the first time he could remember.

It turned out that money was just the thing that had been missing from his life, and he was soon living the existence he'd always dreamed of, enjoying the fruits of his labor. Rachel was the latest in a string of dalliances, although she had captivated him as few others had, and he'd become increasingly enchanted with her as they'd spent more time together.

Ben slid behind the wheel and cranked over the powerful German engine, pausing to enjoy the throbbing engineering marvel that was his to control. He put the little car into gear and swung into traffic, unaware of the SUV fifty yards behind him that had also pulled from the curb, maintaining a discreet distance as it tailed him back to his condo – where another team would take up the watch, having wired it with hidden microphones and cameras while he'd been out on the town, and had tapped the phone and data lines.

❧❦

"Hey, how are you?" Jet asked, happy to hear Matt's voice after hours in the planning meeting.

"Good. Just getting up. Slept in. How are things on your end?" he inquired.

"Don't ask. How about you?"

"No drama here. Just another mundane day. Going to hit the bank, tote around ten million in stolen diamonds, and maybe do lunch. The usual."

"That's about what I figured."

"And you? Have you saved the world yet?"

"No, but I did get to talk to Hannah a few minutes ago. She says she's bored."

"What does she do all day?"

"She has our housekeeper waiting on her hand and foot. Goes to the park and plays with a bunch of other kids. Watches cartoons. Does projects Magdalena comes up with. Today they're making a collage from magazines."

"Why don't you have her doing college prep courses or something more challenging?" Matt asked.

"She's two and a half," Jet said.

"Hmm. That's right. But it's never too young to start. Can't you get her a job on a construction site, or welding, where she'll learn a skill?"

"I think in Uruguay you can't put them to work in the steel mills until they're three."

"What a backwards country. Not like Thailand. They're driving cabs by the time they're three here."

"I know. I still remember how they drive."

Jet and Matt chatted easily, the give and take playful, and when she signed off she felt better than she had all day. The connection with her daughter had been reaffirmed, and she could almost see Matt's wry grin as he wisecracked with her.

She set the phone on the side table and turned off her bedside lamp, trying to get comfortable in the lonely bed, and found herself staring at the ceiling, as she had the prior night, her mind worrying over all the things that could go wrong, and already had. Two hours later she was still awake, and she resigned herself to another long night, the tension from anticipation of the pending operation buzzing in her brain like a hive of angry bees, wishing she was back in Uruguay with Hannah, Matt by her side.

Soon, she thought to herself. She just needed to get through this, and then things would return to normal.

Whatever that meant.

At two thirty a.m. she finally drifted off, her breathing soft, the few hours of rest she would get a meager preparation for the ordeal that was to come.

CHAPTER 19

Jet watched the skyline of Nice, France drift up to meet her as the Falcon 20 business jet the Mossad had chartered descended toward the airport. She would clear French immigration and then immediately make her way to the commercial passenger terminal, where she was booked on a commercial plane bound for Tunis and then Benghazi, departing in two hours.

Her newly minted Italian passport was waved through with hardly a glance by the immigration official at the private terminal, and soon she was waiting to board the flight, which was only half full, mainly with businessmen.

The trip was smooth, the time on the ground in Tunis minimal, and Jet took the opportunity to call Hannah again, knowing that the time was rapidly approaching when she might not be able to touch base with her for days. Once she was in the thick of the mission, she'd be devoting all her focus to the job. As Jet assured her daughter that she loved her, a wave of despair washed over her, the possibility that it was the final chance she'd ever have to talk to her at the forefront of her thoughts.

Benghazi customs was more involved, the visa process taking an hour in spite of the Mossad's reassurances that all had been taken care of, and for a time Jet was worried that something had gone badly wrong. Eventually a document was procured and she received her thirty day visa, but not before she had begun to wonder whether the incompetence was an omen of how the rest of the mission would go. These sorts of last-minute operations were the bane of every thinking operative's existence, and Jet was more sensitive than most, having had a methodical, thorough case officer in David, who would have declined putting his assets on the line for something this tentative.

She took a taxi to the hotel, where a room had been reserved for her — at least that part of the operation had gone according to plan. After unpacking, and donning an abaya, hijab, and niqab — the robe, head scarf, and veil favored by the devout in Libya — Jet activated the cell phone she'd been given and placed a call to the local operatives, who confirmed that they were in position on the small residential street. She told them that she'd be there shortly, then called the contact who would be providing equipment and logistical support and arranged to be picked up outside of the hotel, thirty yards down the block, in ten minutes.

A battered dark brown Renault sedan arrived five minutes late, driven by a paunchy local man in his mid-forties who introduced himself as Luther, sticking to code names. He pulled into traffic before reaching under his seat and withdrawing a SIG Sauer semi-automatic pistol, which he handed to Jet. She checked the magazine and slapped it back into place, then slid it under her robe, into the waist of her pants.

"No suppressor?"

"Sorry. I checked everywhere, but nothing."

"What's the situation here?"

"Still very dangerous. The new regime is trying to establish order, but there are roving groups of gunmen who call themselves militia, but in truth are insurgents opposed to the puppet government that was installed after Qaddafi died. It's not a good situation, although things seem like they've calmed down some. The new government is trying to clamp down on them, but it's easier said than done."

"And the team at the location?"

"In place, but there's been no activity other than lights going on yesterday evening. So someone's inside."

"Or they have the lights on a timer."

Luther didn't respond, nor did she expect him to. His role was to provide her whatever she needed in terms of gear, not to act as a sounding board for the operational details.

"How about the F2000?" Jet asked, referring to the FN assault rifle she'd been told he could get.

"I'll have it in an hour, along with several spare magazines."

"And the night vision goggles?"

"I'm still working on that. Hopefully should have them by tonight. It's far easier to get a bunch of Kalashnikovs or some grenades than the goggles – just not much call for them compared to ordnance, I guess. If you'd wanted some RPGs, I could have thrown a rock and hit ten of them. Welcome to Africa."

The neighborhoods quickly deteriorated as they moved farther from the city center toward the target's house in a district near the old Italian "freedom square," and when they finally ground to a stop a block away, the area looked about as seedy as anything she'd expected – more a slum, reeking of disrepair and rot, than a residential zone. Half-built cinderblock dwellings lurked next to small walled compounds with iron bars on every ground floor window and door. A few starving dogs roamed the dirt road, nosing for sustenance as a small troupe of local urchins kicked an ancient soccer ball back and forth near a dilapidated corner market. An odor of decay and the stench of poorly functioning septic tanks permeated the air, and she was reminded of some of the worst areas in Yemen. The sense of danger seemed to be as much part of the local makeup as the graffiti adorning the dull gray walls.

"They're in the Peugeot on the left," Luther said. "The target is across the road sixty yards further along on the right – it's got a dark brown border painted across the top of the wall. You have my number – call me if you need anything, and I'll work on the night vision gear in the meantime."

Jet nodded, adjusted her headdress, exited the vehicle and began walking slowly to the market. She bought some bottled water and a package of local crackers, and then carrying the plastic bag with her purchases, set out in the direction of the watchers.

When she shuffled past them, she was disheartened to note that they were as conspicuous as imaginable, right down to a set of binoculars around the neck of the man in the passenger seat. She made a mental note and continued along her way, ignoring them, and slowly approached the target house.

Jet immediately spotted the small security cameras mounted on the front, behind the ten-foot-high walls, on the first of the two buildings in the compound. She knew the layout from the satellite footage, but the cameras were a nuance that would only be picked up in person. The building next to the target was a half-completed construction, and a crew of workers was mixing mortar and running conduit, their battered pick-up truck parked in front, resembling more an abandoned vehicle than a functional conveyance. Her eyes roamed over the structure with precision as she moved past it, continuing her shambling gait until she turned the corner.

There was nothing particularly noteworthy about the house – just another in a long line of unremarkable dwellings. She carried on circling the block until she was on the opposite side of it from the target, and confirmed that the compound backed onto another walled house, also heavily fortified, as were all the homes in the neighborhood. Yet even with the situation of living in a de facto war zone, each home had a satellite dish for television reception. Apparently, some things took precedence over relocating somewhere safer – if there was such a place in Libya at the moment.

Random groups of loitering men stood, watching her go by, their gazes aimless, and she saw the telltale shape of a rifle leaning in one of the doorways. At least the presence of weaponry wouldn't be out of place, she mused as she extracted her cell phone and called the director.

"The surveillance team is a joke. They couldn't be more obvious if they'd painted the car bright red and mounted antennas on the top."

The director ignored her opening salvo. "I'll have two seasoned operatives there in a few more hours. By nightfall. They'll be under your orders and can help you with whatever you plan to do."

"That's nice, but I prefer to work alone, as I've made abundantly clear."

"Yes, but on this one, I'm afraid your preferences need to take a back seat. These are experienced field agents. Just deploy them as you see fit."

Jet decided not to fight with him – she'd keep the new arrivals out of trouble and do the ingress herself, exactly as she intended, regardless of what the director wanted. It was her ass, not his, and she wasn't feeling especially cooperative after seeing what had been dispatched for surveillance.

"You're the boss. I also don't have any of the gear I need to take the house. Promises, but nothing besides a pistol. Needless to say, that's not boosting my confidence, either."

"I'll make a call."

"Please do that. I'm going to continue making rounds here to size up the situation, but I think I already know how I want to do this. If your equipment boy can come up with the necessary weapons, I could go in late tonight. I see no reason to wait, do you?" Normally she would be on site for a few days to watch the house herself, but given that nobody had entered or left, she wasn't sure that would do any good beyond wasting time nobody had.

"No, not given the urgency. I'd say minutes count."

"That's what I thought. Hopefully, the surveillance team hasn't tipped the targets off, although it's too late to do anything about that now. Still, I'm going to have them move farther from the house, and get a van so they aren't in plain view of any passers-by – not that there are a lot of people out for a stroll. As it is, though, this is pure amateur night. I can't believe these are active field assets."

"They were doing different kind of work in Tripoli. More administrative espionage. Data, developing a network, that sort of thing."

"Great. So I have file clerks playing at being spies."

"Look, that area of the world isn't exactly our normal stomping grounds. With the latest escalation of armed attacks, many of the embassies have pulled their staff out. There are at least two dozen terrorist entities actively working in the country. It's suicide for anyone to stay in position for any length of time."

"That's not really going to matter if we don't find the nuke, is it?"

The director didn't respond to her observation, silently conceding the point. "Just do the best you can. A simple home invasion should be pretty routine for someone of your skills. Do what you have to do and then report back. I'll make some calls about the gear. Is there anything else?"

"If it's of any interest, I have a bad feeling about all of this."

"Fine. But the house still needs to be taken. If you're not going to do it, I'll have my two agents do so when they arrive. They're qualified."

"If you have someone who can pull this off, why am I here?" she fired back.

"Because just like you, I have a bad feeling, and I need the best I can get. I'm not delusional – I know the odds of the nuke being in there are slim. But we need to know for sure, and I want to narrow my odds of a screw-up."

Jet took a deep breath, forcing her annoyance away. "I'll do it. But nothing about this mission so far is even remotely positive. We've got substandard operatives, we've got almost nonexistent logistical support, and so far a near-zero on equipment. This all needs to turn around, and now, or it's doomed for failure."

"I understand. I'll make the calls. The operatives should be there soon – they'll contact you when they're in the vicinity."

Jet hung up and scanned the street, and then her eyes found the back of the building that was under construction. The crew would be finished for the day in another half hour or so, at which point, hopefully, the building would be vacated for the night.

That would be her launching point.

She just hoped that she would have at least a slim element of surprise. At the rate things were going, she wasn't hopeful. Still, she had a job to do, and one way or another, by the following morning they would know whether they'd found the nuke, or whether the entire exercise had been in vain.

An outcome she was becoming increasingly convinced was most likely.

CHAPTER 20

Bangkok, Thailand

The late morning traffic was still a snarl downtown – a constant state of affairs for a city that had woefully inadequate street planning and an ever-growing number of cars. An endless procession of daredevil motor scooters, their engines buzzing like a agitated hornets, darted in and out of the stalled cars, narrowly avoiding collisions as their operators jockeyed for openings.

Matt took in the entire crazy ritual with a smile. At least some things were constant, and Bangkok's insane traffic was one of them. The contrapuntal cacophony of horns accompanied his footsteps as he edged into the column of vehicles and then made his way to the other side of the street, jaywalking with a cheerful carelessness mirrored by dozens of other pedestrians on their way to whatever destinations called to them.

He rounded a corner, and the bank towered in front of him, one of countless new chrome and glass buildings that had sprung into being over the last twenty years as Bangkok had gone on a tear, its nearly non-stop construction adding to the congestion from thousands of workers now having to commute to the myriad monoliths that dotted the skyline. Matt checked the time – he wouldn't need all the slack he'd cut for himself, but with Thailand, you never knew what would happen next, and sometimes a routine errand like visiting his safe-deposit box could unexpectedly take hours instead of minutes.

Once inside, he approached one of the seated bank officers and announced that he would need to get into the vault. The older woman was courteous and efficient, and after his palm was verified by the wall scanner, she escorted him to the safe-deposit room and left him to his task, assuring him that all he needed to do was push the green button on the wall intercom if he required anything further.

Matt moved down the bank of locked compartments and stopped at one of the larger ones, then removed a key from his wallet and slid it into the lock. It opened with a soft click. He extracted the long drawer and reclosed the compartment before carrying the container to one of the adjacent rooms. After shutting the door behind him, he scanned the chamber for any indication of cameras. Thankfully, like the other room he'd used there, it was just four seamless walls and a ceiling, with no surprises evident.

Matt slid a steel chair from beneath the metal table and set the box down, then lifted the lid and removed one of a dozen black velvet bags. Smiling to himself, he pulled a ladies' coin purse from his pocket and unsnapped the top, then turned his attention to the black sack. He undid the drawstring and tapped out fifty-five diamonds, each four to six carats, D color, VVS1 and IF clarity. After doing a quick mental calculation, he removed another dozen, and then scooped them into the coin purse before removing six more and placing them into an envelope he'd bought on the way there.

His project completed, he stowed the still-bulging pouch of stones back into the box and slid the coin purse and envelope into his front pocket as he rose to carry the drawer into the vault room.

Two minutes later he was back on the street, anonymous in the throng, looking nothing like a man who had ten million dollars in his cargo pants. Glancing at his watch, he figured that he easily had time for a leisurely lunch and a trip back to his hotel to stash all the stones except the ones he planned to sell. He wove his way through the hodgepodge of cars and retraced his steps to his room. After locking the diamonds in his room safe, he set off for a Chinese restaurant near the buyer's offices, where he'd eaten a few times.

Navigating the streets of Bangkok felt as natural as breathing for Matt, and he wondered absently as he meandered down the sidewalk whether he would ever get Thailand out of his system or feel nearly as comfortable anywhere else. After spending decades there, he'd grown used to the customs and idiosyncrasies. A shapely young Thai woman almost collided with him, and as he apologized for his carelessness his thoughts gravitated to Jet, and he imagined himself with her, somewhere in South America. Maybe he could get used to Argentina – a country he'd never visited, but was game to try. At this stage of his life the future was a blank canvas – for the first time in forever he wasn't either hiding from someone or on a mission.

As he saw the sign for the Golden Moon restaurant, Matt realized that he had absolutely no idea what to do next – and that he was comfortable with that, as long as he was sharing his time with Jet. True, they were an odd pairing, but he had resolved not to question things too closely and instead follow his gut and see where it led. After all, he had plenty of money, and his enemies were either dead or in disarray, so he could afford to be directionless for a while.

He pushed through the restaurant doors and surveyed the large dining room as a waiter approached him. The lunch crowd hadn't appeared yet, so he took a table near the rear and ordered, then waited the longer-than-usual time it took to prepare it, reminding himself again where he was. Bangkok functioned at its own pace, and everything took longer than it should. It was just part of the charm that made the place unique.

Once he had finished, he placed a call to his buyer to see if he could move the meeting up an hour since he was running early. Niran sounded overly cheerful when he came on the line, but agreed to Matt's proposal, assuring him that he had the cash and could do the transaction whenever Matt wanted. They agreed to meet in an hour, and then Matt disconnected, pleased that his errands were almost finished. Perhaps he'd fly to Phuket and spend a couple of days on the beach. He was on no particular schedule, so maybe some relaxation away from everything would do him good.

The taxi dropped him in front of the jeweler's building – one of the most prestigious boutiques in a city that boasted enormous wealth. Matt entered the cool showroom, nodding to the fashionably attired sales people he passed, and walked to the rear of the shop where a stunning young woman pouted at him from behind a glass display case.

"Something special for a lady friend?" she asked in perfect English, flashing a smile as bright as a solar flare.

Matt shook his head, taking in her expensive blouse and a fitted black dress that clung to her like a second skin.

"No, I'm here to see Niran. I have an appointment. Could you tell him Ralph is here to see him?" he asked in equally flawless Thai. She reappraised him and then turned to a wall phone and dialed a two digit extension before whispering into it.

"Niran will see you now. Please follow me," she instructed, and then buzzed open the little half door by her perfectly toned thighs so he could trail her into the administrative offices.

They walked down an onyx-floored hallway, and she offered another megawatt smile as her glittering eyes flitted to the armed security guards framing the front entry. Matt strode behind her, admiring her fluid stride, as smooth as if she was gliding on ball bearings. He edged past her as she beckoned to Niran's door.

"I know the way. Thanks," he said, then grasped the lever and twisted it as she spun on stiletto heels to return to her sales duties. He stepped into the spacious office, and an obese Thai man wearing a garish red and orange Hawaiian shirt and white linen pants, sweating in spite of the frigid air pumping from the air conditioner, rounded an enormous desk to greet him.

"My friend. It's been too long. May I get you a refreshment? Something cool to drink? Water or a soda...or perhaps something stronger?" Niran asked, eyeing Matt like a wolf eyes a lamb.

"I'm good. Thanks for seeing me early. I've got a ton of stuff to take care of today. You have the money here?" he asked, in the customarily brusque manner he affected when doing these transactions.

"But of course. In the safe." Niran gestured to a glass-topped table on one side of the room with a scope, a scale and a variety of gemological instruments on it. "Please. Take a seat and let's get a look at what you've got for me today."

Matt did as requested and removed the envelope from his pocket, then slid it across the table to Niran. "As always, they're top of the color and clarity scale. Probably worth more like one point two wholesale, but everyone's got to make a few bucks, right?" Matt said.

Niran studied the stones greedily, trying to mask his delight, and after a few minutes carefully examining each, he nodded. "It's too bad the market's been so soft lately. They're beautiful. But I'm not sure they'd bring what you think they would."

Matt leaned back, smiling, relaxed. "That's a shame for you then, my friend. As I said, I have others that would be more than happy to buy them at the offered price. Perhaps you'd like to take only half, and I'll find a home for the others? To mitigate your risk, of course."

Niran's face tightened. "I didn't say that I wouldn't take them. It's more a question of value..."

"As always. Look, I know they're worth at least twenty to thirty percent more than I'm asking. I know that because this is my business, and I'm not a stupid man. If making that margin – assuming you flipped them to a wholesaler and didn't double or triple your money selling them retail – isn't enough for a day's work, then no hard feelings, it's time for me to get going, and I wish you nothing but success in your future endeavors."

Niran sighed noisily. "You drive a hard bargain, my friend, but for you, I will pay more than I should. Nine-fifty. It's the realities of the new marketplace. Since the economic crisis…"

"Nine seventy-five, or I'm wasting my time, you pirate." Matt fully expected to take a small haircut, and he frankly didn't care about the final number that much – it was still a hell of a lot of money.

Both men grinned as Niran considered pushing back one last time; and then sizing Matt up, thought better of it.

"Fine. Rob me. Just take my money and leave me destitute. I don't care. I'll do this out of friendship. Nine seventy-five it is. Love is blind," Niran said with an exaggerated eye roll. Matt watched him carefully as he put the diamonds back into the envelope, stood, and waddled to the safe.

It took less than five minutes to verify the number of hundred dollar bills in the brick-thick stacks using the automated bill counter. Once Matt was done, he returned the rubber band-wrapped bundles to the chocolate-colored leather satchel in which Niran had carried them and rose, his business with the Thai merchant concluded. He looked at his watch, confirmed that he had adequate time to make it to his other bank to deposit the funds, and said his goodbyes. Niran buzzed the showroom, and the same Thai woman returned to escort Matt to the exit, offering another brilliant flash of teeth as she showed him out.

Back on the sidewalk, he crossed the street and made for the intersection. Thirty seconds later he'd flagged down a taxi, and after giving the driver the address of his bank, he reclined into the seat and closed his eyes for a moment, another milestone completed.

A red Yamaha motorcycle pulled from the curb where it had been parked eighty yards from the jeweler. The rider eased the powerful bike into the dense stream of vehicles, the black tinted glass of his helmet shielding his eyes from the sun as he took up a position behind the car, following at a safe distance as the taxi progressed in fits and starts toward the financial district.

"I have him," the rider said in Thai, speaking into a tiny helmet microphone as he shifted gears and goosed the throttle, swerving to avoid the fender of a limousine that was intent on changing lanes.

"Good. You know what to do."

CHAPTER 21

Benghazi, Libya

Jet performed her final equipment check, the FN F2000 bullpup assault rifle loaded, night vision goggles functioning reasonably well. The two new Mossad operatives next to her were alert and seemed competent, their young faces already toughened by training and the demands of covert field operations.

It was midnight, and the lights in the house had gone out two hours before. They'd been watching from down the street in a stolen green van, and other than an occasional vehicle or a hastily moving pedestrian anxious to get home, the dirt road was deserted, the lights also off in the surrounding buildings. A black and white cat, more skin and bones than anything, darted from the heaps of fresh garbage rotting by the few wooden light poles, and Jet watched its progress through the goggles before flipping up the viewing screen and facing the two men.

"Okay. We'll do this exactly as I laid out. I'll go into the construction site and neutralize the night watchman, then radio you. Adam, you wait by the front gate, and Levi, you stand by with the engine running – we might need to make a very fast getaway. Avoid shooting unless there's no other option. Even with the suppressors, these things will make a racket, and we're in a quasi-war zone." Luther had come through with not only the F2000 rifles, but also silencers for all their weapons.

"So you're going in from the construction site, and then when you give the word I'm to breach the front gate and come in after you to extract any survivors. Are you sure you don't want me to come in with you? Levi can still keep the van running, and duck out to blow the gate on our signal," Adam suggested.

"Negative. I want to go in alone. With any luck I can secure the house before they know what hit them, and you'll be in a better position to help from the road. We have to be in and out as quickly as possible – the militia is still in control of this sector and we'll have to avoid them. Just stick with the plan, with no variation. Do you understand?" she asked, her tone firm.

Both men nodded. Adam clearly wasn't happy about his role, but he'd been ordered to take his commands from Jet, and he knew better than to argue – the instructions came from the very top.

Jet studied their faces. "Give me three minutes to get situated. I'll radio when I'm about to go in. Adam, get into position immediately after. This is going to go down fast. Any questions?"

"No, I'm playing chauffeur, and Adam will hold the door. You get all the fun," Levi said, trying to keep his tone light, but a faint buzz of apprehension evident in his voice as he spoke.

"Correct. Ladies first." She checked her watch. "All right. This is it. I'm going in. See you in a few," Jet said, then flipped down her goggles and opened the rear doors, scanning the empty street before she stepped down onto the hard-packed dirt, virtually invisible in the shadows in her head-to-toe black long-sleeved top and pants.

She listened for any hints of movement in her proximity, but only heard the dull roar of an occasional car from the larger streets a few blocks away. Satisfied that she was unobserved, she trotted to the construction site next to the target. A chain link fence ran across the front of the lot, and a gate barred her way, held shut by a chain with an ancient padlock clasped through the link ends. Not wanting to cause any more noise than necessary, she decided not to shoot it off, and instead took a running start and threw herself as high as she could and gripped the top with her gloved hands. She was up and over in seconds, the fence clattering against the steel support poles, and when she landed in a crouch inside the perimeter she froze, ears perked for any indication that she'd been spotted.

She heard a rustle from the second story of the construction site, and a man's voice called out shakily in Arabic.

"There's nothing to steal here. I have a gun. Don't mess with me…"

Jet was moving before the second word was out of his mouth. She crept on catlike feet to the interior of the building and paused near a load-bearing wall, controlling her breathing, waiting for the watchman to come to her. He was an amateur, one of the construction crew earning extra compensation by staying at the site all night, and she was confident he would make a mistake that would be his downfall.

Her opportunity arrived sooner than she'd expected when the watchman hesitantly groped his way down the dark concrete stairwell, his gun rifle barrel leading, the expression on his face one of fear. The hapless guard couldn't see her in the gloom, and when he got to the final step she swung out of the darkness and delivered a series of brutal strikes, the last of which, below his ear, knocked him unconscious. He dropped to the floor in a heap, and she reached into a pocket of her cargo pants, withdrew a syringe, and injected the contents into his leg. She had three more syringes for any captives, and Luther had assured her that whoever got a shot would be out for six solid hours.

She took the steps to the second floor two at a time, and in moments was peering at the house from one of the windows that had been roughed into the bare cinderblock wall. The target was dark, with no indication of anyone being awake. After another scan of the compound and the road beyond, she retrieved a radio from her belt and murmured into it.

"I'm going in. Get into position. I should be inside in a minute – two at the most. I see the cable for the front security cameras, so I'll cut that before I move in. Remember. No heroics, and stick to the plan."

Jet didn't wait for a response, choosing to turn down the volume and slip the radio back into place. The yard was almost as bright as day in her goggles, illuminated in the distinctive eerie green she knew so well, and she glanced at the wall below her and the side of the target house before making her move. She lowered herself until her feet were hanging above the perimeter wall, and then abruptly swung her legs to the side, creating momentum before she pushed off with her feet. She sailed through space and caught the top of the wall with her hands to stop her fall. Jet used the energy from the drop to bounce; then she swung a leg over the wall and straddled it, looking down into the compound from her perch.

The clouds above her parted and the moon came out, shining down on her position, and she squinted to allow her eyes to adjust to the unexpected light. With a final glance in both directions, she estimated the distance from the house to her landing spot she'd need to cover when she dropped into the compound, and took two deep breaths before tensing her upper body in preparation for the main event.

❧❦

Adam approached the iron gate of the perimeter wall, his weapon clenched close to his body, keeping to the shadows cast by the walls of the other homes, in the hopes of evading the cheap cameras' limited fields of view.

He was almost to the gate when he froze at the sound of a large motor revving from one of the nearby streets, and then was nearly blinded by approaching headlights as a flatbed pick-up truck with five armed militia on the back rounded the corner and lurched down the pitted dirt road toward him.

Darting to the side, he ducked behind the carcass of an old Nissan sedan that had been almost entirely stripped, hoping he had acted fast enough to avoid notice by the gunmen. He'd almost convinced himself that he'd evaded detection when a voice screamed from the truck.

"You. Behind the car. Come out with your hands up, now, or we'll open fire."

The truck slowed as it crept forward, and when it was twenty yards away one of the men yelled again.

"Come out now, or you're dead."

He'd read the reports on the warring militia that acted as the vigilante justice in some areas of Benghazi and cursed the analyst who had assured them that this district appeared to be too close to the town center to be under their control. He momentarily debated trying to bluff his way through, and then caught himself – he was wearing night vision goggles and had a high-tech assault rifle with enough ammunition to level a battalion.

The night exploded as the men in the truck made good on their promise. Blasts from their Kalashnikovs erupted in a flurry, the slugs pounding into the metal chassis and the wall behind him. Any hope of stealth lost, he returned fire, the higher-pitched popping of his suppressed F2000 almost inaudible over the din of the larger-caliber Russian rifles.

Two of his rounds struck a gunman firing over the roof of the cab, who tumbled against the others, and then another burst from Adam's weapon shattered the windshield and killed the driver. The horn blared as his head dropped against the wheel, and then additional shooting directed at the militia erupted from the van, where Levi had made a judgment call and decided to even the odds and support his pinned-down partner.

The crossfire from the two Mossad agents made short work of the amateur soldiers, and ten seconds later the battle was over, the local gunmen either dead or dying. Adam jogged to the bullet-riddled truck, jerked the door open, and pulled the driver out, dumping his corpse onto the dirt. The body hit the road with a muffled thump after the wailing horn fell silent, and the peaceful quiet of the street returned as lights came on in the surrounding buildings.

৵৽

Jet was dropping into a crouch near the house when she heard the truck's rumble at the front of the compound, and when the shooting started she instantly knew that whatever well-crafted approach she'd hoped for had just gone out the window. She withdrew a folding combat knife from her back pocket and hurried to the camera cable, her heart pounding in her throat. Kneeling, she sliced through the wire with a single swipe, and then threw herself to the side when the house door flew open and the ugly barrel of an assault rifle poked out.

A moment went by and she realized that the shooter was blind in the dark. Anticipating his next move, she switched off the night vision goggles just as the exterior lights turned on, followed by the harsh bark of gunfire from the house. Bullets shredded the ground around her as she rolled and simultaneously fired at the doorway, taking cover behind an oversized ceramic pot holding a small tree. Hardened red clay chips showered her from slugs pounding into the planter, and then, sensing a lull, she fired at one of the two exterior lights.

The lamp shattered in a shower of glass and sparks. Silenced gunfire echoed from the front gate, providing badly needed cover for her – Adam had heard the gun battle in the compound and correctly concluded that she needed help. The front door of the house slammed shut as his rounds pocked the walls around it. She shot out the other light and flipped her goggles back down, the darkness providing a slim advantage.

The window nearest the front door shattered and more gunfire exploded from it, but the bullets slammed harmlessly into the structure a few feet to her left – the gunman was shooting blind, hoping to hit something. At the window, she saw the distinctive barrel of an M4 assault rifle poking out and could just make out the outline of the gunman's head in the neon green of the goggles.

Jet squeezed off another burst and the gun disappeared; then an explosion at the street announced that Adam had blown the front gate and was coming in. She heard footsteps pounding behind her and looked up to see him, and then another gun began shooting at them from the house –

114

this one a Kalashnikov, she could tell. Adam returned fire, as did she, and she rolled again, hoping to take better cover at the corner of the nearby building.

Another salvo of shooting burped from the window, and she heard the distinctive whistle of ricochets. She ducked back into the fray and fired measured volleys while she ran towards the front door, Adam continuing to pepper the window with rounds as she sprinted, zig-zagging in the dark.

She slammed against the front façade of the house and waited for a weapon to snake around at her, but there was no more shooting, just the ringing of tinnitus from the defending gunfire. Jet dared a look back at Adam and saw him slamming another magazine into place, holding his fire. She was grateful that he was calm under pressure and had good combat moves – he hadn't wasted any motion getting to her, nor was he shooting indiscriminately, as novices often did in their first firefight.

A clunk sounded from inside the house, nearer the rear, but nothing from the front, from where the shooting had emanated. Adam trotted toward her in a crouch, and then they were both framing the door, weapons at the ready. Jet made a hand signal and he nodded, his breathing heavy. She reached down to the knob with her left hand, her F2000 clutched in her right, and then twisted it with all her might.

Locked.

Adam saw her pull back, and he fired at the lock before slamming it with his boot. The door crashed open and they both held their breath, anticipating gunfire, but were surprised when they were greeted with silence. Jet knelt and peered around the doorjamb, seeking a target, but there was no movement. A body lay by the window in a dark pool of blood, and the cabinets in the kitchen at the far end were splintered from bullets, but there was no evidence of the second shooter. She was just moving deeper into the foyer when she heard a snick – metal on stone, and she barely had time to turn and throw herself back outside before a grenade went off, devastating the living area where she'd been standing only seconds earlier.

Adam grunted in pain. Razor-sharp fragments of shrapnel had hurtled through the door and caught him in the shoulder. His Kevlar vest stopped most of it, but a few shards sliced through along the edge, wounding him. Jet watched from her position on the ground as he tumbled backwards. Her mind worked furiously as she got her bearings. There was no way out of the compound, no back gate or exit, so anyone else in the house was cornered and stood no chance — their first bit of luck that night. The downside was that the gunfire had no doubt drawn every militia unit within five miles, so it was only a matter of minutes, if not seconds, before they'd need to contend with open warfare on the street.

Jet struggled to her feet and was approaching the door again when a massive blast hurled her through the air like a rag doll, the wall in front of her disintegrating as a scorching fireball exploded through the windows and doorway. She landed on her back, dazed but still gripping her weapon, and kept her eyes tightly shut until she could turn off her goggles with a shaking hand. Flames poured from the house, distorting the shapes around her with a spectral orange glow, creating a surreal hell in the front yard as an inferno erupted from every aperture, black smoke spewing into the night sky. She turned groggily and glanced at Adam, lying a few yards away, blood trickling from his ears, his gun on the ground where he'd dropped it.

Jet crawled closer and signed to him that she was going to reconnoiter the house perimeter — the total destruction inside a foregone conclusion. She forced herself to her feet and then spun when she sensed motion behind her, nearly sawing Levi in half with her weapon as he sprinted from the front gate, sweeping the area with his rifle.

"Get Adam into the van. I'll be there in a minute. If more militia show up, take off. I'll fend for myself," she hissed, her face black with smeared soot, the tips of her hair singed.

Levi nodded and moved to Adam, who was grimacing in a combination of shock and pain. Jet didn't wait to confirm that Levi was following her instructions; instead she bolted to the house, this time without bothering to conceal her approach. She ran along one side until she reached the rear section, which was also ablaze, and then, with a glance at the high perimeter wall, crept along the back until she was on the far side of the ruined home.

Fire enveloped the structure, and there was no sign of life — any occupants would have been incinerated. A smoldering beam dropped deep inside the building, a casualty of the flames, and then she heard another big motor revving from down the road to her right — no doubt more militia. She fished her radio from her belt and depressed the transmit button.

"Go, go, go. We'll rendezvous later by the hotel. I'll radio in an hour or two," she ordered, taking in the destruction. The engine noise grew louder, and with a final glance at the gutted home, she shouldered the black nylon strap of her weapon and sprinted for the intersection of the rear and side perimeter walls.

Jet bounded two steps up the rear surface, seeming to defy gravity, and bounced to the side wall. Her hands locked on the top, and then in a move she'd repeated hundreds of times, she pulled herself up and leapt to the second story of the empty construction next door, gripping a concrete window sill until her toes found purchase in a cranny and she hauled herself into the building. She heard the van with Adam and Levi inside tearing off as she prowled across the empty space, her night vision goggles reengaged, and then the sound of men emptying out of a vehicle in front of the blazing compound echoed through the smoke.

Jet moved to the far side of the structure, and after gauging the distance, leapt from one of the windows into space, her feet landing on top of the perimeter wall, her arms flailing to either side as if clutching the air for balance. Then she was running down its length, away from the militia and the dirt road, toward the rear wall, which she knew from her earlier foray backed onto another home on a different street, which would be deserted at that hour, the residents wisely staying indoors lest they become collateral damage in the nocturnal skirmish.

When she reached the next lot, she repeated her high-wire act, and fifteen seconds later dropped down onto the empty, dark dirt road. She hesitated for a moment and then took off at a full run into the gloom, the thumping of her boots on the hard-packed soil echoing the slamming pulse in her ringing ears, the black of her clothes blending with the shadows of the inky Libyan night.

CHAPTER 22

Three hours later Jet was sitting in a sedan near her hotel, studying Adam's drawn features while Levi's eyes darted down the squalid street, dawn still several hours away. Jet was on an encrypted cell call with the director – who, as far as she could tell, never slept.

"That's correct. One confirmed dead, and the rest likely dead in the explosion. The whole house went up. Nothing could have survived," she reported, finishing her terse summary.

"But no sign of the device?"

"No. And unless the satellite picks up a radiation signature from the ruins, it wasn't there. Which was always our worst fear."

The director paused, his breathing heavy as he lit a cigarette. "So where are we?"

"At best, we killed all three of the targets, and the device is hidden somewhere where it will do no harm. Somehow I find that scenario highly unlikely. More probable is that at least one of the targets took off with it and is either en route to, or at, the final destination, wherever that is, preparing to detonate it."

Jet's gaze moved to a black SUV that had just turned the corner and was approaching – the only other occupied vehicle on the street. The SUV accelerated past them and she watched in the side mirror as the brake lights flashed at the next intersection, and then it continued on its way to the waterfront.

"I'm afraid I have to agree with you. Tell me again how this all went so wrong," the director demanded. Jet turned away from Adam and lowered her voice.

"I'll give you a full report later. Suffice to say that the intel we got was flawed – the neighborhood is very much under militia control, and the locals aren't friendly." She didn't elaborate, and didn't want to get into a discussion about how the operative the director insisted she use drew fire while she was silently penetrating the compound. She would put it into the report and he could arrive at his own conclusions.

"All right. The men will remain there. I need you back as soon as possible. Hop on the first plane out this morning. We have another lead we're going to pursue – a technician we've been watching who inexplicably came into some serious money. His spending aroused the attention of some of his peers, who in turn put us on to him."

"Are you going to reel him in?"

"First thing this morning."

"And what about Weinstein?"

"I want to discuss that with you after we see what we get out of the technician. I'm reluctant to bring Weinstein in, because once we do, we've played all our cards, and his disappearance will alert the other members of The Council."

"True, but we're rapidly approaching the point where we have no choice. We don't know when the deadline is, what the target is, or how exactly the bombing will be carried out. That doesn't leave us a lot of options other than finding the nearest fallout shelter and praying…"

"Thanks for the succinct summary. Just get back here as quickly as you can," the director snapped.

"It'll be at least eight hours from the time I board. Everything goes through Europe."

"Very well. Just let me know when you're going to arrive," he replied, and then the phone went dead.

Jet dropped it into her purse and leaned forward to address Levi and Adam.

"You're to stay in Libya. Adam, get whatever medical attention you need, and await further orders. I'd stay away from hospitals or clinics. If it were me, I'd pull the shrapnel myself and stitch it up. I wouldn't trust even the most discreet doctor around here, but it's your call. I'm shipping out at first light."

The two men nodded, Adam wincing, their part in the drama over.

Jet opened her door and was stepping out when the black SUV rounded the corner behind the car and accelerated toward them. Alarmed, she reached into her robe for her pistol as it slowed, a door mounted searchlight flickering on as it drew alongside her. The rear window slid down and she saw the distinctive cap of one of the new government's soldiers, the man's eyes looking her over before he turned and said something to his companions. She relaxed her grip and shut the door, then turned to face the SUV, as any innocent would do, and was rewarded by the window rolling back up and the big truck continuing on its way, the soldiers part of the downtown patrol that secured the area from any insurgents or militia.

She took a deep breath as she moved to the hotel entrance, her nerves still clamoring a protest from the accumulated adrenaline of the night's adventure. Once in the elevator she glanced at her watch – by the time she had browsed online for flights and booked whatever was most expedient and then showered and packed, it would be time to check out and get to the airport. In her room, any hopes of a few hours of sleep evaporated once she saw the flight schedules. She entered in her passport information to confirm a reservation and then moved to the bathroom, anxious to scrub off the sweat and the soot that remained in her ears. Her nose crinkled at the pungent smell of smoke wafting from her outfit, and she stepped into the shower fully clothed and let the spray play over her so her luggage wouldn't smell suspicious if customs wanted to go through her bags.

The water took forever to warm up, and she passed the time scrubbing at her pants and shirt, lathering with soap before rinsing off. Finished with her garments, she stripped them off and luxuriated beneath the hot stream as it washed away the grime from the botched assault. Her ears were still ringing from the explosions, and she knew from experience the tinnitus would take a day or two to diminish. Thankfully the shrapnel had missed her, and other than a few scrapes from being bounced around and her impromptu parkour workout, she was intact, if a little sore from the landing on her back.

When she was done, she brushed the water from her moist hair and donned new clothes, then wrung out her wet shirt and pants before dropping them into a plastic bag. With an eye on the table clock she packed her suitcase and soon was ready to go, having left the weapons and gear in the car. As she waited in the lobby for a taxi, the first slivers of dawn began creeping across the sky, and she was painfully aware that with each new day, their time to stop the bomb was decreasing – for all she knew, D-Day was scheduled for that very morning. If only they had an inkling of where it was going to be detonated, at least they could dispatch personnel. This was the worst of all possible outcomes – a dead end at the house, a nuke in the field, and nothing to go on other than the certainty that it would be used.

The cab finally arrived. The bell captain carried her bag to the curb and informed the driver in an officious tone that their guest would like to go to the airport. Jet eased into the rear seat and closed her burning eyes, wondering how this would all end.

At present, not well, she mused, and then the driver was grinding the gears as they sped down the empty street toward the plane that would carry her north, away from the devastation she'd left in her wake, no closer to her objective than when she'd landed only a few short hours earlier.

CHAPTER 23

Jerusalem, Israel

Ben stood, scarcely half awake, at the counter of the breakfast bar, his hair matted on one side of his head from sleep, a dusting of stubble on his face. He pulled his robe around him as he sipped steaming coffee from his oversized mug, and considered his plans for the day. Rachel was still slumbering in the bedroom, dozing after a late night of frolicking and boozing, and he knew that she wouldn't wake for hours – just in time for a late brunch somewhere expensive. It was the price of admission, he understood, and one well worth paying, given how his life had turned around since he'd started his freewheeling new ways.

He strolled to the living room and punched a button on the remote resting on the stylish glass coffee table. The fifty-inch flat panel television on the far wall flickered to life and he flipped through the channels until he got the business news, then collapsed onto one of the black Italian leather sofas as he lowered the volume to a faint hum. His head was pounding from the beginnings of a hangover, but he figured an hour at the gym would banish the worst of it, and then cocktails with Rachel over brunch would deal with any remnants of the prior night's excesses.

The knock at his door startled him. His condo building was a secure affair, with a twenty-four-hour attendant in the lobby, and nobody could get in without a call to the tenant first. Ben stood, feeling slightly queasy, and carried his cup to the entrance, where he peered through the peephole. Three suited men stood in the hall with serious expressions.

"Yes? Who is it?" he asked, uneasy at the unexpected intrusion.

"Ben Eshel?"

"Who's asking, and how did you get in?"

"Mossad, Mr. Eshel. Open up. We need to speak with you." The speaker sounded annoyed, as if unused to being questioned.

"Mossad? What... let's see some identification," Ben demanded, mind whirling. *What did the Mossad want with him? Perhaps it had something to do with the devices? Or perhaps they were going to chastise him for spending so freely...*

One of the men held up an identity card, and Ben studied the photograph and official crest. He truthfully didn't have the faintest idea what ID the Mossad issued, but the man's demeanor wasn't friendly, and a part of Ben intuited that it would be a bad idea to stall any longer than necessary.

"Okay. Just a second," Ben said as he took a final pull on his coffee before twisting the lock open.

The door swung wide as the men pushed their way in, and Ben was taken aback, knocked off balance.

"Wha—"

One of the men punched him in the stomach, knocking the wind out of him, and the room swayed as he fought for breath; and then everything dimmed and he blacked out.

When Ben came to, he was bound to a chair in a small room. His head felt like someone had played soccer with it, and his mouth was dry to the point he had a hard time swallowing. Some part of his awareness warned him that he wasn't in his condo any longer, and as his eyes flickered open his heart sank.

"He's awake," a voice said from behind him, and footsteps circled as a figure stepped into the light beaming down on him from an overhead bank of lamps.

"So he is," the figure said.

Ben cringed inwardly at the humorless smile the man offered.

"If this is about how I've been spending the money, listen, I'm sorry, and I'll—"

The man seemed to hardly move, and yet the blow, when it came, was like lightning. Pain blossomed from his jaw to his hip, radiating with an intensity that he would have thought impossible. He gasped, struggling to breathe as tears welled in his eyes, the agony worse than if he'd been shot.

"We know all about your spending, Ben. That's not the problem. It's what you did to make the money. That's what we want to talk about. Now here are the ground rules. I'll ask questions, and you'll respond, quickly and honestly. If not, well, this will get unpleasant quickly. Am I clear?" the man said.

"What, and this isn't unpleasant?"

The slap knocked his head to the side, and his cheek burned like fire.

"You don't get it, do you? We know all about what you've been up to. Now no more smart mouth or it'll get worse. Way worse," his captor warned.

Ben blinked back the tears and gave the man a puzzled look.

"What I've been up to? Of course you do. So what's the big deal?" Ben managed, then cringed as if he expected another blow.

Which didn't come.

The man looked uncertain for a split second, and then regained his glacial composure. "You know that we know?" he asked, his voice giving nothing away.

"Of course. I figured you had to. I mean, given what you had me do…" Ben stammered.

"What we had you do?" the man repeated, the adversarial approach replaced with a calm, soothing tone.

"Yeah. I mean, I know it's a state secret and all, but you're with the Mossad, so I assume the information has been disseminated to someone other than those at the top."

"The information," the man echoed.

"You know all this. And you also know I can't talk about it," Ben said, figuring that would be the right response.

The second slap surprised him as much as the first had.

"You'll talk about it. That's what you're here for, and you'll stay here till you do. I'm already losing my patience. You wouldn't like me once I've lost my patience – trust me on that."

Ben looked confused as he bit back a whimper. "Is this some kind of a test? To make sure I won't talk about it? I won't. I swear. I've never told anyone…," he blurted.

The man stepped back and dug in his pocket for a mini-cell phone. He stabbed it on and listened intently, then returned his attention to Ben.

"What do you mean, a test? Do you have any idea what sort of trouble you're in? Let's start with treason, then terrorism."

"But I haven't told a soul. I've never talked to anyone about it, so how can it be treason? What the hell are you talking about?" Ben asked, butterflies of panic fluttering in his stomach.

The man fixed Ben with a steely glare. "How about this – in your own words, tell us what happened. Because you don't seem to get this, at all."

"And you won't hit me any more?"

"Just talk," the man said.

"I...are you officially waiving me of the requirement to stay silent about this?" Ben asked.

"Yes. Officially," the interrogator said, playing along.

"Don't I have to sign something? Get it in writing?"

"Why would you think that?"

"Because they made me sign a mountain of paperwork swearing me to secrecy," Ben stammered, now in full-blown panic mode.

"Tell me about that. You say you signed something?"

"Correct. Official Secrets Act, an acknowledgement that I would never speak about what I did for you upon penalty of death, the whole deal."

The man considered Ben's sweating face. "What you did for us...," he said, almost inaudibly.

Ben's eyes widened as comprehension slowly dawned. He began shaking his head slowly. "No. No..."

"I think it would be best if you started at the beginning, Ben. This is as bad a situation as you can imagine, but you might be able to save yourself if you're completely honest and don't hold anything back. Tell us everything, starting with what you did."

Ben began a stammering account, and the man let him continue, interrupting him occasionally with a pointed question, but otherwise allowing him to finish his narrative. Five minutes later Ben stopped talking, drained, and the man regarded him impassively.

"And this new configuration that you designed is foolproof?" he asked, as if mentally checking off a punchlist item.

"Absolutely. I redid the entire trigger and timer circuitry. What was there was junk. Just ancient technology with mediocre design. It was Neanderthal."

The man was pacing in front of Ben, digesting the details, when his phone vibrated again. He answered it and murmured into the mouthpiece, and then turned to face Ben.

"I'm going to go consult with some people about your story. If you left anything out, now would be the time to tell me. From here, this is going to get a lot worse for you if you did. No lie, Ben. So if there's anything else..."

Ben shook his head. "That's everything, I swear. Look, based on your reaction, I can guess that these people weren't actually the government. So I have no reason to hide anything. I was duped, which means I have as much reason to want to make this right as anyone. I mean, come on…nukes floating around out there, and I armed them? No, I haven't withheld anything. Ask as many questions as you want, and I'll answer them all truthfully. I have nothing to hide."

The man eyed him, then nodded. "I hope for your sake that's true, Ben. I'll be back. Don't go anywhere," he said, and then stepped out of Ben's view.

Ben listened as two sets of footsteps moved away from him and a door opened and closed, and then he was alone, the silence in the room deafening as the implications of what he had done slammed into him with the force of a meteor.

CHAPTER 24

Tel Aviv, Israel

Jet touched down at Ben Gurion airport at four p.m. and was escorted through customs after being met by a Mossad operative. The trip into town took longer this time due to traffic, and she was surprised when they bypassed the tower offices and continued to an industrial park on the edge of town. When the car pulled to a stop in the rear of one of the anonymous buildings, she spotted two men near the cargo door, their suits out of place in the warehouse district.

The director was waiting for her in a large office inside the warehouse. After she entered he closed the door behind her. Once they were both seated at a small round table, he pressed a button on a recorder so she could listen to Ben's confession. When it was over, she leaned back, staring at the ceiling.

The director cleared his throat.

"We believe him. We administered drugs this afternoon, and the story didn't change. Our ex-operatives used their expertise to locate him, then tricked him into believing that they were us. It's actually brilliant. But the bottom line is that he doesn't know much beyond what he did – nothing new. You heard him. They put a sack over his head when they took him to the location where he worked for nearly a year, which was under twenty-four-hour guard. From the description it was a remote complex where someone had gone to great pains to create the impression of a government operation. Serious money was spent. But he has no idea where it was – they drove for hours, which could have been in circles, or to another city. Not that it would do us any good to know at this point. All we really have are descriptions of our ex-operatives, confirmation that both nukes were rendered operational with new circuitry, and the knowledge that the entire gambit was conducted in as professional a manner as we might have done – it's no wonder the poor bastard believed he was working for us."

"Yes, because they had the background, so they were indistinguishable from the real thing. I mean, until they quit, they *were* the real thing, so they knew what they were doing. Are you following the money?" she asked.

"We're all over it, but it looks like a dead end. The funds came through Austria, bounced from Luxembourg, and before that, Hong Kong. It gets fuzzy there, or I should say, fuzzier. All the accounts were set up using shell companies and nominee officers, and from what we can tell, the companies have already been shut down, so these were one-time cutouts that were established specifically for this payment."

"And let's not forget that someone had to come up with a million dollars," Jet said.

"Peanuts to the players in this game. They probably spent ten times that to acquire the devices and fund our three men."

Jet frowned. "What I don't understand is why they didn't just kill him once he'd armed the nukes – seems strange they left him out there as a loose end..."

"They likely wanted to keep him on the bench in case they needed any future modifications or fixes to the devices. After all, he'd be hard to replace, and he had a working knowledge of the new configuration, given that he designed it."

Jet rewound the audio, listened to it again, and then rose, walking to the credenza behind the desk and grabbing a bottle of water before returning to her seat. She took a long pull on it, and then fixed the director with a candid stare.

"What happened in Libya?" he asked softly.

"The short version is that the militia stumbled across the operation and opened up with both barrels. We had to take them out, and in doing so, the targets were alerted. When it became obvious that they were boxed in, they torched the house."

"Do you believe they were killed inside?"

"Anything's possible. But my hunch is there's no way anyone escaped that. It was an inferno."

The director nodded. "What's the long version?"

"The two operatives you sent were somehow spotted by a roving militia patrol, which we were assured by your analysts didn't circulate in that area – so that was an intelligence failure. Obviously, if we had known the area was hot, I would have handled things differently. Anyway, they were forced to engage, and from that point on it was a disaster. I'd already penetrated the compound and was cutting the camera feed when all hell broke loose. The targets began shooting from the house, I returned fire, and it escalated from there. I saw one confirmed dead, and then someone inside tossed a grenade at me. I took evasive action and was preparing to go back in when the house went up. I did a full perimeter search and found nothing, and there was no rear exit, so whoever was in there was prepared to die rather than be caught."

"But you don't know for sure how many were inside?"

"Negative. At least one more besides the dead man, but no way of knowing whether there were more."

They sat in silence as he absorbed her account. The director tapped a cigarette out of a three-quarters-empty packet and stuck it in the corner of his mouth, seemingly absorbed by the simple, repetitive task. He lit it and blew smoke at the ceiling, lost in thought. Eventually he returned his attention to Jet.

"We don't have many options left. We have to assume that at least one of them is still out there, with the device," he said.

"I agree. It's time to bring Weinstein in and put the screws to him. But in the meantime, I want to have a shot at this Ben character. From the tape, I don't get the sense that he was holding out on us, but maybe there's something he forgot that I can extract. Right now we need every advantage we can get. It's a long shot, but hey…"

"Very well. We have him in a room down the hall. Do your worst, and I'll put out the word to get Weinstein. Unless I'm missing something big, we don't have any more alternatives."

Jet rose. "No, you don't. Where's the prisoner?"

"I'll take you to him."

❧

Forty-five minutes later Jet emerged from the interrogation room, tired and demoralized. Ben's account hadn't changed, although he'd remembered a few more details, but nothing that would be helpful in stopping the bomb. He didn't know anything more than what he'd told them, and Jet had gone easy, preferring the soft approach after the director's men had come in hard. He'd been eager to explain how it had all transpired, and a part of her empathized with him – the dumb schmuck had believed he'd been working for his government on a top secret project.

If there was anything positive in the situation, it was that he knew the circuitry by heart, so if they located the device he might prove useful in disabling it. Most of her questions had revolved around the logistics of neutralizing the bomb, once she'd confirmed that he knew little but the technical side; and while his memory had been a little hazy – possibly a byproduct of the interrogation drugs – he'd seemed confident in his understanding and had no doubt that the weapon was now armed. Perhaps the most telling thing to her was how thorough the whole charade had been, right down to the documentation he'd been forced to sign before receiving payment. In reality, he hadn't stood a chance. Not many would have refused a big money offer from their own government to help with devices that would ostensibly be used to defend it from hostile entities intent on its destruction.

When she returned to the office the director was on the phone. He pointed to a chair while he wrapped up the call. When he hung up, he automatically reached for his cigarettes before stopping himself and raising an eyebrow, watching Jet in silence.

"He's a zero," she began, "but we should keep him in custody so if we find the device we have an expert who knows it intimately. Beyond that, he doesn't know anything that's going to help us. The target was never discussed with him, nor was the timing. One interesting thing was that he said it was obvious that someone had been working on the old circuitry, trying to get it operational again, but had failed. That means they've been at this for a long time, and never gave up. Not good for the guys in the white hats."

"No, it isn't. We should have Weinstein in custody within the hour, at which point I'll have him brought here and put the interrogation team on him. When was the last time you slept?" he asked, eyeing her.

"I tried on the planes, but it was rough air."

"Go grab a few hours. I'll send someone when we know something."

"I can question Weinstein, you know."

"Yes, I know you can, but that won't be necessary. I have a specialist who's probably the most persuasive of his kind we have. He'll do well. And depending on how much Weinstein knows, I have an idea of how he can be used to discover what it is they're planning. I don't need you for that, although the offer's appreciated."

"Are you sure? I've got a few tricks you might not have seen, and I'm not officially with your organization, so there's deniability..."

"It's an attractive offer, but I'll pass. Get some rest, and I'll notify you once we've got a lead," the director said, putting an end to the subject.

Jet nodded and made her way to the door. "Good luck."

"Thanks. Hopefully we won't need any, but I'll still take it."

CHAPTER 25

Doha, Qatar

Solomon Horowitz walked cautiously down the jetway to the customs area, the flight from Tripoli via Cairo having taken seemingly forever. An annoyed businessman bumped him as he pushed past in the narrow walkway, causing Solomon to wince and nearly pass out from pain before his vision cleared and he got control of himself. The gunshot wound to his shoulder wasn't terminal, but it was still extremely painful, made worse by the butchery performed by the doctor who had dug the slug out and stitched him up.

The attack on the house had come as a complete surprise, occurring as it had in the dead of night while he and his brother had been asleep. The thought of his sibling, Peter, now dead from an attacker's bullet, nearly stopped him in the jetway, but then he forced himself to continue putting one foot in front of the other. He couldn't afford to break down or attract attention to himself – not when they were at the final stage of an operation that had been a decade in the making. He picked up his pace and emerged into the passenger area, and then made his way to immigration, where his Egyptian passport was duly stamped by a less-than-interested official before he was waved through to the arrivals section.

Taking his time as he rolled his carry-on bag behind him, he emerged from the strikingly modern terminal into the harsh glare of the late afternoon sun, where he stopped at the curb and shielded his eyes with his good hand. A rented Fiat pulled to a halt a few minutes later and he walked to the trunk, which the driver had opened from inside the car, and stowed his bag before circling to the passenger seat, pulling the door closed after him.

The driver, a mid-thirties man with a goatee and a shaved head, nodded at him as he slid the transmission into gear and wheeled into traffic.

"I'm sorry about Peter. He'll be missed," the driver said, his voice quiet.

"Thank you. He was a good man."

The driver shifted gears and accelerated past an overloaded bus that was lumbering in the slow lane. "What happened?" he asked.

"We were fast asleep, and then a gun battle erupted in the street in front of the house. By the time we were up and armed, the walls had been breached and there were shooters in the courtyard. It all happened very fast. Peter got shot within two minutes of the fight's start, so I took evasive action. Lobbed a grenade, then slipped out through the tunnel. I blew the house, so hopefully I took some of the bastards with it."

"Was it an attack on us, or something random?"

"I've been thinking about that. I don't know. My gut says it wasn't random, but then why the gunfight out in front? If it was an attack on us specifically, they would have come in hard and fast. I've thought about it a lot, but other than speculation, nothing makes a lot of sense. But I think we have to assume that they were after us – in which case, they got nothing, and the trail ends at the house."

Both men sat in silence for a few minutes as they jockeyed their way through the stream of cars.

"Well, you're here now. You mentioned you were wounded?"

"Yes. A doctor tended to it. I'm fine," Solomon said. "How is everything set here?"

"All is ready. Tomorrow night we need to go in and get the device, but other than that, everything is awaiting the arrival of the targets. I've selected a perfect site and come up with a viable mechanism for ensuring maximum destruction – the likes of which nobody will ever forget."

"Excellent. Soon the world as we know it will have completely changed. It's been a long time, my friend. I wish my brother had lived to see it, but that wasn't meant to be. Now tell me about the cargo container – the location, the security, and the plan to retrieve the bomb."

☙❧

Bangkok, Thailand

Matt boarded the plane for Phuket and shuffled with the rest of the passengers down the aisle until he found his seat, and then stowed his bag under the seat in front of him. His trip to the bank to deposit the cash had been uneventful, and he'd decided to stay in the hotel for dinner, eating in the room. The meal had been excellent, as he'd expected, given the hotel's reputation, and he'd spent his evening checking on flights for exotic locations, deciding finally on the relatively large beach destination for ease of travel and its host of creature comforts.

Once he arrived, he took a taxi south to his hotel, a five-star resort on the beach, and checked in. The bungalow room was opulent but understated, in keeping with the eco-conscious theme of the area, and he immediately felt more relaxed, the sound of the surf outside his glass patio door hypnotic. He packed the diamonds into the room safe and then changed into beach attire, locked the door, and padded across the sand to one of the three restaurants, his stomach protesting the lack of breakfast that morning in the interests of making the flight.

The day proceeded peacefully, with Matt reclining in a chaise longue in the shade of an oversized beach umbrella, watching other guests explore the water in the cove, no agenda in mind and no pressure to do anything but study his navel. The soft ocean breeze brought with it all the exotic scents he loved about Thailand – flowers, jungle, the sea, suntan oil – and as he settled into the plush cushion, he felt himself relaxing, which was just what he felt he needed most. He'd bought a book in Bangkok the prior day and was halfway through it by the time dusk arrived, alternating his reading with an occasional nap, and when he rose and pulled his white linen short-sleeved shirt on he felt ten years younger, ready for a shower and then a foray into town.

A Thai couple strolled along the sand, she a beauty, watching him make his way back to his room, and Matt hardly registered them as he went inside and tossed his book onto the bed. The pair exchanged glances, and the man slipped a cell phone from his shirt pocket and made a call. Without pausing further, they continued down the beach, apparently celebrating the natural beauty of the island's famous seashore and the miracle of young love.

Matt showered and dried himself, and after brushing his hair back with his fingers, donned shorts and a crème-colored linen shirt. He ran a hand over the two-day growth on his face and considered shaving, but when he caught a glimpse of himself in the mirror he decided that he didn't look half bad, all things considered, and opted to forego the exercise until the next day. Scanning the room, he slipped his wallet and passport into his shirt pocket, locked the patio door, and exited through the main entry, taking his time as he ambled along the rock path to the main lobby, where he'd easily find a cab. The complex was only half full, the season having not yet gotten underway, and it had a rarefied feeling of secluded privilege that made him feel just a little spoiled, especially after having grown accustomed to living in the jungle.

Maybe civilization wasn't so bad after all, he reasoned as he reached the main hotel building, a pair of musicians strumming a tune in the lobby to the delight of a trio of guests sipping cocktails as they waited for friends. He stood listening for a few minutes, declining the server's offer of a drink, and then cursed silently when he felt in his pockets and realized he'd left his cell phone in the room. He looked around the lobby, debating whether to go back and get it, and his thoughts turned to Jet – he didn't want to miss her if she called. Matt reluctantly began the long trudge back to his bungalow, tiki torches illuminating the way. A mouthwatering aroma wafted across the expanse from the formal restaurant, where a band was just revving up an Asian-tinged jazz set that could only fly in Thailand.

Matt reached the room door and was slipping the card key into the lock when he heard an unexpected sound from inside – the muted sound of a power tool. He stopped dead, his head cocked as he stood frozen in place, and then he heard it again, along with the unmistakable noise of metal on metal. His mind raced as he swung around, searching for anything he could use as a weapon, till he spied a pile of beach umbrellas lying a few yards away. Eyes roving over the area in case whoever was inside had an accomplice, he moved to the umbrellas and grabbed one of the wooden rod shafts and jerked it free, then jammed it between a concrete planter and the retaining wall and wrenched it. The shaft snapped, leaving him with a four-foot section in his hand. He returned to the door, where he could hear the clamor still emanating from within.

The card key slipped into place with a soft click, and he twisted the lever handle with his free hand and then burst into the room, surprising the man kneeling in front of the room safe with an industrial drill clenched in his grip. Before the intruder could get to his feet Matt had covered the distance between them. The man twisted and brought the drill up to fend off a blow from the rod aimed at his head. He parried, the pole striking a glancing blow, and Matt swung again, trying to break the thief's grip on the drill.

The intruder lunged forward, now using the long drill bit as a weapon, with which he narrowly missed gutting Matt. Avoiding the attempt, Matt dodged out of the way and then slammed the staff against the man's shoulder – he grunted in pain, but didn't drop the drill, instead feinting to the left and throwing it at Matt with all his might. The heavy steel tool slammed into Matt's abdomen, momentarily winding him and buying the thief a few seconds, which was all he needed. He swept Matt's legs, knocking them from under him, and as Matt tumbled backwards, the burglar leapt up and bolted for the door. Matt fell against the sofa and quickly pushed himself up, but by then the intruder was through the door and sprinting into the darkness. Matt weighed giving chase, but then decided prudence should rule the night, and instead moved to the door, removed the key card, and slammed it shut, taking care to lock it. Gazing around the room, he turned and approached the sliding glass patio door and spotted the thin steel blade the thief had used to jimmy the lock open.

Matt slid it closed and re-locked it, and then, weighing the pole in his hand, leaned down and jammed it into the sliding track, creating an effective block against the door being opened. Breathing heavily, he pulled the drapes together and then strode to the room safe. The drill had mangled the steel but hadn't made it through to the lock. Eyeing the keypad, he punched in the combination he'd chosen and removed the diamonds, then slipped the velour sack into one of the side pockets of his shorts before reaching back into the safe and removing his second passport and a wad of hundred dollar bills. With another glance at the door, he pulled the shirts off the closet hangers and quickly packed his bag, and after two minutes was ready to go.

Staying at the hotel any longer was out of the question – he couldn't afford the scrutiny that a complaint would bring, even though he was the victim. And more alarmingly, one of his identities had been compromised – whoever had planned this incursion had done their homework, which didn't imply anything good. He racked his brain for possible slip-ups on his part, and decided that the only answer was that Niran had anticipated he might be carrying more diamonds and had put someone on to him. The greedy prick hadn't been happy with the outsized profit he was making, and had decided to up his percentage with a little larceny. It was always a danger when dealing with big numbers, but Matt had thought Niran was above that sort of conniving.

Apparently not.

A much more distant possibility was that it was random, but he didn't think so. The thief had been waiting for him to leave, which wasn't typical of the crooks that preyed on tourists. That implied patience and planning, whereas most room robberies, he knew, were with the help of an accomplice working at the hotel, fingering the high rollers, looking for easy scores. Nothing Matt had done could have hinted at an easy money burglary, so unless it had been just bad dumb luck, this was something more.

Whatever it was, he had no interest in sticking around and waiting for the other shoe to drop. It could be that it was over and done with – or the thief could be back to try again, and this time with a gun, or a friend, or both. Matt didn't feel like seeing which, so he picked up the room phone and called the front desk and requested a bellman to come down immediately to help him with his bag, explaining that he'd received an emergency call and had to check out. The concierge was suitably concerned and assured him that a man would be down shortly, and Matt took the intervening minutes to stash the drill out of sight and close the wooden shuttered doors to the closet, concealing the safe behind them.

A polite knock sounded from the entry. Matt hoisted his bag and walked to the small foyer, then looked through the peephole and confirmed that it was a member of the hotel staff. Three minutes later he was signing out as the bellman carried his things to a waiting taxi, and when Matt turned to follow him out he realized that he had no idea where he was going to go. The driver put Matt's bag into the trunk and then slipped behind the wheel, and Matt dropped onto the rear seat and mentioned the name of a famous resort several miles away. The driver nodded and grinned, displaying a spectacular set of decaying teeth, and, then with a wave to the bellman, pointed the cab down the drive.

Matt watched the side mirror for any indication that he was being followed, but the taxi was the only car on the private access way. When they turned onto the beachfront road the driver pulled into the steady stream of traffic, and Matt exhaled, satisfied that he'd gotten away clean. He impulsively changed his mind when they were halfway to the resort and told the driver to take him into town instead, and then considered his options. Maybe it would be a better idea to get the hell out of town, now, instead of lingering. Part of him was still uneasy, and questioned whether it would be smart to remain in Phuket.

Because there was one other disturbing thing about the thief, in addition to his fearlessness and apparent skill.

He was Caucasian.

And while there were plenty of burned-out hopheads banging around Thailand in a drug fog, hoping to run out the clock in a foreign land where their poison of choice was inexpensive and they could sustain themselves by preying on fellow tourists, he hadn't gotten that impression from the intruder. For one thing, the drill wasn't cheap, and a junkie would have sold it long ago. For another, he hadn't shown any indication of being impaired – if anything, his reactions had been cat-quick.

Which meant only one thing. He'd been a pro. And if a pro was tailing Matt, there would be more than one – that was just how things worked.

No matter how Matt sliced it, that spelled danger.

He'd had about all he could handle of trouble finding him wherever he went. It was time to disappear and leave a cold trail. And he had a few ideas of how best to accomplish that, especially after dark in the nether reaches of Thailand. After all, it wasn't like he hadn't done it countless times before.

CHAPTER 26

Tel Aviv, Israel

The cell door opened and two suited men entered. Ben looked up and cringed inwardly, anticipating another round of interrogation. He was surprised when the heavier of his two captors stopped in front of him and fixed him with a stony gaze.

"I have good news and bad news. The good news is that we've decided we believe your account, and that you acted in good faith when modifying the bombs."

Ben exhaled a loud sigh of relief. "Thank God. You have no idea how sorry I am that I did any of this." He paused. "What's the bad news?"

"You're going to remain a guest of the Mossad for a while. We might need your expertise if we can locate the device, and we can't take a chance that you get hit by a bus. So you'll have to forego your playboy lifestyle for a bit."

Ben considered the implications. "Are you going to keep me in this damned cell?"

"No, we'll move you to a more comfortable location. But you'll be confined to house arrest with guards until the crisis is over."

"House arrest!"

"It's better than being charged with treason, wouldn't you agree?"

"I suppose so," Ben conceded glumly. "How long do you think this will take?"

"I wish we knew. Hopefully not long. But this isn't a negotiation. And ironically, you'll be required to sign all the secrecy documentation you did before – only this time, the genuine article. This can never be spoken about, to anyone."

Ben nodded. "I understand. Mum's the word. Not like I've been posting it on the internet or anything. So when can I get out of here?"

"How about now?"

Ben's face broke into a grin for the first time since he'd been taken into custody.

"It's about frigging time…"

⋙⋘

Jacob Weinstein was just settling in for the night when the knock at the door echoed through his lavish home. His housekeeper answered it, and a few moments later three men were standing in his bedroom, their expressions more than signaling how much trouble he was in. The lead man was the older agent from the prior meeting. His icy smile sent a chill down Jacob's spine.

"You were warned. Put your clothes on. You have thirty seconds. After that, we'll drag you out of here in your underwear. I sort of hope you try me on that," the agent said, and Jacob knew he was lost.

"This is prepost—" he tried, but the Mossad man cut him off.

"You now have twenty-six seconds," he said, checking his watch.

"I want to speak to my attorney," Jacob tried a final time, mustering as much outraged conviction as he could while facing three seasoned Mossad operatives in his silk pajamas.

"Twenty. You'll have a better time in a cell with the boys in your jammies, I think, so keep talking."

Jacob didn't need any further convincing. He threw off the covers and made for the closet. He'd slipped a shirt on and was pulling on a pair of blue suit trousers when the agent snapped his fingers.

"Time. Get him," the agent ordered, and the other two operatives moved toward him.

"Please. I need shoes," Jacob pleaded.

"Should have thought of that when you were mouthing off." The agent's eyes strayed to the slippers Jacob had been wearing. "Put those on. You're lucky I'm in a good mood."

Jacob was horrified at the prospect of being forced to appear in public wearing his slippers, half dressed, his hair sticking up in all directions, but a glance at the agent silenced any protest forming in his mind. He trudged to his slippers and wedged his feet into them, and then an operative took his arms and held them steady while the other slapped on a set of cuffs, the snick of the locking mechanism as loud as a rifle shot to Jacob's ear. The reality of the situation couldn't have been better underscored than by that sound, and Jacob's heart sank as he realized that all his work, all his money, would be lost in the witch hunt that was to follow.

"I still want my attorney," he managed, and then froze when the Mossad agent smiled again, this time with what appeared to be genuine merriment.

"Jacob Weinstein, you are charged with treason – a capital offense in times of war, which it will be pretty soon if your bomb goes off. You have no rights, and should have no expectation of anything but death at the receiving end of a firing squad. If it was up to me I'd have you stoned, like the old days, but unfortunately it's not. Then again, I plan to lobby for an exception, and you never know – given the heinous nature of your crimes, I may just get it. So shut your mouth and stop your whining. You disgust me enough as it is."

The men led him downstairs while the housekeeper stood with a fourth operative who was taking her into custody – they weren't taking any chances of Jacob's plight being communicated to anyone. She would be detained until the crisis was over, with no contact allowed with the outside world.

The team led Jacob to a black van parked by the service entrance and loaded him into the back. The two silent operatives took seats on the bench next to him, with the agent taking one across from him.

"Did you really think you would get away with this? I gave you a chance and you spit in my face. Now we'll see who's all high and mighty by the end of the night. I've seen battle-hardened true believers cry like newborns after the interrogation team gets through with them – assuming they live through it. You? You're old and weak and soft. My guess is you'll be spilling your guts before they're done with the cattle prod to your genitals, much less the rest of it."

The man saw the reaction he was looking for in Jacob's eyes – pure, unadulterated terror. That was good; the desired response. He would break much faster if his mind worked against him, playing the horrific scenarios in his head. It was all part of the drill, but he was enjoying his role, perhaps more than in most cases. That this wealthy industrialist – who had made fortunes more vast than he could imagine – would plot to create a terrorist event that could bring the country to the edge of disaster was more loathsome than a suicide bomber or a rabid cleric spewing hate and intolerance. This man had benefited in every way by his associations and his position, and he had betrayed them all.

The van rolled onto the street and wound its way from Jerusalem to Tel Aviv, Jacob turning increasingly white as the journey continued. The prisoner was clearly panicked, which was the whole point to the exercise – they needed him to be pliant when the interrogation began.

Eventually they pulled to a stop outside the darkened warehouse where Ben had been questioned, and the rear doors swung open, held by two somber operatives, their suit jackets bulging from their concealed weapons. One of them muttered into his cuff, and then the men in the van unloaded Jacob and began walking him to the rear entrance.

Gunfire exploded from the gloom; the man holding Jacob's right arm went down with a groan. Another burst echoed from the between the buildings, and the agent fell forward in an explosion of blood. The other operative holding Jacob released him and drew his pistol. The rapid burp of an automatic weapon shattered the night again, and he fired at it even as he was hit and fell into a heap at Jacob's feet, blood soaking the white shirt beneath his suit. The two remaining operatives crouched and shot at the assailant, but the incoming fire was too much to overcome, and in seconds they too were lying dead.

Jacob spun around, his eyes searching furiously for the threat, and then a black-clad man came running at him carrying an MTAR-21 assault rifle, a trickle of blood running down his right cheek from where a bullet had grazed him. Jacob froze, waiting for the death shot, and then the man whispered at him.

"Come on. Can you run?"

"What?!"

"*Can. You. Run?* We're going to be swarmed with operatives any second, so make up your mind."

As if to highlight their predicament, two men appeared in the building's doorway, and the black-clad man crouched and emptied his weapon at them, hitting them both with a sustained burst before ejecting the spent magazine and slamming a fresh one in place. His gaze swept the parking area before returning to Jacob.

"Last time I'm going to ask."

"Yes, I...I think so..."

"Good. Let's go," the man said. He tugged Jacob's arm and sprinted for the shadows behind another of the massive buildings. Jacob hesitated for a second and then followed him, anxious not to be left behind. After a final look at the corpses all over the lot, he ran behind his rescuer, the dim lights behind him fading as he picked up his pace.

"Over here," the man called, and Jacob saw him standing near a black Mercedes G550 with no plates. "Hurry. We're out of time. They'll have helicopters here soon, and then we're dead."

Jacob approached the vehicle as the man cranked over the big engine, then leaned over and opened the passenger door for him. "Now. Man, you're slow. Do you want to be tortured and killed? Move, damn it," he hissed.

Jacob pulled himself into the seat and then got the door closed – difficult to do with his hands cuffed, but he managed. His rescuer floored the accelerator and they surged forward, cutting across a dirt field, bouncing over ruts, and then slammed through a chain link gate and merged onto an empty access road that paralleled the freeway in the near distance to their left.

"Are you all right?" the driver asked, eyes locked on the road in the darkness, running without lights by the faint glow of the moon.

"Ye...Yes, I think so." Jacob paused and took in the man's bleeding profile. "Who are you?"

"A friend. The group hired me to extract you. They got a tip that you were to be taken tonight, but there was no time to warn you. Sorry about that. You're lucky I made it before they got you inside. Nobody ever walks out of there. Nobody. It would have been impossible to save you then, so this is your lucky night."

"It doesn't feel like it."

"That's because you didn't make it into the building. Trust me. You narrowly missed your worst living nightmare in hell. I used to work for them. I know."

"You're ex-Mossad?"

"No, I'm a dentist and you're late for your cleaning. What the hell's wrong with you? What do you think?"

Jacob jolted as they hit a particularly nasty rut, his mind churning. "Where are we going?"

"Someplace safe. We need to get you out of the country. They'll be scouring the Earth to find you."

"But–"

"No buts. Do you want to live? If so, you'll do exactly as I say. Now stop being an idiot and listen up. First, what did they tell you?"

"Not much. That I was being charged with treason."

"That's it? And what did you tell them?" he demanded as he veered left down a drainage ditch.

"Nothing. I told them nothing."

"Jacob. This is very important. You didn't tell them anything about the bomb? Not even a little hint to make things easier for you? You can be honest with me. Really. I understand what you have to do when in a crisis situation, more than most. What did you tell them?"

"I told you – nothing."

"You expect me to believe that? My instructions are very clear – to get you out of this mess, and verify how much you told them so we can take evasive action. But you have to help me, Jacob."

"How do you know about the bomb?" Jacob asked, suspicious.

"I'm part of the team that's going to deal with it, you dumb bastard. Now answer my question – did you tell them where it was to be detonated? Or when?"

"No! How the hell could I? I don't have any idea where it's going to go off. All I know is that it'll be soon. How would that help them?" Jacob spat, seething at the man's tone.

They hit another bad pothole, jarring them both, and the man twisted the wheel to the left again.

"They're going to be all over us, Jacob, so I need to be able to trust you, and know you aren't going to crumple on me in the clinch. Don't you dare lie to me. I'll find out eventually, and if you're lying to me, there's no place you'll be safe. Ever."

"I swear I'm telling you the truth! How could I tell them what I don't even know myself?"

"So you say. You must have some suspicion, some clue. What did you tell them, Jacob? Shit. Get down. Duck out of sight," the driver ordered, his brow furrowing. Jacob obeyed, slouching down into his seat so his head wasn't above the door panel.

"Can you reach the lever on the right side at the base of the seat? If so, drop the back as far as it'll go and stay down."

Jacob strained as the rough terrain jostled the vehicle when the man increased his speed, and his groping, cuffed hands finally found the handle. He reclined with a jolt, almost prone, and the driver nodded, his eyes still on some distant object.

"Last time, Jacob. What did you tell them? Look at you. You aren't bloodied. Why wouldn't they have already started on you? Because you talked. Now so help me, you tell me what you said, or I'll dump you off here and you can take your chances with their dogs and patrols."

"God damn it! I told you, I didn't tell them anything! Shit, if I did, it would be pure guesswork. An invention. Nobody knows where the bomb's going off except for the inner circle of The Council. Didn't they fill you in?" Jacob snapped.

"They don't tell me everything. Just what I need to know," the driver said, and then jerked the wheel. They pounded over some ruts, and then the way smoothed out.

"How much longer until I can sit up?" Jacob asked, his back beginning to cramp from the position.

"A few minutes. Stop complaining. I'm going to make a phone call, and tell The Council what you said, and verify that you don't know the details of the operation. You sure you don't want to change your story?" the driver asked, fishing a cell phone from his pocket as his left hand gripped the wheel.

"Positive. They'll confirm it. I'm not worried," Jacob said.

"All right, it's your funeral," the driver said, and then his eyes widened and he dropped the phone into his pocket. "Oh, shit. Hang on," he warned, and then they were twisting and being knocked to and fro as he negotiated a particularly rough patch of terrain. The jostling went on for some time, and the big motor groaned as the driver modulated the gas to better manage the difficult ground.

Eventually, the vehicle began to slow, and then lights illuminated the cab as the tires found pavement.

"Are we clear?" Jacob asked, but the driver didn't answer, his attention elsewhere. Jacob debated asking again, and then his rescuer stomped on the brakes.

"Okay, you can sit up now," he said, and Jacob was fumbling for the handle when his door flew open and strong hands pulled him from the seat. He barely had time to react when he saw that they were back at the industrial building, the dead men miraculously walking, apparently no worse for their experience. "Amazing what a few blood squibs can do, isn't it?" the driver chuckled, seeing the look of shock on Jacob's face.

"He doesn't know anything. I think he's telling the truth," the driver said to the agent, his shirt still stained crimson, splatters of theatrical blood still staining his profile. "But take him into the interrogation cell anyway. I'll start with a drug cocktail, and then move to torture – we need to be sure."

Jacob's eyes widened as he heard the final words, and he struggled in a panicked frenzy when he realized that his ordeal was only beginning. The driver shook his head as two operatives half dragged him toward the door, and then he turned to the agent.

"This may turn out to be a big waste of time. Hope the old man has a plan B for him, because my money says he doesn't know much more than we do."

"Only one way to find out," the agent said.

The driver looked at the distant lights on the freeway, his expression pensive.

"You got that right."

CHAPTER 27

Eight hours later, the interrogation concluded. Jacob had been telling the truth – all he knew was that there was a bomb, and that it was going to be used sooner rather than later. For what precise purpose, or where, he wasn't privy to, and while he had been told to anticipate something shortly, he had nothing more solid about the timeframe.

The director watched the last of the video of the questioning and sat back heavily in his chair, thinking. After a few minutes, he called Jet and explained the situation, and told her he would have a car pick her up in half an hour.

When Jet arrived she looked rested, a long night's sleep having worked its magic, and when the director briefed her on what he wanted her to do, she nodded.

"Are you serious about the deal?"

"That's why I want you to make the offer. Something about deniability, I think you mentioned?"

"Ah. Crafty. I like it. I was going to say, he deserves no mercy, but it sounds like we're on the same page there," she said, an edge to her normally calm voice.

The director pointed to the door. "Like minds think alike. Just get him to play ball."

"That's my specialty. Or one of them. Consider it done," she said, standing.

"I'll be listening."

"I would expect nothing less," Jet said, then exited the office and walked down the hall to where two operatives were guarding one of the steel doors. She stopped in front and the taller of the pair unlocked it, offering a wan smile. She didn't return it, preferring to stare straight ahead as she mentally prepared for what was to come.

Jet entered the cell and moved around the chair until she was just a few feet from Jacob and regarded him without expression. He raised his head, his skin pasty, groggy from the lingering effects of the drugs, and looked at her. His eyes registered surprise at the presence of an astoundingly beautiful woman, but then the light faded from them.

"Jacob Weinstein, I'm here to offer you a deal. I have a proposal for you, and I want you to listen carefully so you get it all the first time. Do you understand? Can I get you something? Water? A trip to the restroom?" she asked, and he became more attentive.

"I could use both," he said simply, sounding defeated.

She walked behind him and knocked on the door. A few moments later it was unbolted, and she ordered one of the guards to uncuff the prisoner, take him to use the toilet, and bring him a liter bottle of water.

When Jacob returned he looked better, although still a shell of the powerful man who had been lying in bed only a short time before. He accepted the water with trembling hands and drank greedily from it, dehydrated from the drugs as well as the near-constant sweat of fear. The guard let him drink, and then sat him back in the chair. He was about to re-cuff him when Jet shook her head.

"I don't think we'll be needing those. There's been enough barbarism for one night," she said, cocking an eyebrow as she locked eyes with Jacob.

The guard appeared to hesitate and then shrugged, deferring to her. He handed Jet the cuffs, then returned to the door and left.

"Mr. Weinstein, I want you to carefully consider the position you're in, as well as my suggestion for how you can extricate yourself from it. You are guilty of treason. You've admitted it. We have it on tape. Your guilt is not subject to debate – you're guilty. The penalty for treason is life imprisonment, but in this case, it will be death. There's no way for you to escape that fate – no lawyering, no amount of money, no connections will allow you to dodge it. Do you understand? In fact, they'll probably just haul you to the nearest field and put a bullet in your head rather than having to suffer the public humiliation of one of the country's most respected citizens being branded a traitor."

Jacob nodded silently.

"The only way that you can atone is to help us avert the terrible event you've put into motion. But you don't know enough to do so. Which means there's only one way to help – you need to call a meeting of The Council and find out what's planned, and when. If you refuse to do so, you'll die. Probably before the end of the day. Nobody will mourn you or notice your passing – you'll simply cease to exist. Your legacy will be lost, and you'll be just another forgettable businessman who made a few bucks and then faded into history – into obscurity. You'll die cold and alone, probably in a drainage ditch over in the field you drove through, and your remains will rot buried under a thin blanket of mud. But before that happens, they'll proceed to physical torture you can't even imagine. You'll beg for death before they're done. Am I getting through to you?" she asked, her voice melodious to his ear, her cadence almost hypnotic.

Jacob nodded again, and then answered, "Yes."

"What I'll need you to do is make a call, or calls, and convene a meeting. You'll be wired, so we'll hear everything you say. You need to find out what's planned. That's it. Once you do, we'll take the rest of the members into custody, and only you will leave a free man. That's the only deal being offered."

He glared at her. "You want me to betray the men I've worked with for decades – to build a better nation? Because that's what all of this is about. Building a stronger country. A country that isn't divided, filled with recriminations and acrimony and self-doubt. That's why I did all this."

"Mr. Weinstein, save the filibustering for someone who cares. You don't even know what it is that you've done. You're so deluded that you've gone along with a plot, and you don't even know exactly what the plot is. For all you know, they're planning to detonate the bomb in downtown Jerusalem to stoke outrage over terrorism and prod the government into laying waste to millions of innocents. You're in way over your head, and the destination – the only end point for you on this road – is death before nightfall, after hours of unspeakable agony. I'm offering you a way out. Help us stop whatever atrocity these madmen are planning. And then walk away, free and clear. The country doesn't need brinksmanship or Armageddon to prosper. That's delusional thinking, and I think part of you knows it."

Jacob appeared to consider her words, and Jet gave him time. He needed to arrive at the correct conclusion himself, without too much prodding. She deliberately took a few steps away from him, allowing him to regain some self-respect.

Carrot and stick. *Betray your friends like you betrayed your country, or be executed and forgotten.* Momentary unpleasantness exchanged for survival. An irresistible offer.

It wasn't a lock, but she had seen what she had aimed to establish in his eyes – a glimmer of hope, and then of calculation. She paced for a few moments, and then stopped and faced him, addressing him by his last name again, a part of her tactic.

"Mr. Weinstein, time's wasting. Your office will begin wondering where you are soon, and that could trigger a defensive reaction within your group if they have you under surveillance, which they very well might. So it's decision time. Do you help us put an end to this craziness, or do you suffer the unspeakable and then die a pointless death? Oh, and just in case you're feeling virtuous, you should know that while you were drugged you divulged the names of the other members of your little circle. So if you decide that you're not going to play ball, we'll be moving to the next in line, and they'll get the offer…and you'll get the bullet. At this point all you'll be doing is saving us a little time. It won't affect the outcome at all. Because one of them will talk – just as you did – and then we'll still have the information we need, only you'll be history. This is your only chance. Choose wisely." She fixed him with an unwavering stare. "Make your decision – what's it going to be?"

Jacob closed his eyes as if in prayer, and then gazed up at her with the look of the eternally damned, a haunted expression on his face, no defiance left in him.

"How is this going to work?"

CHAPTER 28

The restaurant was closed for a private event, the owner having given the staff the night off when he'd received the call late that morning requesting the premises for a meeting. The rule was that if any of the nine members of The Council wanted to meet, the others had to make arrangements to do so as soon as possible. When Jacob had made the calls, agreement had been assumed, and it had merely been an issue of timing. The event had been set for five p.m., and as the hour approached a steady stream of expensive vehicles arrived at the rear door, disgorging their occupants before disappearing so as not to attract untoward attention.

Jacob was the last to arrive, and he had fortified himself with several single malt Scotches and a half a Xanax before having his car take him to the restaurant – one of dozens owned by a prominent Council member, who also controlled a significant portion of the local commercial fishing fleet. Jacob strode purposefully to the service entrance, as had the others, and the surveillance group a block away in a hastily commandeered office could detect the clicking of his heels as he made his way into the recesses of the brick building to a private dining room on the second floor.

Jacob nodded to the assembled men when he entered the room, and then took a seat at the large round table. He examined their faces, studying them, and saw both resolve and fatigue – men whose lives had been long battles, with no quarter offered nor expected, a Who's Who of the financial might of the nation. David wasn't among them – Jacob had brought him into the information loop many years ago, but he wasn't an official member of The Council, lacking the experience – and the bankroll – to be an equal.

"Gentlemen, a meeting has been convened due to the special request of one of our group. As the member calling the meeting, Jacob will now address the gathering. Jacob?" the oldest member, Eli, said in a gruff voice that still resonated with authority, honed over an illustrious career as one of the most famous attorneys in the land, and later, one of the larger residential real estate landowners.

"Thank you all for coming. I wanted this meeting because it occurred to me that we're now very close to our ultimate ambition coming to fruition, and yet I have literally no idea what it is, precisely, that we're about to do. I know, as do you all, that it involves the detonation of the second device, but beyond that and assurances that it's for our mutual good, I'm in the dark, and I've been waking up in the middle of the night, unsure that I'm comfortable with not knowing what's planned. Therefore, I'm proposing that the security committee brief us all – today, at this meeting – so that we know what to expect and how our money has been spent. Given that last week we were told that the event, whatever it is, is imminent, I can see no reason to keep the inner circle out of the loop any longer. So I propose a vote, by a show of hands. I want to know what's being done in my name."

"Before everyone votes, I should let you know that our contractors – no, our partners in this affair – were attacked in Libya only hours ago," Saul, the head of the security committee, said, *sotto voce*.

"Attacked? Related to our matter?" Jacob demanded. "And when were we going to be informed?"

"Jacob. Relax. We don't know that it had anything to do with this. Early reports suggest it might have been insurgents – the house was in Benghazi, and that's seen more than its share of violence in recent months," Saul assured him, sounding reasonable. "There's no hint that this involves our operation. But it *is* an indication of how vulnerable we all are, even now."

"What it tells me is that these men shouldn't have been living in a war zone," Jacob snapped back. "Yet another aspect we knew nothing about. I had a phone number for them, but if the security committee had told me that they were in Benghazi, I would have told them to move – immediately. Saul, I'm saying that the time for silence is over."

"Until the detonation, I think it's a poor idea for anyone to know more than they do," Bernard, another security committee member, said. Bernard was a perennial curmudgeon, so nobody took his grumbling tone personally. "We've waited this long. What's a few more days?"

"Bernard, what harm could possibly come from you sharing with the members when and where the detonation is to take place, now that it's practically happened? Don't you trust us? Is there anyone here whose loyalty or ability to keep a secret is in question?" asked Rubin, one of the other members, bristling at the implication.

"It's not about secrecy, necessarily. If someone did something stupid, like taking large options positions in anticipation of a major disruption of oil supplies, it could be backtracked to them and endanger our existence moving forward – at a time when our solidarity will be even more necessary than ever," Saul said.

"Then let's pass a resolution barring any of our members from investing based on the knowledge. That's simple. I trust my fellow Council members to honor that. The question is, do you, and if not, why not?" Jacob said, turning the objection around on Saul. He could sense the sentiment in the room going his way; he didn't want to belabor the point, so he decided to close with his strongest argument. "Look, I've been a member of The Council for over twenty years. We've never had a security breach, and all the members have always conducted themselves in a manner that's above reproach. I, for one, am confident that everyone in this room will preserve our secret. That being the case, I dislike being treated like an idiot child who can't be trusted to know the truth. Especially after putting millions of my own money into the project. Frankly, I understood the need for compartmentalization before, but at this juncture, the reasoning is just insulting."

He sat down, his point made, and then cleared his throat and tapped his pen against the side of his bottle of Perrier water, calling for attention.

"I propose a vote. First, on banning any investment based on foreknowledge. All in favor?"

The vote was unanimous.

"Before we vote on the security issue, may I just remind everyone how close we are to a success we've all been waiting for over thirteen years to achieve? Why endanger it now? Be patient for just a little while longer. I urge you all to take the high road on this," Saul said, trying to turn the tide.

"Right. Because only Saul, Bernard, and Russ can be trusted," Jacob said, naming the three members who knew all the details – effectively driving a wedge between them and the other members. Framed in that manner, how could the others not be insulted, especially when their money had flowed generously, and without question? Jacob sensed his win, and tapped the bottle again.

"And now, a show of hands. All those in favor of the security committee informing us of the details of the impending detonation?" Six hands shot up, with the three members of the security committee abstaining. Under the rules of The Council, a majority of seven would be required, and for a moment Jacob's heart sank. Then, slowly, Russ' hand rose, passing the vote.

"There. It's decided. Saul, time to spill the beans. What are you up to?" Jacob asked, the moment of his ultimate betrayal at hand.

Saul shook his head in defeat. "I think it's a terrible idea to tell you anything," he protested.

"We understand that. But the vote has been cast. Now tell us," Jacob pressed.

"Very well. Tomorrow, at ten-thirty a.m. local time in Qatar, the device will be detonated at a brunch that kicks off the annual Arab League meeting – a special assembly attended by not just the delegates but the heads of many of the countries, including Saudi Arabia and Iran. The leaders of virtually every Muslim country will be there, so in one fell swoop the funders of global terrorism will be eradicated. This will accomplish two things – first, it will disrupt the flow of money to those who have been working to destroy us – Hamas, Hezbollah, and all the rest. And second, it will create a situation where we will likely be blamed, irrationally, of course – forcing at least a limited war with our belligerent neighbors in which we can seize necessary territory and deal swiftly and finally with those who would love to see our beloved nation destroyed. It will create a new order for the region, and enable us to take a leadership role."

The room was silent at the audacity of the undertaking. Most had been imagining a strategic strike, perhaps against Iran, but to kill all their adversaries in one blow... The Council was composed of ultra-hard liners for whom there was no middle ground. Most had been in combat, defending the country, and had little patience for the diplomacy that had, in their view, eradicated the nation's resolve. The plan made perfect sense – if one condoned butchering tens of thousands as well as assassinating the heads of state of virtually every other country in the region.

"How will it be done? What's the mechanism?" Jacob asked in a hushed voice.

"I don't know. Nobody does. Our partners in this were adamant that they control that part of it, in complete secrecy. We had to agree on the target and fund them, but beyond that, they're the implementation side, and the less we know, the better," Saul explained, and Bernard nodded beside him.

Jacob's stomach did a flip at the information.

Nobody knew how to stop the bomb.

And it was going to go off tomorrow morning.

৵৽৽

The director gasped as he heard Saul describe in calm tones the insane scheme that would throw the Middle East into chaos. He turned to Jet, afraid to miss even a single syllable as the meeting was broadcast to headquarters from the surveillance point, and listened in horror as Saul described how the actual details weren't known to anyone in the room.

"They're mad. Absolute lunatics. If this succeeds it'll ignite the region and mean war – possibly world war," he whispered.

"Yes, the most dangerous thing in the world is a bunch of rich old men who feel that many dying is an acceptable tradeoff for whatever their agenda is."

"It has to be stopped."

Jet nodded. "I agree. But have you noticed how those advocating killing always believe that God is on their side, and that they're just doing what has to be done to combat an even greater evil?"

"All due respect, spare me the philosophy. We have to stop this. Whatever it takes. Good Lord…it's happening tomorrow…I need you to get ready to fly to Qatar. I'll assemble a support team. Lou, get the situation room briefed and ready – find out what assets we have in Qatar, and the best way to get a team in without alerting the locals," the director said, turning to his second in command.

"You need to tell Qatar," Jet said flatly. "This completely changes the stakes."

"I'll brief the cabinet within the hour. I don't disagree, but there's more to this than just warning Qatar. For one thing, they hate us. For another, it will achieve almost the same effect even if they abort the summit – we'll look like monsters, even though this is a rogue group and in no way officially sanctioned. We'll be painted with the same brush and demonized in the eyes of much of the world. There are a lot of things to take into account…"

"Wait. You mean to tell me you're going to consider the political fallout, instead of just the actual fallout of allowing a nuke to take out the entire Arab world's leadership? Tell me how that's any less insane than planting the nuke in the first place?" she fired back, momentarily forgetting who she was talking to in the heat of her outrage.

The director looked like he'd been punched, and then replied frostily.

"Thank you for your thoughts on geo-political realities. I'll pass them on to the cabinet. Might I suggest that you temper your passion and stick to the mission? We need to stop this event from occurring. That's the easiest fix."

"Yes, but right now all we know is that there's a bomb that will vaporize the Middle East's leaders that's set to detonate tomorrow morning, and we know nothing else about it. How would *you* suggest we go about stopping something that we can't find?" she snapped back, furious at his arrogance.

"I'd say you should come up with a plan, then. We don't have much time. You have any and all resources you wish – so make it happen."

She choked back her anger and nodded. "Fine. First thing, get every satellite under our control focused on Qatar. Do we have any that can detect radiation?" she asked.

"That's a secret. But yes, we do."

"Get them pointed at Qatar as well. The more eyes we have on it, the better our odds of spotting something. And if we have any operatives in the capital, let's have them relay anything they hear, no matter how insignificant. We have about twenty hours to discover a lead and turn it into something we can use." She gave him a dark look. "You realize that if I go in and can't stop this from happening, that getting out, assuming I'm not in the blast zone, is going to be close to impossible, right? I didn't sign up for suicide."

He studied her face, nodding. "I understand you have a daughter. Don't ask how I know. Remember, my job is to know things. I can appreciate how you would want to be around for her, but I'm afraid I have to insist you follow this through. At worst, I'll make a personal commitment to extract you, no matter what the cost. You may have to go to ground there for a little while, but I'll get you out. You have my word on that."

"And what about if I'm caught in the blast?"

"Don't be. If you haven't stopped the device by ten-fifteen, get the hell away from the meeting zone."

"That's cutting it close, isn't it?"

He checked his watch. "I need to get going. I'll have my men round up these traitorous Council scum and interrogate them. You don't need to concern yourself with them anymore. Get ready to move out after you meet with the situation team in…two hours. I'll need an hour with the cabinet, and then I'll return. Start without me if I'm not back. Lou, she's to be accorded every respect. Whatever she says, goes. Clear?"

Lou stiffened, practically saluting. "Yes, sir."

"Send the men in and take the so-called Council to one of our larger facilities. I don't want them talking to each other. Put interrogators on the three security committee men and get everything they know. Use whatever means are necessary. I don't care what you have to do – it's possible that this 'Saul,' or one of the other two, was holding something back. Find out. Now, if you'll excuse me, I need some privacy. I have to make some sensitive calls," the director said, and moved to the door. "I'll be in my office if anything comes up."

"What about Jacob?" Jet asked.

"What about him? I never made any deal with him. You did. He can spend the rest of his life with the others. I'd say he more than earned it," the director snapped, and then stalked from the room, the stink of nicotine trailing behind him as he left to inform the government that the unthinkable was about to happen.

CHAPTER 29

Doha, Qatar

The dry air was still, the aftermath of an afternoon dust storm having left a thin film of grit on everything in its wake. Towering buildings thrust relentlessly into the starry night sky, the glow from their lights illuminating the financial district enough to give Las Vegas at its most garish a run for its money. The city was at rest at one in the morning, the never-ending construction taking a necessary breather; the massive cranes towering above the endless array of skyscrapers were motionless, awaiting the dawn of a new day.

Nearby Dubai was famous for its world class hyper-development, but Doha had similar aspirations and was making up for lost time. An idyllic seaport with white sand beaches, tranquil turquoise Persian Gulf water, and virtually limitless oil revenues, the tiny nation was hell-bent on rising with the dawn of the twenty-first century.

Solomon and Joseph had parked several miles away and stolen an inflatable dinghy with an outboard engine to make their approach to the darkened port. Countless cargo ships and support craft for the oil rigs out in the Gulf hulked along the concrete waterfront embankments, their heavy steel forms pulling gently at the lines securing them as a lazy surge pulsed in the harbor. The throb of the outboard sounded like a jet on takeoff to Solomon, but he knew that his nerves were close the surface and that nobody was likely to pay any attention to it.

Joseph killed the engine as they neared their destination, and then dropped the oar tips into the water and began rowing toward the huge ships. A few minutes later the small craft glided to a stop at the base of a corroded steel ladder rising from the water, and Solomon tied the bow line to it, securing the boat for a quick getaway. They had considered other means to get into the container storage area of the busy port, but ultimately discarded them as too risky – a sea approach was the least likely to be detected.

Solomon pulled himself up the rungs, grimacing at the pain radiating from his wounded shoulder. Joseph followed him up. Both men wore black and were invisible in the darkened yard, where hundreds of shipping containers sat inside, awaiting transport to their ultimate unloading points. Joseph pulled a small device from his pocket and switched it on, waiting a few seconds for the screen to illuminate, and then he zoomed in and studied a blinking dot with coordinates immediately below it.

"We're about two hundred yards away. Follow me," he whispered, and then took off at a cautious jog in the direction of the target container. Solomon followed, trusting Joseph, who was the technology guru, to interpret the blip and get them to their destination.

Joseph stopped at a row of forty-foot containers stacked three high, and then shined his small flashlight beam on the identifying number of the bottom one and nodded to Solomon as he produced a pair of bolt cutters to cut the anti-tamper bolt. The hardened pin's head snapped off with a soft *crack*. He eased it free, raised the handle, and swung the door open.

Inside were dozens of wooden crates containing air conditioning compressors and power transformers, as well as machinery and parts for maintenance of the cranes that dotted the city's growing skyline. Joseph directed his beam on the boxes and then climbed inside, searching for the one that contained the device.

Halfway to the rear he stopped and smiled to himself. The red hand-written lettering for a five-ton compressor was exactly as he'd been promised – innocuous unless you were looking for it. Moments later he had pried the top off and slid it aside. He retrieved a flathead screwdriver and began dismantling the compressor casing. When he had it loose, he lifted the gray metal outer grills, placed them next to the crate, and unscrewed the inner top portion of the cooling fan. After a few more seconds he heaved the case out, his arm muscles bulging at its weight, and then set it next to the lid and switched his flashlight off.

Joseph grabbed the case handle and was moving from his position when the crate lid shifted and fell with a bang against the steel container wall, the noise like a fifty-five gallon drum smacking cement. He froze; and then a dog began barking. A big dog. Nearby.

He made it the rest of the way to the doors in a few long moments, and closed them as Solomon eyed the row of containers distrustfully. Joseph's eyes met his, radiating a silent apology. He handed the case to Solomon and pulled a silenced pistol from his backpack.

"Get going back to the boat. I'll slow whoever comes looking. Can you carry that?" he whispered, concerned about Solomon's ability to maneuver with the heavy case, given his wound.

"I'll manage," he responded, as he gritted his teeth and hoisted the strap over his good arm. "Let's split up. Make some noise and hopefully they'll go after you."

Joseph nodded. "I'll be back at the boat in five minutes. If not, leave, and we'll meet at the house. If you hear any sirens or anyone but me approaching, get the hell out. The device is more important than anything else."

"I know. But it's not going to do me a lot of good without you, so be careful."

"Can you find your way back?"

"I think so. I'll just keep going till I hit the water, then look for the dinghy. Now get out of here."

Joseph chambered a round in the pistol and strode off to the next row. He took another look back at Solomon, then ducked around the corner and was gone.

A flashlight beam blinked in the distance, sweeping down the aisles formed by the stacked containers, and Solomon took that as his cue to get moving. He heard a clatter nearby – Joseph creating a diversion, hopefully drawing any pursuers away – and squinted in the darkness as he trotted toward the water. Another noise, this time further away, was followed by a shout, and he picked up his pace as he toted the bomb, the weight slowing him more than he liked.

He heard the sound of full-speed motion behind him, then a fur-covered form slammed into his back and he fell face forward. The case pounded against the concrete, bouncing twice before it skidded to a stop five yards away. Solomon was barely able to stop his fall with his hands; a stab of blinding pain shrieked from his good shoulder accompanied by a low growl as a large German shepherd sank its teeth into him. He rolled to the side and pushed the dog off, swinging his fist at its head, and landed a blow that seemed to do nothing but infuriate the animal, which then went for his legs. Solomon stifled a scream as the dog latched onto his left calf, and he kicked his free boot at the slavering beast, breaking its jaws loose with a grunt.

The dog was leaping for his throat as Solomon held his arms up to defend himself when a pop sounded from in the gloom, and the dog whined mid-air as a slug tore through its back. The stunned animal landed a foot from Solomon's bleeding form – he rolled away and looked up to see Joseph sprinting from the shadows, silenced pistol in hand.

A light appeared behind Joseph and he spun and fired three times at the guard. The flashlight fell to the ground with a crash, followed by the wounded security man, his revolver clattering harmlessly at his side. As Solomon struggled to get to his feet, Joseph moved to help him, pulling him up while listening for any sounds of pursuit.

"Shit. The damned dog got me good," Solomon hissed, limping as he made his way to the case, holding his shoulder where blood was streaming from the bite.

"Just move. I'll take the bomb. Head for the water – it's just past that next row, to the right. Go," Joseph instructed, assessing Solomon's condition and instantly making a judgment call.

Solomon didn't argue, and staggered in the direction Joseph had indicated. Joseph waited, head cocked, anticipating more guards, but didn't hear anything, and after a few moments he approached the battered case and lifted it, gun gripped tightly in one hand as he carried the deadly device in the other. He increased his speed to a jog, and was just rounding the corner when his eye caught a glimmer of light at the far end of the aisle – more guards, and not too far behind. His only hope was that they didn't have more dogs, and that finding the wounded man would delay them long enough for him to make it to the boat and get clear of the area before they sounded a general alarm.

Once at the water's edge he ran as fast as his legs would carry him with the additional weight to contend with, and made it to the boat as Solomon was tying a piece of cord around his leg to staunch the blood pulsing from the shredded flesh.

Joseph slipped the pistol into his backpack and swung himself over the rail, clutching the side of the ladder with an iron grip, and lowered himself to the waiting tender. Voices were now audible from the container area. He placed the case in the bow, untied the line from the ladder, and pushed off.

"Move to the rear. I need to sit on the middle bench to row," he instructed, and Solomon inched to a position next to the outboard. Joseph dipped the oars into the water and spun the little craft around, then pulled with all his might for the inky water beyond the large cargo ships.

Two lights raced along the waterfront as the remaining guards hunted for the intruders, but by the time they made it to the ladder the dinghy was already on the far side of a five-hundred-foot-long cargo ship, whose rusting hull neatly concealed the boat as it continued its journey to the far side of the harbor.

Joseph waited until they were nearly at the port mouth before he started the engine and gave the motor as much throttle as it could take, and soon they were skimming along the calm sea toward the lights of the hotel near where they'd left the car.

Once ashore, they wasted no time hauling the case to the vehicle and placing it in the trunk.

"Damn. It looks like it was hit by a truck," Solomon said. "I'm sorry. The dog…"

"What's done is done. I'll check it when we get back to the house. Let me go deal with the boat. I'll be right back," Joseph replied. He closed the trunk lid and returned to the tender at the water's edge, stabbing the blade of his folding combat knife into the inflatable hull with a hiss. He watched it deflate for a few seconds, then pushed it away from the shore with his foot. Hopefully it would sink out of sight – not that it would matter as of morning tomorrow.

He returned to the car and got behind the wheel, then turned to consider Solomon. "You look like shit. I'd say the dog almost won that round."

"I don't disagree."

"How's the shoulder?"

"I'll live. I may need a doctor for my leg. We'll see when I get to the house. Maybe we can stitch it – hopefully it didn't get an artery. Hurts like a bitch, though."

The boat burbled air into the water behind them as it drifted, sinking slowly, the motor and fuel tank too heavy for it to stay afloat. Joseph muttered noncommittally and then backed out of the lot, traversing the dark asphalt in silence before he hit the lights as they rolled toward the seafront road that would take them to their safe house, his mind already on the possible ramifications of a damaged bomb only a scant few hours before it was scheduled for detonation.

CHAPTER 30

The French-flagged Citation business jet touched down on the runway in Nicosia, Cyprus, and after refueling and taking on three passengers, hurtled down the runway and into the starry sky. Jet watched the glowing lights of the island disappear beneath her before pulling down her window shade and closing her eyes, hoping to get a couple of hours of rest before arriving in Qatar in the wee hours of the morning.

The Mossad contacts in the capital had scrambled when the director contacted them and told them he needed to get some operatives in, and the money that had been required in order to get the immigration officials to turn a blind eye had been jaw-dropping; but then again, nobody was in a bargaining mood. Security had never been higher, in anticipation of the arrival of the heads of state for the Arab League meeting, and even with her Italian passport and the fake papers of the other two specialists, getting visas on a few hours notice had been nothing short of Herculean.

In the end, cash had won out, and the flight had been cleared for arrival at four a.m., with visas good for a week awaiting Jet and her two companions – the Mossad's top field operatives, now that her team was history. Jet had read the men's limited dossiers she'd been allowed to peruse, and had been heartened – while they didn't have nearly the qualifications of the members of her old group, they'd both been involved in enough successful operations to warrant confidence.

The planning session had dragged on endlessly, and as the hour had grown later, the attendees had agreed that they would get Jet onto the ground as the satellites were being repositioned, and pass on any intelligence that came in after to her in the field. As it was, until she touched down, the Mossad presence in Qatar was limited to intelligence gathering moles and a station head who would get them whatever equipment they needed. They couldn't chance bringing anything in on the plane, especially given the heightened security surrounding the conference.

Jet was frustrated by the lack of hard data they had to work with; other than knowing the bomb would be detonated at ten-thirty, they had practically nothing to go on. A contact in the government offices had secured a comfortable retirement by agreeing to provide a back door for the Mossad's hackers to get into the immigration database and scour it for the errant operative's entry records. The members of The Council had been taken into custody and were being interrogated, probably brutally, but as of right now, no new information had been forthcoming. Jet's only hope was that one of the security committee knew more than they had let on, and that the combination of extreme torture and drugs would yield something they could use. The director had made it abundantly clear that he wasn't concerned about whether any of them lived past sunrise, so the interrogation teams had carte blanche, and Jet's experience told her that they were using every means at their disposal.

The Citation hit a patch of turbulence as it reached the coast of Lebanon, and the pilot climbed in an effort to find a smoother altitude. While it would have been faster to fly from Tel Aviv, a private jet arriving from Israel would have been a red flag for Qatar, and no matter how much money changed hands, everyone on board would have been held and interrogated. Cyprus, on the other hand, raised no eyebrows, and because the plane was French flagged there was no connection to Israel – Jet had flown in over an hour earlier on a Lear 35 that had deposited her in the private Nicosia arrival lounge with no questions asked, and spent her time on the ground online before the French charter had arrived to take her to her final destination.

The only thing she'd brought other than a robe and veil and a change of clothes was a notebook computer, and concealed within it, an earbud and the associated comm gear. Hopefully their contact on the ground would be able to supply them with whatever they needed, although at this point that was a question mark – they had no target, no strategy, just an imperative to get into position in Doha and pray for a break.

Two hours later they began to descend and Jet came back to full awareness, her effort to catnap having been more or less successful once the ride had calmed down. The pilot's voice droned over the intercom and alerted them that they would be on the ground in fifteen minutes, and an uncomfortable silence settled over the cabin, the dull roar of the turbines the only sound as they banked on approach from over the Persian Gulf.

At the airport they were escorted through customs by a tall, dignified, sleepy-looking man in a military uniform who dispensed with immigration formalities by handing the clerk a sheaf of visas, freshly prepared by his office for the esteemed guests from Cyprus. Once their passports had been stamped, the officer said his goodbyes and departed, leaving them standing outside the private aircraft terminal staring at an empty access road.

Jet powered on her cell, and instantly her phone vibrated. She listened to the voice mail message and then hit redial, and was soon greeted by the director's deep and distinctive voice.

"Our man will be there any minute. He'll take you to a safe house and equip you, by which time I'm hoping we have something more. One of the interrogators phoned a few minutes ago to tell me that his subject knows more than he let on. Something about how the bomb entered the country. It may be nothing, or it may be critical. I'll call you when I know the details," he said.

"Fine. Right now we're standing around outside the terminal, fully exposed, with our thumbs up our bottoms. Let's hope your man here is just contending with traffic, because this isn't getting off to a great start."

Jet disconnected the call, both annoyed that their contact hadn't seen fit to be more prompt, and hopeful that they were catching a break from the questioning. The two operatives who had joined her on the plane ride, Aaron and Eric, looked at her expectantly, and she gave them the update as a pair of headlights rounded the long curve that led to the terminal. A silver Honda minivan pulled to a stop at the curb and the driver rolled down the passenger window.

"Open the side door and get in. Toss your bags next to you. Sorry I'm late," he said in Arabic. Jet gave him a black look and then slid into the passenger seat behind him. The others piled into the back, and soon they were rolling down the road, leaving the airport.

"What was so important that you left us waiting?" Jet asked.

The driver peered up at the rearview mirror and caught her glance. "The police had a checkpoint over by the port. They said there was a shooting. Didn't really seem to know what they were looking for, but it clearly wasn't one humble local on his way to work," he explained, his tone calm and reasonable. Jet immediately felt remorse for her attitude and quiet cursing of the man. "I'm Isaac, by the way. We'll be at the house in fifteen minutes, and then you can stretch out and check your gear. I wasn't able to round up a lot on such short notice – pistols and a Kalashnikov."

"What about ID?"

"As requested, I doctored up a few official identification cards making you members of the police force. They'll get you in and out of situations where there isn't a lot of scrutiny, but you're dead in the water if someone radios it in." Isaac glanced at the frowning faces of the group in the mirror. "How long will you be needing me?"

"All day," Jet said, not wanting to share anything more with him. If the bomb went off, the less he knew, the better. Which at this point was a very real possibility.

"I got a couple of cars for you to use, too. The communiqué indicated I should give you every courtesy, and specified you would require weapons, identification and vehicles. Do you think you'll need anything else?"

"How are you set for computer gear?" Aaron asked.

"Got a laptop and a workstation with two thirty-two inch monitors. State of the art."

They saw the flashing lights of the roadblock in the distance, off to their right, and Isaac gave it a wide berth, choosing secondary streets until they arrived at the house – a modest affair in a working-class neighborhood on the southern end of town. He reached up and pressed a garage door remote, and the heavy iron plate gates swung open, enabling him to pull the van into the walled compound and then close them behind him, effectively sheltering the house from any view from the street.

It was five in the morning by the time they got settled, and Jet was anxious to get going. When her phone vibrated she almost jumped. She hurried to answer it, stepping into the kitchen for some privacy as the men joined Isaac at the computer.

"The bomb entered the country by cargo ship. The container was removed from the ship the day before yesterday. At least we now know how they got it in," the director said, without preamble.

"Are they going to detonate it there?" she asked.

"Negative. Apparently, that came up during a cursory discussion of the planning. It's too far away from the brunch location."

"Well that narrows it down, doesn't it? To something close to the target?"

"Not necessarily. They could be planning to detonate it in a plane, a drone, a nearby car..."

"Then we're really no closer than we were."

"Correct."

"Is it possible it's still in the container?"

"Almost certainly not. The captive was sure that they were going in to get it either last night or the night before."

"Shit." Something tugged at Jet's awareness. "On the way from the airport, the local contact said there was some sort of a roadblock by the port. A shooting. What do you want to bet that was related?"

"I'm not feeling much like betting at the moment. I'll have the techs see what they can pull from the police servers. Now that we're in the immigration system, should be a piece of cake. Oh, and we have a photo of the tech man – Joseph. He entered on a work visa three weeks ago. Sponsored by a company affiliated with one of The Council's members, as was the shipping company that brought in the container. No doubt the address on the application is a fake, but it's something you need to follow up on."

"Send the photo and the address to the operational email account. We have good access here."

"There's one more thing. The facial recognition software also flagged a new arrival. Came into the country day before yesterday on a tourist visa. Traveling on an Egyptian passport. I'll be sending his photo over as well."

"Who is it?" Jet asked.

"Solomon. The older of the two brothers. My guess is that you killed the younger one in Libya during the attack."

Her mind churned as she digested the news. "Where did he fly in from?"

"Cairo."

"Which would be one of the hubs if he had been at the house during the attack. He would travel from either Tripoli or Benghazi…"

"That occurred to us. We're already tracing the passenger manifests, but I'm not sure how much good it will do. Still, we now have two of the targets in Qatar. As if we needed any further confirmation this was going to happen."

"How's the questioning going?"

"I'm not hopeful. One of the three already succumbed to a bad heart. I've given instructions to push the other two to the limit. We're down to only a few hours now. Believe me, if we hear anything, you'll be the first person I call."

The phone went dead. The director, as was his custom, simply hung up when he finished imparting whatever info he had. Jet considered this latest wrinkle – two ex-Mossad operatives to track down, rather than one.

She moved back into the living room, where the computers were set up, and instructed Isaac to go to the encrypted e-mail box and pull up and print out the photos. As she watched the images spill from the high-resolution printer, she had a sinking feeling in her gut – there was no time to find the bomb if all they had were some immigration photos.

Which meant that in just a little while, the fate of the world was going to change, forever, unless they got very, very lucky. And of the many things she'd been feeling since taking on this assignment, lucky wasn't one of them.

CHAPTER 31

Phuket, Thailand

The roar of the local bus outside the bar sounded like a runaway locomotive to Matt, who had ultimately decided to spend the night awake, moving among dozens of watering holes, never remaining in one spot for very long. Twice he had spotted possible watchers, and both times had evaded them by sneaking out the rear exits, knowing even as he did that he was probably being paranoid.

Whatever the case, the week of relaxation on the beach in Phuket had gone from an idyllic reward to a tense game of cat and mouse as he was pursued by unknown adversaries. The most likely explanation for the thief was that Niran had sold him out to a gang that would split any profits – or perhaps it was a well-equipped opportunist, but Matt doubted it. The most remote likelihood, but by far the most worrying, was that his old nemesis, the CIA's drug-running cabal, had gotten a whiff of him, either from Niran or from someone at the bank, and put a team on him.

But Matt hadn't stayed alive as long as he had by being careless or hoping for the best, and now he was in a state of high alert, watching for real or imagined threats behind every tree and vending machine. Fortunately for him, the nightlife in Phuket was non-stop and the carousing continued until dawn, catering to swarms of drunken Australians and Americans out for an adventure with one of the friendly natives.

At the final bar of the evening, he'd grown tired of his unrelenting counter-surveillance. After buying several beers for a tiny little thing in a plaid schoolgirl's skirt and a white silk blouse tied just under her breasts to better show off her flat brown belly, he agreed to accompany her to a nearby hotel that asked no questions and rented rooms in three-hour intervals.

Matt pretended not to speak the language and inwardly smiled when his new date told the bar Mama-san that she'd hooked a live one, and he cheerfully handed over the bar fine – compensation to the club for the money it ostensibly would have made if the girl had remained there instead of going off with him. She took his hand and led him into the night, walking confidently on a trip she'd undoubtedly made countless times before, in spite of her apparent teen age – also an illusion, but a carefully crafted one. He knew that she had probably been in the business for several years, and being as attractive as she was, serviced two to three patrons a night on a busy weekend. But her placid face and feigned naïveté were convincing, and he was quite sure that many an inebriated young man had fallen for her act.

She led him to a seedy single-story motel with a sporadically blinking neon sign promising 'Paradise Palms,' and he obligingly paid for the room, nodding as the old man behind the counter warned in broken English that he needed to be out no later than eight a.m., as though there was going to be a rush of post-breakfast patrons eager to use the facilities.

The room itself was everything he had imagined from the exterior – relatively new due to the reconstruction following the tsunami that had nearly wiped the resort from the map, but already sliding into disrepair, as was so much in Thailand. He set his bag down on the only chair, a scarred wooden job that looked like it had taken more abuse than the rusting fishing scows off the beach, and turned to his escort, who was humming to herself as she slipped off her blouse, revealing pert girlish breasts, one with a small tattoo of a scorpion on it that was probably her nod to truth in advertising. She gave him a beaming smile and then darted into the bathroom before he could say anything, and Matt relaxed when he heard the shower start – she was a conscientious one, his new schoolgirl friend.

He peered out the front curtains at the darkened courtyard and caught a flicker of movement in the corner of his eye, off to the left. He struggled to get a better glimpse of whoever was out there, but it was too dark and he couldn't make anything out. A part of him argued that, given the business model the motel had, it wasn't unexpected that there would be constant traffic on the grounds; but another urged caution and was clamoring a warning. It could be danger – someone who had followed from the bar, even if that seemed impossible to him.

Matt erred on the side of caution, and extinguished the lights before taking another glance outside. *There.* A man off to the side, maybe fifteen yards away – standing, watching Matt's room door, and on a cell phone. Perhaps it was all innocent, another satisfied motel customer phoning home, or someone working security at the late hour, but Matt wasn't interested in finding out the hard way that he was wrong.

The bathroom door opened and his new friend strutted from the bathroom wearing only high heels and a smile, and then hesitated, seeing the lights off and Matt still fully dressed.

"Come on, sexy man, I so hohney, don't make me wait…," she purred in a velvet sing-song, the words delivered with a kind of bored professionalism, and then she stopped when she saw Matt shake his head and remove a wad of baht from his pocket, peel off several large denomination bills, and hand them to her.

"What's wrong, lovah man? I need you, baby," she tried again, uncertain what was happening.

"No thanks, young sister. I'm afraid I don't feel well all of a sudden," Matt replied, this time in Thai, and her eyes narrowed at his unaccented command of the language.

"You don't want a girl? Maybe I can make you feel better, huh?" she said, sidling up to him, but then something about his expression stopped her.

"No, I think this was a bad idea. I'm sorry. It's not you. It's me. Too much beer and too many years. Get dressed – I want to get out of here. This place stinks," Matt said, his speech plodding and slightly slurred.

The girl did a quick assessment of the amount of currency in her hand versus what she stood to make if she was able to coax her suddenly agitated paramour into an entanglement, and decided that she was getting the better end of the deal if she just walked away. Keeping to her pidgin English act, she offered a professional smile.

"Okay, sexy man, maybe you come back tonight and I show you paradise, yes?" she offered, hoping to hold onto the business – especially in light of his generosity without her having had to do anything. He nodded and offered a tired smile, and she went back into the bathroom and was dressed in thirty seconds.

Matt walked her to the door, and she offered him a chaste peck on the cheek before he opened it – a surprisingly tender small intimacy from little more than a girl, who had been parading around in her birthday suit like a seasoned stripper only moments before. Matt watched her slip out the door, and then he closed it, cursing the cheap lock, and stepped to the other side of the sagging bed to check the back window. He pulled the curtain aside and found himself staring at iron bars, the dim light of an alley struggling to shine through the caked grime obscuring the glass. That wasn't going to be a way out. He next padded into the small bathroom to gauge his chances, but his heart sank when he saw that there was only a tiny ventilation window, also barred, and also facing the alley.

Returning to the room, he surveyed the meager furniture – an ancient chest of drawers, the bed, a bedside lamp, a chair. Not much to work with, but maybe, just maybe, enough from which to fashion a weapon – presuming he was right, and that they, whoever they were, would be coming for him before first light.

He didn't have long to wait. Half an hour after bidding the bar girl goodbye, the flimsy lock jiggled a few times and then released with a soft click. An unseen hand turned the knob, and then the door inched open, the room black as pitch, the form on the bed unmoving.

A slight figure slipped in, the distinctive outline of a pistol leading, and Matt waited another second to see whether there was more than one assailant before slamming the chair leg down on the intruder's head. The pistol tumbled onto the tiled floor, and Matt delivered another devastating blow. The figure collapsed, unconscious.

Matt remained where he was, anticipating another attacker, but after a few moments of silence he scooped up the pistol and studied it. He knew the weapon – an Ed Brown Custom Classic .45 caliber 1911, popular among the wealthy and the prosperous criminal element in Thailand. After checking to ensure that the magazine was full, he cleared the chamber, seated the bullet back into the magazine, then slapped it home before loading a round. The gun cost at least four thousand dollars, which ruled out any chance that this was an opportunistic robbery – petty thieves weren't in the habit of toting around Ed Browns to roll tourists in dives.

Pausing motionless, he listened for footsteps, but after thirty seconds the grounds were quiet. Confident now that nobody was going to follow the first attacker in, he knelt and squinted at the unconscious figure's face – a young Asian man, probably local. Judging by the blood streaming from his hairline he wasn't going to be doing much pursuing in the near future. Matt rose, and after expertly searching him, finding only a slim wad of local currency and a cheap cell phone, he hefted his bag and slipped the pistol into the waist of his shorts, hiding its bulk with his mini-duffle.

He slipped through the doorway and glanced around, his darkness-accustomed eyes roving over the surroundings, and when he saw nothing, he made for the far end of the courtyard and the exit that led out onto the street. Matt had gotten across the expanse and was pulling the iron gate closed behind him when he sensed someone approaching from his right. He spun and then relaxed when he saw that it was only a local girl, walking from the main street. She smiled at him as she neared, and he almost missed the tell-tale glint of steel from the stiletto as she lunged, trying to eviscerate him with the razor-sharp blade. He stepped back and turned sideways, presenting as small a target as he could, and the knife slashed through his shirt as he brought his hand down against her wrist, simultaneously whipping the pistol from his shorts and slamming it against her temple.

She stumbled and dropped the knife, but then surprised him by winging a kick at his head, even as blood trickled down her face from the gash he'd put in her skull with the weapon. The kick got him in the neck as he instinctively pulled away, and everything began to fade – she'd managed to get him near enough to the carotid that he was momentarily stunned. He shook off the daze as she dipped her left hand and retrieved the knife; she was about to make another run at skewering him when he rabbit-punched her in the face, breaking her nose. Her eyes welled with tears and fury, and then he spun and delivered a brutal kick to her chest, knocking her backwards. She lost her balance, stumbled, and went down hard, and he heard the crack of her head splitting as the back of her skull struck the sidewalk.

She convulsed several times, jerking like a beached fish, and Matt didn't stick around for the inevitable. The pair had been working as a team, and he had no way of knowing whether there were more, or if these two were the night shift after the safecracker had run off. The girl had been good – almost too good, he thought, as he moved down the sidewalk. Better than an amateur, with an adept command of Thai martial arts and unexpected tenacity.

Whoever had sent them after him had paid top dollar, but they'd underestimated his abilities, as well as his field instincts. If the man survived his beating, he'd be out of the game for a long time, so he no longer presented a threat. The girl was history – he'd seen those kinds of convulsions before, and he knew what they meant.

Matt slowed as he neared the corner and checked his watch – five-thirty, so maybe another forty minutes to go before dawn. The inevitable police would take their time at that hour, but it would still be wise to put some distance between himself and Phuket. There was a good chance that the motel clerk might give them a decent description, and even if every other person in town seemed to be a middle-aged Caucasian man on vacation, he didn't want to press his luck any further than he already had.

He glanced around the building's edge and, seeing nobody on the larger street, hesitated for a moment and then opened his bag to retrieve another shirt – this one a light-green short-sleeved dress shirt he'd acquired in Bangkok. He pulled it on and stuffed his current one into the sack; then, with that flimsiest of disguises, made for the bars, where he was hopeful he could get a cab to the airport and from there another headed north. He knew the country well enough to know that trying to board a plane in Phuket was a bad idea, but if he could make it to the mainland – a town with an airport, like Krabi – he could get out of the area and go to ground someplace more remote.

Which, at this point, as he rubbed his neck, sore from where the woman's shoe had gotten him, sounded like a good strategy, given how badly his attempt at a beach holiday had gone.

As he approached the nightclubs, the disco music still pumping from the tireless speakers, he smiled. Last time he'd decided a beach in Thailand was a good destination they'd burned down his house and killed everyone around him. This time had also rendered a poor result, although not as dramatic.

Maybe, he thought, next time he'd stick to the jungle.

So far that had proved the safest choice.

And right now, safety sounded pretty good.

CHAPTER 32

Doha, Qatar

The dingy walls of the safe house seemed to seep despair as dawn's rays brought the tense group no closer to finding the bomb than they had been two hours earlier. Jet paced the rough tile floor, her usual calm marred by an anxiety that was palpable as the minutes ticked by with no further contact from headquarters.

When the phone rang, Jet lunged for it on the dining room table, now the epicenter of their ad hoc situation room, and stabbed the call activation button.

"I have news. A radiation sensor was triggered at the port at about the same time a guard was shot. So the bomb is hot – we have no idea how much radiation it's leaking, but it is, which means that we may have a shot at locating it using our satellite. We have the ability to locate minute amounts of radiation if we know what we're looking for. In this case, Ben, the technician, confirmed that the business end was uranium, so we're calibrating the satellite to look for any traces in Doha. It'll be in position in twenty minutes, and we should get several good hours before it's orbited out of range again."

"How long until you have something?" Jet demanded, her words laced with impatience.

"If there's anything to be had, I would think within the hour. But this isn't an exact science. This is all very new stuff, and it's not a hundred percent. Usually we would be looking for something larger. I just wanted you to know that we're on it," the director said.

"What about the local authorities? Aren't they freaking out with the Arab League meeting happening today and a radiation sensor sounding the alarm?"

"Apparently not, although it's hard to tell for sure. The attack on the guard is being treated as a robbery issue. We only found out about the radiation sensor just now, and nobody's made the connection. Remember that there are innocent things that could set one off – poorly shielded

176

medical containers with radioactive sources being by far the most common. Qatar doesn't have the same concerns that a port like New York does, so the sensors aren't nearly as sophisticated. According to the report, the government will have a hazmat team going into the container area today, but it's a big place with hundreds of possible suspects."

Jet snuck a look at the men and then walked down the hall to the bathroom.

"You haven't told them, have you? The Qatar government?" she whispered.

The director sighed, weighing how best to answer her direct question. "It was decided at a higher pay grade than mine that a group of our most prominent citizens scheming to nuke the Arab leadership into oblivion could be misconstrued. *Would* be misconstrued. So no, nothing's been said. We're depending on you and your team to stop this in time. If not, it's a Russian device, and will ultimately be traced back to the Russians. We have plausible deniability."

"But you don't need deniability. You're doing everything in your power to stop it."

"That's not how politics works, my dear. Nothing is straight lines." The director sounded exasperated, unaccustomed to having to explain himself to anyone, much less female subordinates. "There are more considerations than I'm able to discuss, but the decision was made at the highest level."

"It's a stupid, dangerous decision," Jet snapped, furious at the old men running the government for risking countless lives, as well as the stability of the region. "Surely having a nuke explode is worse than a PR problem."

"I don't disagree, but it's out of my hands. At this point you're our only hope. If the worst happens..." The director paused, and then cleared his throat. "I don't expect you to be happy with the decision, but it was made, and there's no going back now. I'll call you as soon as we have something on the leak."

Jet stared at the dead encrypted phone, shaking her head. The enormity of the situation was like a monstrous weight over her head – her government had betrayed her trust with this idiocy, and now the world would pay. She wondered how many innocents would be immolated by the blast – people who had never harbored any hate in their hearts, who were guilty of nothing but being in the wrong place at the wrong time. Children like her Hannah, just starting out in life...

The ramifications infuriated her, but there was nothing to do. She wasn't responsible for the crisis, but she would certainly be part of the solution – if any was to be had.

Jet choked back the rage she felt, the broiling in the pit of her stomach eating at it like acid, and took several calming breaths before going back to the men and filling them in on the new radiation detector development.

⌖

"It's cracked. You can see where the lead shielding has a hairline fissure in it," Joseph reported, leaning back from where the bomb sat on the dining room table.

"What about the circuitry?"

"Everything appears to be functional, but there's only one true test. It'll either work, or it won't."

"Damn it. This is a disaster. Isn't there any way we can be a hundred percent sure?" Solomon demanded.

"No. But I *can* be sure that we're getting irradiated the longer this thing is around with that crack. And I, for one, would like to live to tell about our day of victory," Joseph said.

"Can you repair it?"

"I don't see any reason why not. The truth is that it's more of a safety issue for us than a functionality issue. Whether or not it works is going to come down to whether there are any microscopic cold solder joints – something we can't fully verify without detonating it. I've checked what I can with my instruments, and I'd say it's still viable, but now that it's been dropped–"

"Joseph, I can't tell you how sorry I am," Solomon interrupted, his face pale from blood loss as well as the pain of having his bites cleaned and sutured without anesthetic.

"Enough, already. Let me think for a second. I'll need to jury rig something with lead. I don't want to risk the device itself, or I'd just melt the existing shielding to repair it." Joseph trailed off, thinking about where he could get some lead to make the repair. At six a.m. in Doha, it wasn't like he could just head to the nearest hardware store and ask them if they had any lead available to repair a bomb.

"Can't you just scrape some from the rest of it, then melt it down and pour it into the crack? There has to be more lead than necessary in that thing. And it's not like we need it to shield the uranium for the next fifty years…"

Joseph contemplated Solomon's suggestion and then leaned back and smiled. "You're not just a pretty face after all, are you? I would have gotten there, eventually. I'm just tired."

"I know the feeling. I'd gladly trade you whatever fatigue you have for the dog bites."

Joseph frowned. "I felt bad about the poor dog. He was just doing his job."

Solomon nodded and took the seat next to him.

"As are we all, my friend. As are we all…"

CHAPTER 33

The promised hour turned out to be more like an hour and a half, but when the call came in at seven forty a.m. the news was the most positive that Jet could have hoped for.

"We narrowed it down and have a location. It's a house in the Abu Hamour district, near the big animal market." The director's voice was excited for the first time Jet could remember.

"Can you send everything you have? This is going to be a seat of the pants operation, but I don't see that we have much choice in the matter. We're going to have to go in. Am I missing something?" Jet asked, hating that they were going to have to do an incursion in broad daylight with zero surveillance or information on what to expect.

"It's on its way. But the bottom line is that we have a defined radiation signature coming from the structure, so unless someone is enriching uranium in their bathtub, that's our target."

"I'm presuming that we have full discretion on how to handle this?"

"Absolutely. All I care about is that you stop the bomb from going off. I don't really care how. Once you have it, we'll take it from there, but how you get it is up to you."

"Okay, then, we're going to move out as soon as we've got all the recon. Do you have satellite imagery for it?"

"That's a different bird. It'll take a few minutes to get it up on line – it's just now hitting the point in orbit where we'll get images. The technicians are scrambling to bring it live. Any second now."

"Damn. Isn't anything going to go our way on this one?"

"At least the one with the radiation detector was in position this morning. That's something."

"I suppose so. Anything else?"

"Good luck. You know the stakes."

"I haven't forgotten them."

This time when the line went dead, it was Jet who terminated the call. She strode into the living room, where everyone was gathered around the monitors, studying the odd-looking thermal imagery that highlighted the radiation as a bright blip on the overlaid map.

"We have a go. You're looking at the target. I want to move out in five minutes. Isaac, what can you tell us about that neighborhood?"

Isaac shook his head. "It's a residential area. Middle class mostly, shop owners and managers, construction supervisors and the like. I've only been through it a few times, but it's very much like this one – nothing special."

"I don't suppose you have any surprises for us, like some decent assault weapons instead of this Russian junk?" Jet asked, eyeing the well-used AK-47 by the door.

"On short notice, you're lucky you aren't going in with daggers and slingshots," Isaac said with a shrug. "I only had a few hours to round these up. It's not like anyone gave me sufficient time. And I still don't know enough about what you're doing to be dangerous."

Isaac had been kept out of the loop, other than being informed that the group was targeting terrorists. He didn't know about the nuke, nor that their adversaries were ex-Mossad. The director had kept the need to know very tight; if the bomb went off, the fewer that knew what had actually happened, the better.

"Trust me, you have as much information as you want to. How long will it take to get us there?"

"At this hour? Maybe twenty minutes. You want to take one vehicle, or multiples?"

Jet considered the question. "You drive the van, we'll take the two cars. I have no idea what we're walking into, so might as well err on the side of maximum flexibility."

Isaac nodded and stood, jingling his keys. "I have a pistol as well. Hopefully I won't have to get involved in the shooting, but if you need help with this, just let me know and I'll do what I can."

"If all goes well, you'll just be keeping an eye out on the street so we aren't disturbed. But it's never a bad idea to be packing," Jet said.

Aaron and Eric checked their weapons as Jet studied the directions, and then they bundled the assault rifle into a rucksack along with a pair of bolt cutters. Jet fixed the earbud into place and the others followed suit, and the group moved outside, Isaac taking the van and Jet taking one of the cars while the men took the other.

The streets leading out of the area were congested with commuters bound for work, and Jet found herself frequently being cut off by drivers who seemed completely unfamiliar with turn signals or basic rules of the road. Isaac seemed utterly unfazed by any of it, gunning the van into seemingly impossible openings with the fearless dexterity of a Formula One champion. The flow lightened as they moved north, parallel to the seashore, as most of the traffic headed for the downtown districts and the towering buildings that housed many of Qatar's largest businesses.

When they drew closer to the target, Isaac murmured into his earbud. "The house will be up on the right, two blocks, number 193. How do you want to do this?"

"Pull past it and let's get a look at the parking near it," Jet instructed. "If it won't look odd, park within a hundred yards and begin surveillance. I'll slow down, so we aren't in a motorcade, and park further away. Gentlemen, see if you can find a spot around the corner, preferably on the next street over, so you can watch the back."

The homes were typical of the region – high walls on the lot perimeters to act as a barrier against robbery, ornate iron gates protecting the driveways and entrances, the construction basic with few frills. The properties were smaller than the safe house, perhaps sixty feet wide by double that deep; an area without pretensions, where the residents worked long hours to pay for their dwellings. She hung back as Isaac braked and swung the van to a stop near the far corner, then backed into a space between two junker vehicles that looked like they were on their last legs.

She kept her speed constant as she drove by the target, noting that there were no cameras in evidence – just the ubiquitous satellite dish on the flat roof, along with air conditioning compressors and a propane tank, presumably situated there to discourage theft. The street itself was quiet, any children already in school, their working parents on their way to the job. Once she was past, she made a right turn on the next street, noting Isaac reading a paper as he watched the house in his side mirror, and then drove slowly around the block, looking for anything they could use to their advantage. As she was approaching the target's street again, her cell vibrated.

"We've lost the signal," the director said, his gruff voice taut.

"What do you mean, lost it?"

"The satellite stopped picking anything up about twenty minutes ago. We first thought it might be some kind of atmospheric interference, but not now. The signature disappeared, and the satellite has been confirmed as fully operational."

"Isn't that impossible? I mean, it's radioactive. How do you stop something from being radioactive just like that?" Jet demanded, coasting to a stop near the corner.

"We're still detecting a trace – background radiation from the house – but other than that, nothing. I don't know what to say. It was there, then it just stopped being there."

"Shit. Where does that leave us?"

"I can't make the call from here. You're on the ground, so I'll defer to your expertise. But my gut says go in hard, and do it now. Time's not our friend, and we know that the device was there until a few minutes ago. Ben, the technician, says that it's possible that they opened the shielding for some reason, and then closed it back up. So there's still a good chance that they, and the bomb, are still inside."

"What about the visual sat feed?"

"That's why we thought it might be an atmospheric glitch. It's taking longer than we thought to bring it online and grab the stream. The techs say the data's still there, so they can recover the small window of time since the radiation emission went dark, but it'll take a few more minutes – hopefully only a couple."

"All right. I'm signing off. I'll report back once we've taken the house. If you know any good prayers, I'd start saying them."

"Believe me, I exhausted my repertoire hours ago."

Jet punched the call off and considered the new information. A bad situation had just gotten far worse. At least as long as the satellite was picking up the radiation emission, they knew that the nuke was in the house. But twenty minutes was a lifetime without any sign of it, and her unease soured her throat as she tapped the earbud on.

"We're going in. I'm heading straight to the entry gate – if the lock is the usual for this level of place, I should be able to get it open in half a minute, tops. Aaron, I want the rear of the building watched. I saw an alley running between the houses for garbage collection. You have two minutes to get into position. Eric, you come up the street behind me. Give me thirty seconds of lead time. Isaac, stay put. But if you see anyone but us come out the front door, check in on the comm line and then follow them. If we all go down, you're the last link. You'll need to call headquarters and get instructions. Okay, everyone, I'll be making my approach in one minute. It's show time."

Jet caught a glimpse of her emerald eyes in the rearview mirror as she pulled on her veiled headdress – the bourga and shayla worn by devout Muslim women in Qatar, along with the ubiquitous abaya – the long black robe that served as perfect cover for toting a Kalashnikov. She double-checked the magazine in the assault rifle and chambered a round before doing the same with her silenced pistol, more a reflex than a necessity given that she'd already done so a half dozen times at the safe house. Satisfied that she was as ready as she would ever be, she patted her front pants pocket, where she carried the lock picks Isaac had given her, and then took a deep breath and exited the car. With a measured glance in both directions, she moved to the trunk and withdrew a bulging sack, then proceeded down the street carrying an opaque white canvas shopping bag filled with paper towels and water from the safe house, her date with a suitcase nuke and ruthless enemies only footsteps away.

CHAPTER 34

As she rounded the corner she spotted Eric near a corner market at the far end of the block, across the street from Isaac, where he'd been dropped off by Aaron and had raced for the alley to get into position. Jet took her time on approach, senses tingling, wary of any observation. So far she didn't detect anything, but that didn't reassure her – they'd had zero time to do any reconnaissance, which made this the very worst kind of operation right from the get-go. Even now the crosshairs of a sniper rifle could be trained on her head from one of the curtained windows of the two-story structure, a nervous finger tic away from vaporizing her skull. Her pulse pounded in her ears as the acrid taste of bile tickled her throat, and she choked it back as her eyes scanned the street, then the houses, her steps slow, befitting an older woman burdened with a thankless day's chores and a future of endless more.

She spotted the gate twenty yards up on her right and slowed further, now shuffling more than walking. In the gutter, sheltered from the sun by a dull gray pick-up truck, a mangy cat arched its back as she locked eyes with it, and for a moment everything seemed to freeze in her awareness, synthesized into that one second, the insanity of the pending nuclear devastation suspended as she considered the sad, frightened animal, and it looked back, seemingly into her core, an unspoken message in its glittering eyes.

A car backfired down the street, the report sounding like a cannon to her ears, and the spell was broken; then she was alone, the rifle clutched in her left hand, hidden by the folds of her robe, the barrel held tightly against her body as she set down her shopping bag a few steps from the door.

To any observer, Jet would have appeared to be pausing for a rest, leaning against the wall by the gate, catching her breath as the sun's baking rays beat down on her. Few would have caught the fleeting movement as she fished the picks from her pocket and, with her body blocking the gate from view, set to work on the lock, all her concentration focused on the tumblers, everything else filtered out.

The picking seemed to take forever, and then the lock gave with a soft click, just as footsteps clumped across the road at an unhurried pace – Eric, right on time, the only other figure on the street, a serious young man with a spring in his step. She gathered up her grocery bag, and when he was a few feet from her, she pushed open the gate and darted inside, followed immediately by Eric, who drew his pistol once he was in the courtyard. Jet set down her bag and whipped the AK-47 into firing position, finger on the trigger, then ran to the side window as Eric took the front door. She peered inside through a space between the heavy drawn curtains, but saw nothing except a darkened empty room, no sign of life in the living room or the kitchen.

"The front room is clear. I'm going to try the rear door – it'll have one," she whispered as she inched along the side of the house. "Wait for me – I'll be back in a few seconds."

Jet took cautious steps, eyes roving over the windows, and then she froze as she approached the kitchen window, her foot inches away from a nearly invisible strand of monofilament strung six inches off the ground, running from the perimeter wall to a junction box on the side of the house. Her eyes narrowed as she studied the box, then she lifted the bottom of her abaya and carefully stepped over it, marking an X in the soil to the side of the line before proceeding even more carefully, each pace hesitant, watching for anything suspicious.

There.

An almost imperceptible rise, a slight bump in the dirt, the surrounding earth marginally lighter in color – no doubt a land mine triggered by either a pressure plate or the tripwire. Not a particularly crafty device, but crudely effective against a trespasser in the dark. If they'd tried to go in a few hours earlier, they would have been hamburger – the only thing that had saved them was the morning light.

She tapped her earbud and murmured, "The place is rigged. Mine on the side. Tripwire. We have to assume the entire exterior is like this. I'm coming back to the front. There's a fifty-fifty chance they've wired the rear door and any of the windows – I would have."

"What about the front door?" Eric whispered.

"Also probably wired. I'm going to give you the AK, and then I'll scale the side of the house and try the second floor. Worst case, there's got to be a way in from the roof."

She retraced her steps and avoided the trip wire, then fixed Eric with a steely gaze as she handed him the Kalashnikov.

"Time for a little workout. Don't touch the door. I have a bad feeling about this whole deal," she said, then spun and sprinted for the side wall next to the house. Her boots struck the coarsely finished mortar and she moved laterally a few yards up before thrusting herself away, toward the house. Her fingers caught a second-story molded concrete windowsill. She paused, then heaved herself upwards, the soles of her Doc Martens fighting to grip on the rough mortar as the muscles in her arms knotted from the effort. The left toe of her boot found a slight indentation and she pushed herself higher; she then swung her legs to the side and, using the momentum, hurled herself at the small second-story balcony that had attracted her attention.

Eric watched her progress, a black-clad ninja defying gravity, and then returned his focus to the door when he saw her alight on the terrace, the weight of the Kalashnikov in his hands slim reassurance given what they were up against.

Jet squinted through the drapes at an empty bedroom, spartan, occupied by only a bed and a floor lamp. Her hands felt along the perimeter of the glass door frame as she pored over every inch of it before trying the handle, twisting it gingerly.

Locked.

But she hadn't been decapitated by a concealed grenade, so net positive.

The picks made short work of the largely cosmetic lock, and in seconds she was easing the glass door open, pulling it toward her, and slipping inside, her pistol now steady in her hand.

The rich smell of recently prepared food wafted up from below through the partially open bedroom door. As she drifted through the space like a ghost, nerves close to the surface of her skin, she didn't detect anyone – whoever had been in the house wasn't there any longer. Jet crept to the next door and listened for a few moments before cracking it open – a bathroom. Empty. The one beside it held another bedroom, also uninhabited. Ditto for the last.

Her hopes sank as she slipped down the stairs and quickly confirmed that the lower floor was also empty, although vacated so recently that the odor of breakfast still hung in the air like a taunt. She tapped her earbud.

"They're gone. No sign of them. I'm going to come out the front door. I'd back off from it if I were you – I see a keypad," Jet advised, then approached the crudely mounted box adjacent to the doorjamb. Her gaze followed the wire up to the ceiling and across to a potted plant on a molded ledge in the corner. She looked the box over, the contact points on the door mounted without finesse, and then flipped out a butterfly knife and sliced through the cable. They hadn't expected anyone to tackle disabling it from the inside, obviously. Another bit of luck – if losing track of the nuke that would change the world order could be considered in the same sentence as luck.

She unlocked the deadbolt, opened the door, and without pausing fished out her cell and dialed the director as she motioned to Eric to stay put.

"It was empty. But they couldn't have left long ago. Pull the satellite data and go back in time," she said.

"No indication of where they were going?"

"None. Unfortunately they didn't have a map of the city pinned to the wall with a big red star for the detonation site. Just some lukewarm coffee."

"We're live now, so let me see what we can get."

"I'm not going anywhere."

She told Aaron what had happened and advised him to pull his car around to where Isaac was waiting. Eric came inside, and she shut the door so as not to arouse any suspicion on the off chance the bombers returned.

Her phone vibrated again.

"We've pulled the data and we're going over it now." The director paused. "Wait. There. Twenty-three minutes ago. There's a van in the driveway. Two men are leaving the house. One of them is carrying something. Putting it in the back of the van. Now he's closing the door. Going to open the gate. The van is backing out. Damn. Some noise in the feed. Never mind. It's back. The van is pulling out of the driveway and he's closing the gate again. Wait – freeze that." The director hesitated. "I'm going to send this image to your phone while we're tracking them real time. Stand by."

A few moments later her phone vibrated again and she opened the file she'd been sent. A grainy black and white image of a tiny van. She zoomed in and then her breath caught in her throat. She held out her hand to Eric, showing him the picture, then raised the phone to her ear.

"Can you enhance that image? It's too blurry for me to make out."

"We're already working on it. In the meantime, we've acquired them and we're tracking the van. It made its way onto one of the main roads, heading east. Haloul street. Get going, and stay on the line. They're not that far ahead of you."

"Far enough, unfortunately."

CHAPTER 35

Jet ran to her car, trailed by Eric, Aaron staying in touch on the comm line to wait for instructions. She popped the trunk and he dropped the rifle in. She started the engine and the little car revved as he threw himself into the passenger seat; then she tore off, working through the gears as she held the phone and the wheel with her left hand.

"We're fast-forwarding through the footage. So far they're headed straight for the financial district near the diplomatic area," the director reported.

"That's not surprising. The big breakfast is on the grounds of the Four Seasons. The closer the better if they're going to be guaranteed to take the whole place out."

"How are you doing?"

"We're on the road, going as fast as we can. I don't want to attract any cops, so I can't do Mach two down the street, but I'm pushing it. Isaac is following us with Aaron. But it would really help if I knew where we were going."

"I know. We're doing the best we can." The director's voice was muffled for a few seconds as he had a hurried discussion with someone in the background. "All right. It looks like they stopped at a high rise at the edge of the diplomatic area."

"When?"

"Three minutes ago."

"What's the address?"

The director gave her the information, which she repeated for Eric's benefit. "They drove around to the rear of the building. Hang on. We're accessing the records on it. It's listed as still under construction, but it looks pretty far along to me," the director said.

"That's got to be where they plan to detonate it. How far is it from the hotel?"

"Less than half a mile. Easily close enough to vaporize everyone at the breakfast. Remember the briefing."

"I do. All too well."

"There. They're walking into the building, wheeling a cart. They went inside. How far away are you?"

"I'm guessing no more than ten minutes, if we're lucky. Anything on the image?"

"Not yet. Working on it."

Jet stopped talking as she swerved around a plodding semi-rig and almost hit an oncoming cargo van passing illegally, speeding toward her in her lane. She stomped on the brakes and struggled to control the car as the wheels locked up, screeching on the hot asphalt as she stood on her horn. The other vehicle careened back into its lane just before she would have struck it, and she caught a fleeting glimpse of an angry bearded face making an obscene gesture at her, and then she was past it and flooring the gas again.

"What happened?" the director barked, obviously agitated.

"Crazy driver. I need to concentrate on what I'm doing. I'll call back when we're close."

She redlined the engine as she pulled past another truck and slammed the shifter into fourth gear, focused on the erratic traffic. A few minutes later an ocean of red brake lights blocked the road, the traffic snarled as they got nearer the diplomatic area. Slowing, she checked the mirror to confirm that Isaac was still behind her, his maneuvering of the van nearly miraculous given the speed at which they had been hurtling down the crowded road.

Tall buildings thronged the skyline as they drew nearer the coast, and once close to their destination their progress slowed to a crawl. Jet hit redial on her phone and the director's voice boomed in her ear.

"Are you watching the time?"

"I've never been more aware of it in my life."

"We're getting down to the wire."

"Tell me something I don't know."

"The breakfast starts in an hour."

"We'll be at the building in five minutes."

"That doesn't give you a lot of time, I know. But we know they're inside. The van is still there."

"I'm thinking that we use our fake credentials to get past whatever security they have – will that stand up?"

"The men will have to take the lead on that. You can't. Remember where you are. I don't think it's believable if you're with them."

"Then how the hell am I going to get in? No disrespect, but I need access to the building if I'm going to stop the bomb from detonating."

"All I can say is improvise."

"Got it. Nuke going off in an hour, and the plan is to wing it." Jet hung up, shaking her head, and then the target building loomed ahead of them, easily thirty stories tall.

She tapped her earbud. "Aaron, we're going to go in, scope out the security situation, and figure out a way to search the building."

Aaron's voice came in loud and clear. "Sounds good. How are we going to do that?"

"I have an idea."

❧❦

Jet followed Aaron and Eric into the lobby of the office tower, and the two security guards behind the front desk looked up from whatever they were eating. The older of the two stood and shook his head.

"I'm afraid we're not open. This is a construction site," he intoned, not unfriendly but still firm, a practiced authority in his voice.

"Yes, I know. I'm here to show the space to my clients. They're looking for offices, and I was told the building is selling out fast," Eric said, offering his best real estate salesman's grin, as phony as a pole dancer's smile.

The two security men exchanged glances. They weren't prepared for anything besides checking the IDs of construction workers and lounging behind the counter all day.

"I don't think you're allowed up. Like I said, it's still a construction zone," the guard tried again.

"It looks pretty done to me," Eric said, trying another toothy display. "We understand that it's not completely finished. That's the whole point of showing it before it is – to be able to pick the floor we want. My clients are most anxious to see the space. I'd hate for the building owners to miss out getting a landmark tenant because of a misunderstanding. We won't be but a few minutes."

The younger one rose, uncertainty in his eyes. "We were told to only allow workers in. I'm sorry..."

"That's fine. I'm quite sure that they didn't mean to stop me from showing the available space," Eric replied, his tone confident and reasonable.

"If you'll wait a bit, I'll call someone and see if we can allow it," the older one said, and then his eyes widened when Aaron pulled his pistol from his jacket pocket and stuck it under the guard's chin.

"We tried this the easy way. Now let's do it the hard way. Both of you – stand completely still or I'll blow your heads off."

Eric moved from behind the guard and unholstered the older man's revolver. He slipped it into his jacket and rounded the desk to the younger man, who had his hands in the air at the first sign of a gun, and disarmed him.

"All right. Two men came in here a few minutes ago with a cart. Where did they go?" Aaron growled. Neither man responded. Eric withdrew his weapon from his waistband at the small of his back and held it high so they could both see it. When Jet lifted her robe and whipped the Kalashnikov out, it was obvious to the two hapless security men that the situation far exceeded their four hours of training.

The younger man was practically shaking at the sudden display, and the older one swallowed hard before answering.

"I…I don't know. We just check IDs. They go wherever they're supposed to once we let them in."

Jet stepped closer, the muzzle of the Russian assault rifle as menacing as a live cobra. "How many workers are in the building right now?"

The older one closed his eyes for a moment. "I don't know. Maybe forty? It's almost done. Not much left–"

"How many more guards?" Jet demanded.

"More? None. Just us."

Aaron nudged the older man in the chest with his gun. "I'm taking over security for the day. I'm guessing you have a storage room somewhere back there, or a bathroom?"

The younger man's eyes darted to the left as the older man's shoulders slumped. "Please. Don't hurt us. This is just a job," he begged, a bead of sweat trickling from his temple, teasing its way down to his chin.

"Do as I say and nobody gets hurt. I want you to cuff your hands behind your backs. Don't make me ask twice," Eric ordered.

The two men removed their handcuffs from their web belts and did as instructed, and then Aaron waved his gun at the doors behind them. "Which one?" he asked, and the older man indicated with his head.

"First one on the left is the security office."

"Move."

Thirty seconds later Aaron emerged and nodded to Jet. "They're not going anywhere. I disconnected the phone and duct taped their mouths. Now, how do you want to do this?" he asked.

"Somebody needs to stay down here while we're searching the building. You're it, Aaron. Eric and I will go floor to floor." She rounded the counter and leaned the AK-47 against the back of the reception desk, then checked the time. "It's probably best if I don't cause a panic with the remaining workers. Aaron, you take the rifle." She glanced at the bare counter. "This is a big building, and the device could be anywhere. Did you see any security monitors in the back room?"

"Nope. I don't think they've got that part finished yet," Aaron answered, taking a seat behind the desk. "Do you want me to check IDs if anyone comes in, or turn everyone away?"

"Turn them away. Tell them that there's a contamination inspection going on – someone complained about something. Whatever. But I want as few people in here as possible."

Aaron nodded, and Jet made for the elevator bank with Eric.

"Where do you want to start?" Eric asked, stabbing the elevator button. Three sets of stainless steel doors faced them, the nearest one humming quietly as it descended to the ground level.

"You take the bottom fifteen stories, I'll take the top. At a minute or so per floor, we should be able to completely search the building and be done within thirty minutes of detonation. We'll stay in touch via the comm channel."

Eric shook his head. "Wouldn't it be a better idea to start at the top floor and leapfrog down, alternating floors?"

"That's exactly what I would expect if I were them – they were trained using the same playbook we were, so they might anticipate that. And given the distance to the target, the device could be anywhere in the building. The speculation that they would shoot for an upper floor is just that – guesswork."

"Then what you're saying is that any way we slice it, we're screwed."

"Welcome to government work. I'm thinking we start with the middle floors because it's unorthodox, and that's about the only advantage we have at the moment – our ability to be unpredictable. Put yourself in their shoes – what would you do?"

Eric nodded. "You're probably right. They haven't made any stupid mistakes yet."

"Which is why we're going to do this my way. Are you ready?" she asked.

"I'll start at the fifteenth and work down," he confirmed as the closest elevator slid open with a hiss.

"I'll work up from there," she agreed, glancing around the lobby one final time before they stepped into the elevator, precious seconds ticking away in their race to stop a nightmare.

CHAPTER 36

Jet was prepared for anything when the elevator arrived at the sixteenth floor. Thankfully her robe provided cover for the pistol in her hand, its long suppressor unwieldy but necessary if she was to avoid drawing the police when she came across her quarry. She found herself looking out over the city and the Persian Gulf beyond it, the view as breathtaking as any she'd seen. The polished marble floors gleamed in the natural light streaming in through the floor-to-ceiling tinted windows, the entire space open, the layout of the final interior walls still to be completed to the ultimate tenant's specifications. She did a fast walkthrough of the area, her muffled footsteps echoing in the ghostly quiet space as she inspected the oversized electrical panels in one of the corners, and then went back to the elevator and took it to the seventeenth floor.

This time, her arrival was met by three workers framing out an office, using aluminum studs and drywall, who looked as mystified by the apparition of a woman as if she'd been a circus bear riding a unicycle. All three stopped what they were doing and stared, their eyes following her as she repeated her search. The heaviest of the men put down his level and frowned slightly at Jet.

"Can I help you?"

"I'm looking at the space. Considering renting it."

"Not this floor. It's already taken. We're building it out."

"Ah. I must have hit the wrong button."

"The next one up is also taken. We've got crews working on it. But I think most of the upper floors are still available – nobody has told us to do anything up there yet."

Jet nodded her thanks after a quick glance at the junction boxes. She was dying to ask whether the men with the cart had been through there. "Say, I met two very helpful men pushing a cart downstairs. Have you seen them? I wanted to thank them."

The workers gave her a blank stare.

"A cart? No. Sorry," the heavyset foreman said.

She moved back the elevator. The stainless steel panels glided open on their freshly oiled tracks and she pressed the glowing eighteen button. Once the doors had closed, she tapped her earbud.

"Two down. Nothing. How are you doing?"

"Zip. I ran into some workers, but nobody's seen anything," Eric said, murmuring. "I'm at thirteen. This floor looks empty."

"You're checking the electric panels?"

"Of course. Be hard to miss a suitcase-sized container there, wouldn't it?"

"Gotta go," she said and tapped the earbud off as the steel doors slid aside again. The scene from below was repeated, walls in various stages of finish, an electrician running wiring as other workers laid out the final floor plan, and she used her mistaken floor explanation with similar results. Nobody knew anything about two men with the cart.

Satisfied that the area was clean, she re-entered the elevator and repeated the process on the next three levels, the eighteenth with a skeleton crew working and the final two empty. As she completed her hurried inspection on the twentieth floor, growing increasingly impatient, her phone vibrated. She held it up and waited while the screen pulsed, and then an image popped up – the van picture, digitally enhanced.

Her eyes widened as she studied the photo, then she tapped her earbud again as she entered the elevator.

"I got the van image. It's the elevator manufacturer's logo. They're posing as elevator technicians," she said.

"Wait. One of the elevators is stopped up at the twenty-eighth floor. Two below the roof," Eric said as he studied the glowing floor indicators. "I see yours at the twentieth, and the third one is at the lobby. I've been using the stairs."

"That has to be it. The twenty-eighth. We're running out of time – the bomb has to be up there."

"I'll get moving now and meet you in the stairwell at the twenty-seventh, and then we can go in together."

Jet pushed the button and waited for the doors to slide shut again, her pulse accelerating at the news. Finally, they had the break they'd been looking for. She just hoped that they could find the device before the clock ran out for good.

❧❧

"We have a problem. Company." Solomon's voice was distorted over the radio speaker, but Joseph could still make out the tension in it.

"What! How do you know? Who is it?"

"Mossad. I saw that one of the elevators was stopping at each floor and thought it was suspicious, so I activated the intercom to see what I could pick up. They know you're up there. And I presume they're Mossad because they were speaking Hebrew."

"Damn. How the hell—"

"It doesn't matter. I'll do what I can. I'm going to cut the power to all the elevators so they'll be stranded. How's it going with the timer?" Solomon asked anxiously. He had taken up a position in the basement elevator room just in case of this sort of eventuality – they'd agreed that between his shoulder and the dog bites, he would be more useful behind a switch than staring over Joseph's shoulder as he armed the bomb.

"I only need a few more minutes, so their efforts will be in vain. I verified the rest of the circuitry, and it looks good to go. I just need to tweak one of the connections that looked iffy and set the timer, and we're out of here."

"Let me know when it's done and I'll disable the elevator control panel. Just a little insurance. Hope you don't mind walking down twenty-eight flights."

"Down's the easy part. And I'll be motivated."

CHAPTER 37

The lights shut off inside the elevator and it shuddered to a stop halfway through its rise to the twenty-seventh floor. For an instant it jolted, the whole car seeming to vibrate, and then the car dropped and went into freefall. Jet's last thought as the elevator plunged was that something had gone horribly wrong, and that she loved Hannah with all her heart.

Her stomach lurched as the car plummeted, hurtling toward the bottom of the shaft an impossible distance below, and then the emergency brakes engaged and it ground to a stop, the sound of metal on metal deafening in the enclosed chamber.

Jet stood motionless for a small eternity, gripping the metal handrail that circled the interior walls, her heart caught in her throat, afraid to move lest she somehow shake the elevator loose and it resume its drop. When it became obvious to her that it had stopped for good, she waited until her eyes became accustomed to the complete darkness and then fumbled her phone from her pocket, pausing before pressing one of the keys to illuminate the screen so she could use it to see. She studied the ceiling and spotted a panel that looked like it would hide an emergency access door, and after memorizing the location, she pocketed the cell and pushed herself up onto the steel railing, bracing her feet against it as her fingers felt for a grip.

The plastic panel shifted to the side, and when she groped above it she felt the cold metal of a handle. She twisted it and the mechanism unlatched, allowing her to push the hatch open, and then her hands moved to the edges of the aperture, searching for a hold.

The elevator shuddered, slipping a few inches, and she lost her footing and fell, hitting the floor hard. Cursing, she willed herself up and repeated her ascent, this time finding a suitable grip. She pulled herself up until her torso was through the hatch, then shifted her hands and eased her legs out.

Once she was standing on the elevator roof, she gazed up to where dim light was entering at the top of the shaft through ventilation slits. Jet forced herself to take a moment and close her eyes, and when she opened them again she could make out more detail – including the motor that opened the two doors for the level just above her. She reached up and pressed against the pair of panels, and they slid open relatively easily – when the power was off, the electric opener disengaged, so there was only token resistance. She remembered from a prior mission when she'd deliberately cut the power to an elevator in South Africa so she could gain access to a target via the shaft. Jet wedged her arm into the space and pushed the doors wider, then climbed through the gap onto the marble floor, never happier to be on solid footing.

That level was empty, and after a cursory confirming look she ran to the emergency stairwell on the far side of the building. She wrenched it open and heard the echo of footsteps ascending above her. When she tapped her earbud, the noise abruptly stopped.

"I'm in the stairwell below you. Twenty-first floor," Jet whispered.

"Why? You need exercise?" Eric asked, keeping his voice low.

"Hardly. Problem with the elevator. They may be on to us. The power's off. Hard to believe that was an accident. I'll be right up. How close are you?"

"Twenty-fifth."

Jet stopped talking and took the stairs two at a time, her robe billowing behind her as she practically flew up the steps. When she made it to Eric a fine sheen of perspiration glistened on her cheeks behind the veil. Standing on the landing with him, she pulled the headdress off and hurriedly stuffed it into one of her cargo pant pockets beneath her robe, then gazed up at the remaining flights.

"Same plan as before. Except that they're expecting us, so go in low and fast," she warned in a whisper.

"You want to lead, or should I?"

"Doesn't matter. Whichever you like."

"I'll go first," Eric said.

"Better pick up the pace. We're running late. Let's hope they haven't decided to make the end of the world a little early. That could ruin everyone's day."

Eric nodded, turned, and resumed his climb, Jet only a few steps behind him, both of their weapons now out in the open, rounds chambered, ready to engage. When they arrived at the twenty-eighth floor landing they were preparing to breach the door when silenced gunfire from above shattered the stillness in the confined space, the staccato popping of a sound-suppressed automatic weapon unmistakable.

Ricochets gouged chunks from the concrete above their heads as the shooter rained slugs down on their position, and an errant round tore the top of Eric's skull off, drenching the wall behind him with a spray of blood and bone fragments. Jet was already throwing herself to the side as his body dropped like a sack of cement on the steps in front of her. Dodging lower, she reached out with her free hand and tried to stop his slide down the stairs even as she brought her weapon up and returned fire at the muzzle flashes two stories above. Ten shots spat from her pistol as she pulled the trigger as rapidly as she could, hoping to hit the gunman with a stray, and then Eric's body jerked as more slugs pounded into him, his bulk shielding her from a hail of certain death.

Her awareness narrowed to where there was nothing but her and the shooter as she answered the gunfire with her remaining rounds, and then ejected the spent magazine in a fluid motion and slapped a fresh one into place. Another eight shots coughed from her pistol, and the last elicited a pained grunt from above, followed by the faint creak of hinges and a loud slam. The stairwell fell suddenly silent, and Jet rose cautiously from her position, ears alert for any hint of another onslaught. When she was sure the shooting was over, she leaned forward to feel in Eric's jacket for his spare magazine. She retrieved his gun and mounted the steps, holding both weapons in front of her, ready to empty them at the first sound or movement.

Jet reached the top floor in seconds and studied the two metal doors — one leading to the penthouse, the other to the roof. She slowed her breathing as she searched for any tell-tale signs of which the shooter had gone through, and then her eye drifted to the corner of the penthouse entrance, where a small crimson droplet glistened on the floor directly below the handle.

Now sure her quarry was on the other side of the penthouse door, Jet debated her options — if she tried to follow him, she'd almost certainly be greeted by a barrage she wouldn't survive. But the bomb was ticking away and she was running out of breathing room, and as unpleasant as the idea of certain death was, she didn't see a lot of options.

❧❧

"I'm hit," Joseph hissed into his radio, breathing heavily as he staggered across the floor to a wooden crate by the massive glass exterior wall.

"How bad?"

"Bad enough. Gut."

"Shit. I'm coming up."

"No. Get out of there. It's too late for anyone to stop it now. But you aren't going to survive if you're not at least a couple of miles away. Kill the guards and create as much confusion as you can, then move. I'm not going to make it down thirty stories of stairs with a bullet in my stomach."

"You can if I power on the elevators again."

Joseph shook his head, fuzzy from the pain. "Fine. But they're still up here, following me. I need to deal with them before I can bail out of here."

"Radio me when you're done. I'll hit the electric in three minutes," Solomon said, and then Joseph turned down the volume and took cover behind the crate, crouching low, blood trickling down his leg onto the floor as he faced the exit, his silenced MTAR-21 trained on the door, waiting for his pursuers to throw it open and walk into their own death.

He was surprised when a female voice called from the stairwell, the words dampened but still audible.

"There's nowhere to run. It's over. Surrender and tell us where the bomb is, or you'll be dead within minutes."

"I'm already dead. Why don't you come in here and put me out of my misery?"

"It doesn't have to end like that."

"Do your worst. You're too late. The bomb's going to go off, and there's nothing you can do to stop it. Nothing. I may die, but the world will change permanently. In the scheme of things, my sacrifice will be worthwhile, whereas yours will have been pointless – trying to interfere with something you don't even understand. So come on. Let's get this over with. Take your best shot."

He waited, but she didn't respond. Which was fine. If the situation were reversed, he would also take his time, waiting for him to weaken before rushing the door. Or better yet, he'd wait for his nerves to work against him, for him to weaken and grow impatient, act impetuously and do something stupid. As long as he was in the penthouse, they had him in a controlled environment, and they could have someone searching for the bomb while they sat, exactly as he was sitting, a gun pointed at the exit door, playing a deadly game of cat and mouse.

But he wasn't going to react the way they thought. He was willing to die, and every minute they stalled was another minute closer to when none of it would matter anymore. Just to reinforce his response, he fired a burst into the door, his bullets thumping into the steel with belligerent fury.

Let whoever wanted to go to paradise first come through it. He was more than ready for them.

⤛⤜

Jet pulled herself up the ladder in the dark from the twenty-ninth story, her body tense as she rushed her ascent. She'd darted down to the level below even as the bomber in the penthouse was giving his little speech. Seeing no viable alternative, she'd pried the elevator doors open and then swung herself into the void, ignoring the seemingly endless abyss beneath her, focusing instead on the objective above.

A few moments later she reached the penthouse level. Bracing herself against the ladder, she pulled the nearest of the two outer elevator doors with a powerful tug. When the panel slid soundlessly open, she threw herself through the gap, landing in a roll on the marble tiles as she whipped both pistols from her robe and leveled them at the surprised figure by the window. For a split second she registered his shocked expression, his body fully exposed from that angle, and then he was bringing his weapon around and she was shooting, the two weapons bucking rhythmically as she emptied them.

His torso jerked like a marionette as he staggered backward against the now-shattered glass wall, and then he was falling, weightless, his last conscious impression the patchwork of listless clouds drifting across the placid blue sky as he dropped at nearly two hundred feet per second toward the concrete's cold embrace.

Jet stood and walked to the yawning chasm in the glass and looked down, taking in the bloody lump on the concrete sidewalk surrounded by glittering shards, and then pirouetted and raced for the stairwell door, an eye on her watch as she ran.

Behind her, the elevator panel blinked twice, and then one of the floor indicator lights moved from twenty-eight to twenty-seven. The radio by the crate lay silent, but even if the volume had been turned up there was nobody to hear Solomon's alert that the power was back on, followed by a strident demand for an update.

❦

Downstairs in the elevator room, Solomon tried again, murmuring into the radio one final time. When he didn't get any response, he assumed the worst and shut off the electrical power to the elevator controller console. With a final look at the silent radio, he moved to the far wall where a fire extinguisher and an axe rested in a red metal case, and pulled the wooden handle free. Gripping the chopper with both hands, he returned to the console and delivered a powerful blow to the control cabinet beside it, destroying the electronics inside and eliminating any ability to operate the elevators remotely. He knew the emergency backup power hadn't been connected yet, so he didn't need to worry about the computer returning the cars to the ground floor – they would remain where they'd stopped, frozen in place for the duration. Anyone trying to move the elevators would be out of luck.

His last act before leaving was to hack apart the thick cables below the power switch, cleaving them with two swings of the heavy steel blade. Stepping back, he studied his handiwork with satisfaction, then dropped the axe and made for the exit, his final errand to kill the security guards before making his escape.

CHAPTER 38

Jet tapped her earbud as she wheeled into the stairwell from the penthouse, taking the steps at a run. The bomb had to still be on the twenty-eighth floor – that's where the bomber had been working and where the elevator had been stalled. She cursed as she sidestepped Eric's body on the bloody stairs and threw the exit door open. When no gunfire greeted her she hurried into the room in a crouch, her reloaded weapons sweeping the area; the partially constructed office walls offered plentiful places for an accomplice to be hiding or for the bomb to be stashed.

Wary of a trick but sensing no threat, she did a methodical grid search of the offices, confirming that she was alone.

And that there was no bomb.

Which was impossible. It had to be there.

Her eyes roved over the space before settling on the bank of elevators. The last one on the right had been stopped at that floor. The indicator lights were dark, but she crouched down and placed a hand on either door and pushed outward, and as before the polished steel panels inched apart, allowing her to slide the left one open. She peered into the darkness and saw the car stopped a story and a half below.

Jet swung into the shaft and eased herself down the service ladder that ran along the side. Once on the roof of the car, she pried the service hatch open and held her phone inside, again using its screen for scant illumination, noticing as she did that it had a dent in the case from where she'd fallen on it in her earlier elevator escape.

The screen's dim light caught a flash of blue aluminum on the floor. There, in the corner – a metal suitcase, its contents capable of turning the building into a supernova unless she was able to stop it in time.

She slipped the phone into her pocket, slid her legs through the hatch, and lowered herself in, supporting herself with her arms. Counting the seconds in her head, she dropped down beside the case and retrieved her phone, then stabbed the screen to life before holding it up and studying the bomb. Her eyes roved over the latches searching for an obvious booby trap; seeing none, she unclasped first the left, then the right, and swung the top open.

A timer with a digital readout blinked neon red digits at her, with four and a half minutes remaining on the display as it counted down. She swallowed hard, then raised her phone to her ear and hit the call button, and when the director answered on the second ring, gave him the abridged report.

"I've got the device in front of me. It's got four minutes to go on the timer. Get the technician on the line, now. This is cutting it way too close," she spat, a bead of sweat running down her forehead.

Twenty seconds went by before a younger voice came on the line. "This is Ben. Tell me exactly what you see."

Then the signal cut off, the phone crapping out, damaged from her fall. Grimacing, she slammed it against her leg twice and then tried again.

"Repeat. Didn't get the last part," she said.

"Tell me what you see."

"There's a timer with a digital readout. Next to it is a circuit – no, two circuit boards, with what looks like four wires disappearing underneath them. And there's a battery outside of a long gray casing; the bomb casing—"

Ben cut her off. "Did you say wires? There shouldn't be any wires. Are you sure?"

"I know what I'm looking at."

"That's impossible."

"I'll take a picture and send it to you. Stand by," Jet said, then pointed the phone's tiny camera lens at the device and closed her eyes as the flash went off. She checked the image, took another close-up of the timer, and then pushed send.

There was silence on the other end of the line, and when Ben's voice came back on, he sounded far less confident than he had before.

"It's been modified. I don't know exactly why, or how. It's impossible to tell from here without dismantling the casing for the circuit board, but that will take too long, and there's no guarantee of a quick workaround," he said.

"How about just unplugging the battery?"

"No – it's set up so that if you do that it'll detonate. There's a secondary lithium battery that acts as a backup inside the charge detonator. The bomb is basically that explosive element, and the two uranium sections – the bullet and the target. The charge explodes, the two sections collide, and the reaction occurs in a split second."

"Thanks for the dissertation. How do I stop it?" Jet asked between gritted teeth.

"I'm thinking. Let me study this for a minute…"

"In case nobody explained this to you, every minute counts. Why can't I just take it and throw it in the ocean?"

She heard the director mutter something in the background.

"Because you wouldn't get there before it went off. You wouldn't even make it to the lobby in time. And immersing it in a sink or tub won't work – it's water-resistant. Now stop talking. I'm thinking," Ben said, his voice sounding slightly panicked. Jet decided it wasn't the time for assertiveness and bit her tongue, allowing him some breathing room. After what seemed like forever, he came back on the line.

"You see that long chip in the socket next to the timer? With the 89-whatever number printed across the top? That's the timer controller. If you pull it, assuming they haven't done anything to it, it should stop the clock."

"And what if they have?"

"I…I don't know."

"Shit. This is the best you can do? Something that *might* work? What about clipping one of the wires, like in the movies?"

"I don't know what those wires do. And unfortunately, this isn't the movies."

"Put the director back on," Jet ordered, seething.

"I'm here. I put you on speaker," the director said.

"I now have just over two and a half minutes. And no way of stopping the damned thing from exploding. What do you want me to do?" she demanded, an edge to her voice.

"Take a deep breath, and then…." The latter part of his instruction broke up, distorted so she couldn't make him out. She shook the phone in frustration – *of all the times for the damned thing to be shorting out* – then held it up to her ear.

"What did you say?"

"I said pull the chip."

Jet eyed the device distrustfully and brushed sweat out of her eyes before reaching into her back pocket and flicking open her knife. She looked skyward and offered a silent prayer, then carefully slid the tip under the chip and levered it out of the socket, wincing as she did so.

The display flashed on and off several times.

"It's blinking," she reported, and then nearly choked as the display resumed its countdown.

"Oh God. It's still ticking. Looks like…I have less than two minutes before it goes off."

"Wait. Clip the–"

"What?" The signal broke up again. She rapped the phone against the floor and then punched at the screen, putting it in speakerphone mode.

"I didn't hear you. What?" she barked.

"I said clip the wire on the–"

Static cut off the last words.

"On the what? Clip the wire on the what?"

"…left of the…"

More interference. She squinted in the darkness at the bomb, the timer's pulsing glow shimmering against the black rubber wiring insulation. *Left of what?*

"Repeat. I didn't get that last part," she said, a deadly calm now settling over her.

Ben's voice was distorted, but she thought she made out the word 'timer'."

"Did you say left of the timer? Nearest the battery?" she demanded, her voice tight.

Nothing. The phone sat as silent as a rock, an occasional burst of static squawking from its tiny speaker, the garbled words unintelligible.

Jet watched as the timer continued its relentless countdown, and prayed for something intelligible to come through the phone. Ten seconds went by, then another ten. She reached over and banged the cell repeatedly, each *crack* as it struck the floor like a coffin nail being hammered. Only white noise emanated from it, and with resigned frustration she abandoned her punishment of the cell and stared at the bomb, its timer mocking all of her efforts to thwart it.

With a deep breath, she slid the knife blade under the wire she thought Ben had singled out, holding either end with her fingers, and pulled up, slashing it. The blade came free, cutting only half the wire's copper core, and she swore, the timer blinking its taunt as it continued its countdown to destruction, now reading only thirty seconds as it blurred toward zero.

Jet blinked sweat out of her eyes. At the current rate she'd be dead before she could exhale her final breath. She slipped the blade back under the wire with a trembling hand and then slashed again with all her might, knowing that this would be her last act on Earth if she'd called it wrong.

The wire severed and the timer froze.

At twelve seconds remaining on the clock.

She fell back against the elevator wall, her pulse pounding in her ears, and glared at the battered phone.

"Did – you – do it?" Ben asked, his distinctive voice choppy, barely discernible.

"It worked," she said simply.

She heard cheering on the director's end, and then the line crackled and dropped out.

Jet exhaled noisily and slowly rolled her head, working the tension out of her neck muscles, and the phone vibrated insistently from its position near the case. She answered it, but the director's words still sounded distorted.

"G – job. Congr – lations."

"Thanks. My phone is damaged so you're breaking up. What do you want me to do with the device?"

"Hand it off to Eric. Your part in this is over," he said.

"I can't. Eric's dead."

Silence.

"What about sshhccrrssshhh?"

She banged the cell on the marble elevator floor again, hating the little device more than she could have thought possible.

"What?" she asked.

"Aaron. What about Aaron?" he asked, then the signal deteriorated from more interference.

"Let me check. Hold on." Jet tapped the earbud and spoke softly. "Aaron. Respond. Come in."

Nothing. Only silence on the comm line.

She tried again, but got no reply.

"I'm not getting anything. Assume he's compromised," she said, suddenly tired.

"Damn. All right. Get – device out – Doha. There's a fort a hundred kiloshshhsh north, near – coast. Al Zubara. It's a mushshhgsh now, but it's desolate. Go now, shhcrrshh I'll arrange –"

White noise hissed from the speaker in an obnoxious burst. She held the phone away from her and hit it again. The call went dead, and when she tried to redial the director, all she got was the dull hum of nothingness.

Perfect.

She tapped the earbud again and tried Aaron, but there was no response.

Jet looked overhead at the escape hatch and quickly calculated that the case wouldn't fit through it. She closed the lid and re-latched it, then stood and searched for a pressure bar release on the interior of the elevator. Finding none, she slid her knife between the doors and then twisted, forcing them open an inch – just enough room to wedge her fingers in. She braced her boots and heaved against the right one until it slid aside with a low scrape. Scowling, she spied the tops of the next floor's doors occupying the bottom three and a half feet of the elevator doorway and knelt down in front of them.

This time it was harder to force them apart, but driven by determination, she managed, using the pressure from her palms to slide them wide. After a brief look through the opening to gauge the distance to the floor, she slid the heavy case to the edge of the elevator and shouldered the carrying strap. Her stomach tensed as she jumped onto the marble tiles, absorbing the heavy case's drop with her legs and back, which shrieked in protest at the impact.

Ignoring the pain, she moved to the stairwell and began the long process of descending twenty-four stories, gripping the handrail with all her might in case she lost her footing, her mind racing over the latest cryptic instructions from the director — take the nuke to a fort in the middle of nowhere.

Maybe he had another operative who was going to smuggle it offshore from there? Bahrain was just across the Gulf, twenty-five miles away. Perhaps the Mossad had more assets on that small island, or it would be easier to put it on a jet from there than Qatar?

Her back spasmed and she briefly stopped to rest, thinking through the logistics of her odd instructions.

The director wanted the bomb transported to Al Zubara. He'd seemed adamant, so that was where she would go. She knew from the map she'd studied during her briefing that there was a major highway that ran north — Highway One. From there she was sure she could find it.

Jet shifted the strap, trying to ease the pressure on her lower spine, and then, her face intent on her task, continued her descent, the stairwell silent except for the soft impact of her boots on the concrete steps.

CHAPTER 39

When Jet arrived at the lobby it was empty, Aaron nowhere to be seen. She inched to the reception desk and her worst fears were confirmed – Aaron had been shot in the head with a small caliber pistol and was lying on the floor behind the counter in a pool of coagulating blood.

A noise sounded from the stairwell doors at the far end of the lobby, and Jet took that as her cue to get out of there. She sped to the front entrance, then pushed through the doors and took measured steps to where Isaac was waiting with the van.

She scowled at him through the window. "Take me to my car. Come on, let's get out of here. Now."

Jet swung into the passenger seat and hauled the case onto her lap, and Isaac jammed the transmission into gear and lead-footed the gas, spinning the wheels as he made a long U-turn before speeding toward the main artery.

"Mind telling me what's going on?"

"Aaron and Eric are dead. Just drive," she said, ignoring his request. Isaac had been kept out of the loop by the director – he wasn't at a high enough level to know much more than he already did, and there was probably a good reason for that.

The van pulled alongside her car and stopped. Jet opened the door and stepped out of the vehicle, and after scanning the street for threats, turned to face him.

"Your part in this is over. You don't want to know anything more, believe me. I'll swing by the safe house later today to get my things. Wait for me there." She moved several feet away, then stopped. "Thank you, Isaac. You did well."

"I wish I knew what it was I did well *at*, but never mind. Mine is not to reason why. I'll see you when I see you. You need anything?"

She shook her head. "No, I'm good. Just keep your head down."

His eyes drifted to the drying blood on the front of her abaya – traces of Eric's last stand. "You don't need to tell me twice," he said with a grim half smile.

She watched as he disappeared around the corner at the end of the block, then opened the doors and placed the case on the back seat, securing it in place with the safety belt.

Jet withdrew the headdress from her pocket and donned it again, then inched the little car onto the quiet street, keeping her speed down so as not to attract any undue attention, an anonymous woman who wouldn't warrant a second glance.

She made good time on the eight-lane highway, the traffic sparse, with only a few large ore trucks and tankers heading north, and then found herself the only car on the road when she pulled onto the smaller thoroughfare headed towards the coast, a blue sign announcing Al Zubara pointing the way.

As she drew nearer she saw a lone vulture, looking forlorn and miserable, perched alongside a road hazard sign featuring a black outline of a camel against a white reflective backdrop. The sight gave her pause and she nearly burst out into giddy laughter, the natural delayed response to the stress in the elevator hitting her like a summer storm.

The fort was plainly marked, a sign in English and Arabic announcing it as closed propped against the empty parking lot gate, the two temporary offices next to it unoccupied. Jet eased the car behind the buildings so it would be shielded from the road and took stock of her surroundings – empty, no other humans in sight. She stepped from the air-conditioned vehicle interior and was immediately assaulted by a harsh, dry wind blowing from the south, carrying with it dust and not much more, the low moan as it passed through the structure's four turrets a mournful lament. The sun blazed down on her as she strode past a ceremonial cannon to the building's sole entrance and pushed against the ornate wooden doors, verifying they were locked before trying the smaller portal cut into the one on her right. To her surprise it opened easily, and she drew her weapon before swinging it wide, cautiously eyeing the interior courtyard before returning to the car.

Jet lugged the bomb to the entry and pushed her way into the fort, then closed the door behind her and bolted it shut. A small dust devil spiraled into the air in the center of the hard-packed dirt yard, and she watched it absently before carrying the case to the nearest doorway and setting it inside the barren room. Shaking off the vague sense of unease that she'd been struggling with since she'd pulled off the road, she took a fast tour of the lower level barracks, confirming that they were empty, and then climbed the stairs to the second level, which was also deserted. She was preparing to enter the nearest turret when she heard the rumble of heavy vehicles in the distance, and then four military Humvees with .50 caliber machine guns mounted behind the cabs came trundling down the road, headed straight for the parking lot and her lone car.

Jet pressed herself against the rampart and watched through one of the gun slits as the vehicles pulled onto the barren track leading to the parking lot before taking up position at the four corners of the fort grounds. Camouflage-clad soldiers dropped from the beds brandishing assault rifles, their bronzed faces somber even from a distance. She felt beneath her robes and withdrew her 9mm pistol and eyed it with grim pessimism. Even in her skilled hands the weapon was no match for a squad of trained soldiers with enough firepower to wage a war.

The diesel engines idled noisily as the gunmen established a perimeter, and then another sound intruded – the thumping of large rotor blades overhead. Jet raced down the stairs and took cover under a heavy stone overhang, wary of an assault from above, and then crept to the fort's wooden gateway and peered through a narrow gap. A Sikorsky Black Hawk helicopter sporting Qatar army markings dropped from the sky and hovered over the parking lot before settling down in the center of the baking asphalt.

The powerful turbine slowed as the side door opened and a figure stepped out, wearing khaki civilian trousers and shirt, a tribal headdress shielding his face from the sand and dust being thrown up by the downdraft. He moved away from the aircraft and marched to the fort entry, then tried the doors, as she had.

Jet heard the rattle of the bolt fighting to hold, and she called out in Arabic, "I have a gun and a bomb. I'll detonate it rather than be taken alive. I don't know what this is, but leave now, or I'll take you all with me."

The figure backed away from the door and responded in Arabic. "Sounds serious. But before you blow us all to kingdom come, perhaps you could take the time to field a call?"

Her brow creased as she moved closer to the gap in the entryway and squinted at the figure standing outside, a satellite phone in one hand, his posture relaxed, apparently unarmed. No obvious threat in evidence, she slipped the bolt open and stepped away, her pistol aimed at the doorway.

"It's open. Just you, come in. Nobody else," she instructed.

The wooden slab swung slowly inward and the man stepped through the door.

"Close it behind you and bolt it," she ordered, the gun unwavering in her steady hand.

He turned, slowly, and locked the door, then faced her, holding the phone out. "It's for you."

"Set it down and back away."

"Yes, ma'am," he said, and placed the phone on the dirt between them. "How far?" he asked, edging backwards.

"That's good," she replied, kneeling, the Beretta trained on his head, eyes never leaving his face. Her fingers groped in the hot dirt until they found the handset. She lifted the unwieldy phone to her ear.

The director's voice boomed from the speaker. "I trust you met our associate, Tom," he said, more statement than question.

"Tom?"

"An American. I think your phone died before you heard my entire message."

"Which was?"

"To go to the fort, wait for the military to show up, and surrender the case to them."

"Hand the device to an American working with an Arab country's military…," she said unbelievingly.

"Correct."

Tom unwrapped his headdress, revealing piercing blue eyes set in a tanned, forty-something face.

"I should give him the bomb."

"Yes. There's more to the story, but I don't have time to explain it all now. Suffice to say it will be well taken care of. Give it to him and get back to Doha. I'll have a jet waiting to pick you up. It's over."

"Fine," she said softly, then stepped toward Tom and offered the phone.

"Where is it?" Tom asked, clear eyes scouting the interior of the fort.

"Behind you. First room."

"You can lower your weapon now," he said with a trace of a smile, and then turned and ducked into the darkened barracks. A few moments later he emerged with the case, the strap over his shoulder, the handle gripped tightly in his hand.

"Pleasure doing business with you," he said, his Arabic flawless.

"Likewise," she replied as she slipped the pistol back into her robes. "That's it?"

"That's it. I leave in the big bird, the bully boys get back into their trucks and take off, and you're free to do whatever you like. Although my advice would be to avoid staying in Qatar for any extended vacations."

"Put like that, how can I resist?"

Tom gave her a two fingered salute, slid the bolt to the side, and opened the door.

"Nice outfit, by the way," he said in Hebrew.

And then he was gone.

The Humvees rolled out of the parking lot and onto the road once the helicopter was out of sight, and Jet watched from the fort as they disappeared into the horizon's distorted heat. Several minutes later she returned to the car, and after thoroughly checking it to ensure that no bomb had been planted to end her part in the mission while she'd been occupied with the American, she cranked the air conditioner, relieved that the ordeal was finally over, but also feeling somehow incomplete. It was surreal – all that, the world on the brink of chaos, only to hand over the nuke to an unknown foreigner.

Eyeing herself in the rearview mirror, she removed the bourga and allowed the cold air to blow on her face, taking a moment to savor the icy draft before putting the vehicle into gear and coaxing it onto the lonely strip of asphalt. The tires murmured to her as she passed the vulture again on her way back to civilization, leaving it to its solitary duty in the uninhabited wasteland.

CHAPTER 40

Jet rolled to a stop on a dusty street on the outskirts of town, a few miles from the safe house, where a weathered sign proclaimed internet access and air conditioning. She stepped out of the car and took care to lock it, and then strolled into the café. After a brief discussion, the proprietor pointed to a phone in a corner of the main room, and she took a seat. A few moments went by and then the man gave her a thumbs-up sign. She closed her eyes, thinking, then dialed the director's number from memory.

"I'm back in town, on the way to the safe house to get my gear. I'm starving, so I'm going to stop for lunch. I presume I'll be safe for that long?"

"The danger's past. Take your time." The director chuckled. "I heard that you made quite an impression on our friend."

"He must not get out much."

"Perhaps. Anyway, it was a job well done."

"Not that well done. Two men dead, and the bombers — one of them escaped."

The director hesitated. "The danger was neutralized. I'm not worried about the last of the traitorous scum — we'll catch up to him eventually." The director cleared his throat. "The jet should be in Qatar in two hours. I'll alert the crew to be ready for takeoff in...how long?"

"I've got to go retrieve my papers and eat, so figure around three to four hours, depending on traffic — it's snarled all over town because of the meeting. I could probably walk across car roofs faster than I'm going to be able to drive there."

"I'll let them know. Safe travels, and again, congratulations," the director said, then hung up. She hadn't expected anything more, and wasn't disappointed. At least he was consistent — she'd saved the world, and all she'd gotten in return were a few grudging words of praise. But now her obligation was fulfilled and she could be rid of his meddling in her life once and for all. The only remaining item was her debriefing, and she was finally free.

The thought cheered her, but then a tickle of anxiety roiled in her stomach. The decisions that had been made had put everyone in the region in jeopardy, and it was only because of a last minute bit of luck that Doha wasn't a smoking crater. As much as she wanted to trust that the same men who had weighed those odds and decided to favor their own interests would honor their commitment to leave her in peace, Jet didn't really believe it.

She knew too much, and there would always be another emergency that they absolutely needed someone to help them with.

Only one solution would be foolproof. She would need to disappear. This time for good, leaving no trace. She knew that it wouldn't be that simple once she was in Israel, so she moved to one of the computers and checked on flights from Doha. She had another ID with her, and once she was on the ground in another country she could become someone else and find her own way home, leaving the whole ugly mess behind her.

A flight bound for New Delhi departed in two hours. She would call right before takeoff and warn the director that she was running late, buying herself another couple of hours, and by the time anyone realized that she wasn't going to show up, she'd be gone, permanently off the radar. The director wouldn't be happy, but he would understand – he'd practically invented the game, and she was just following her operational instincts, trusting no one.

Jet moved back to the phone and dialed another number.

"Well, hello there," Matt answered, and Jet immediately felt the familiar tug of emotion he evoked in her so easily.

"Hello yourself. How did you know it was me?"

"Nobody else calls me."

"Where are you?" she asked.

"In the wilds of Vietnam. How about you?"

"Getting out of Dodge," she replied, preferring to keep things vague.

"Wow. That was quick."

"No point in wasting any time, was there?"

"Guess not. Everything turn out okay?"

Jet took a deep breath. "Routine. How about you?"

"A few surprises. Nothing I couldn't handle. I'll tell you all about it in person. I ran my errand and I'm just loafing around now."

"Vietnam, huh? The old stomping grounds lost their charm?"

"Yup. I got tired of Thailand pretty quickly," he said, a slight edge in his voice.

She didn't press him. There would be time to fill in the blanks later. "Nothing stays the same."

"Indeed."

"Are you near an airport?" she asked.

He paused. "I could be within four or five hours."

"I was thinking. Maybe we should hook up in Singapore. From there we can make our way to South America. We still have a date for that, right?"

"You bet. When will you be there?"

She looked at her watch. "In about twelve hours."

"I'll have to check on flights, but it sounds doable. I may take longer, though. Will you wait for me?"

She debated possible responses, and then smiled.

"Absolutely."

⤬

Back at the safe house, Jet handed Isaac her dead phone and her gun as she was preparing to leave. He accepted them without expression, sitting at his workstation, the screens dark now, the mission finished.

Jet lifted her bag and slid the strap over her shoulder, watching him as he slipped the weapons into a drawer. She was still wearing the robe and the veil, preferring the anonymity, and figured she would get rid of the outfit once at the airport.

"Thanks for all the help, Isaac," she said as she backed toward the door.

"No problem. You know, I never even knew your name."

"Best to leave it that way."

She caught a small movement, a shift, a flicker of his eyes, and she shook her head, fixing him with a hard stare.

"Don't, Isaac. You don't have to do this," she said softly.

He shrugged, a sad expression on his face. "I'm afraid I do. Following orders," he said, then raised a tranquilizer gun from where he'd had it in his lap, out of sight, the desk shielding it from view.

The 9mm parabellum round hit Isaac high in the chest and he dropped the weapon, his eyes registering surprise, the smoking hole in her abaya from the gunshot all the explanation he needed.

219

She withdrew Eric's silenced pistol from the garment and popped the magazine out, taking care to eject the round from the chamber before placing the weapon on the table in front of him.

"I could have killed you. You'll live, but you'll need to get to a doctor for that. I figure you have someone discreet you use. Is that right?"

He nodded, blood seeping from between his fingers as he clutched the wound.

"I'll do a compression bandage. Keep pressure on it and you should make it. Give me the doctor's number, and when I'm safely away, I'll call him and have him come for you." She took a step closer to him, staring deep into his eyes, her gaze unflinching. "That's what I'm willing to do for you. Now, let's talk about what you'll need to do for me. You're going to call your handler and tell him that I contacted you and won't be here for three more hours – I stopped for lunch and to get a new phone. If you say anything else, no matter how innocent it sounds, I'll cut your throat and let you bleed to death. Clear?"

Isaac nodded, and she picked up the handset on the desk. "What number are you supposed to call?" He told her and she dialed it, and then held out the phone. He took it with a hand slick with blood and did exactly as she'd instructed, her eyes boring through him the entire time.

Ten minutes later he was seated in the kitchen, hands cuffed to a length of chain that she'd fastened to a gas line that ran under the cabinets, a bloody makeshift bandage in place. After a final look around, she lit one of the burners and then tossed the still-smoking wooden match on the floor by his feet.

"Just be patient. It'll be five hours before I call for help. The bleeding has all but stopped, so just don't exert yourself and you'll be fine. I've got the doctor's number." She glanced at the chain. "If you try to pull the pipe loose, the room will flood with gas and the burner will ignite it before you have a chance to reach it. So bad idea. Just stay still, conserve your energy, and wait for the doctor."

Jet opened the refrigerator and removed a liter bottle of orange juice, then unscrewed the top and placed it within his reach.

"Keep hydrated. The juice will help replace the blood you've lost. Pace yourself. Here, I'll give you some water, too," she said, reaching into the fridge and grabbing a plastic container before setting it on the floor near him.

"I'm sorry," he said, his tone meek. "I had to do it."

"I know."

Jet moved to where she had left her bag, then approached the front door and gave Isaac a parting wave. "I'll leave this open so he can get to you easily. You should call the director once you're freed and tell him what happened. He won't be that shocked. Probably the only thing he'll be surprised by is that I let you live. Consider it my gift to the agency. Tell him, and use these exact words: *I'm not the enemy.* Do you understand?"

Isaac nodded, pain clouding his eyes, and she knew that he would remember. For the rest of his life.

Jet made her way to the car and threw the bag onto the back seat. She would drive to one of the big hotels and leave the vehicle with the valet, then catch a taxi.

And disappear without a trace, her operational life behind her, finally, on her way to a brighter future, with Hannah – and now Matt – going to a destination where they could be safe, and ultimately, free.

At the airport, she placed a call at the internet café as she was waiting for her flight, much as she planned to do once she landed in India – honoring her commitment to Isaac to contact the doctor. Magdalena's voice answered, sounding slightly out of breath.

"Magdalena. It's me. I only have a few minutes, but I wanted to touch base and tell you that I should be home in a couple more days."

"*Señora!* That's wonderful news. Is everything…did you accomplish what you'd hoped to?"

"Yes, Magdalena, everything went well, and I miss you both. But I have some news. I want you to pack up and take a bus to Colonia, today, and get a hotel there. Please do it now. I'll meet you there in a couple of days, and I'll call to find out where you're staying."

"Oh. Is…is anything the matter?"

"No. But it should be nice on the water, and you've spent a lot of time where you are. A new town would be a good idea, just in case."

"Just in case…"

"Don't worry, Magdalena, everything's fine. I'm just being extremely careful. Could you just please me on this?"

"Yes, *Señora*, of course. I'll get our things immediately and take the next bus south."

"Thank you, Magdalena. This is almost over."

"And…we're safe, right?"

"Of course. Again, there's nothing to worry about. I was just thinking that it would be a good idea for you to move around a little. That's all."

"All right, then," Magdalena said, a trace of doubt still lingering.

"Is Hannah there?"

"*Si*. Let me get her. She's very excited – she played with a puppy in the park an hour ago."

Ten seconds went by and then Hannah's squeaky voice came on the phone. "Mama!"

"Hi, sweetheart. How are you?"

"Good," Hannah said, sounding tiny and a million miles away.

"Mommy misses you."

"Me too."

"Have you been good?"

"Yeth," Hannah assured her in a tone that made clear it was a stupid question. *Of course she'd been good. She was always good.*

"I'm coming home soon."

"Good."

Jet had almost forgotten how limited a conversation with a two and a half year old could be.

"Magdalena tells me you played with a puppy today?"

"Yeth. I love him."

"What kind of puppy was it?"

"A baby dog," she answered tentatively, surprised her mother didn't know what a puppy was.

"What kind of dog?"

She heard rustling as Hannah held the handset against something while she conferred with Magdalena, and then she returned to the conversation.

"A bagel."

"A beagle! Those are very sweet dogs, aren't they?"

"Yeth. Hannah want."

"I'm sure you do, honey. But a puppy is a big step – a lot of work."

"I want. Bagel. Baby bagel!"

"Well, we can talk about it when I get home. I have to go now, but I wanted to say I love you very much, my angel."

"Me too," Hannah said solemnly, and then her tone brightened. "I love bagel, too."

Jet's eyes moistened at her daughter's single-minded determination and she smiled.

"I'll be home soon. Bye bye, honey."

"Bye bye, Mama."

The overhead speaker announced boarding for her flight to India, and she rose and paid the attendant before making her way to the departing gate, a lump in her throat as she walked, visions of Hannah, and maybe Matt, playing in a yard with the cutest 'bagel' puppy the world had ever seen. Jet took her place in line with the other travelers and struggled to mute the emotions surging through her, the internal battle raging behind her placid gaze hidden from the surrounding passengers. By the time she made it to the podium and handed the attendant her ticket she was herself again, a cool, confident woman, self-possessed and in control.

She'd booked a window seat with nobody next to her, the plane only a third full, the traffic typically light on the return trip to India, and as the jet taxied to the end of the runway and began its takeoff run she closed her emerald eyes and pictured her daughter, her Hannah, rolling in the grass with a puppy, safe at last.

For a brief and precious moment, life was good.

ABOUT THE AUTHOR

A *Wall Street Journal* and *The Times* featured author, Russell Blake lives full time on the Pacific coast of Mexico. He is the acclaimed author of many thrillers, including the Assassin series, the JET series, and the BLACK series. He has also co-authored *The Eye of Heaven* with Clive Cussler for Penguin Books.

Non-fiction novels include the international bestseller *An Angel With Fur* (animal biography) and *How To Sell A Gazillion eBooks (while drunk, high or incarcerated)* – a joyfully vicious parody of all things writing and self-publishing related.

"Capt." Russell enjoys writing, fishing, playing with his dogs, collecting and sampling tequila, and waging an ongoing battle against world domination by clowns.

Sign up for e-mail updates about new Russell Blake releases

http://russellblake.com/contact/mailing-list

Made in the USA
Lexington, KY
02 November 2014